A LOVELY BUNCH OF POSEYS

Lily

Alice Addy

Copyright © 2014 Alice Addy

All rights reserved
2021 Edition
The characters and events portrayed in this book are fictitious. Any similarity to real persons, living or dead, is coincidental and not intended by the author.

No part of this book may be reproduced, or stored in a retrieval system, or transmitted in any form or by any means, electronic, mechanical, photocopying, recording, or otherwise, without express written permission of the publisher.

ISBN-13: 978-1499785555
ISBN-10: 1499785550

Cover design by: Katheryn Klein

Printed in the United States of America

DEDICATION

This story is dedicated to the ones we love— Past and present—First and last. Thank you for everything.

CONTENTS

Title Page
Copyright
Dedication
A Lovely Bunch of Poseys   1
CHAPTER ONE   3
CHAPTER TWO   17
CHAPTER THREE   30
CHAPTER FOUR   44
CHAPTER FIVE   60
CHAPTER SIX   72
CHAPTER SEVEN   91
CHAPTER EIGHT   104
CHAPTER NINE   131
CHAPTER TEN   149
CHAPTER ELEVEN   170
CHAPTER TWELVE   185
EPILOGUE   198
Amaryllis   206
About The Author   209

A LOVELY BUNCH OF POSEYS

The Poseys are your typical 1901 family—well, maybe not precisely typical. They have their own special eccentricities, as does everyone else. Through simple, or contrived good fortune, they comprise a beautiful bouquet of turn of the century American life. Mr. Forrest and his wife, Fern, are the parents to a large family of seven girls and one son—all having one thing in common...their beautiful botanical names...each more flowery than the next. Perhaps it was a lovely idea to follow tradition, but living in Garden City, Kansas, on Orchard Lane, well...one can see the difficulties they might encounter. It isn't always easy being floral.

Lily

First love...a time for discovery and a time to cherish. In all its forms, first love can be wonderful, as well as a bit daunting. When a handsome young rogue meets a delicate, hothouse flower, you can expect to have more than a few ups and downs.

❖ ❖ ❖

Lily sat back against the pillows, reliving the moment their eyes first met and her heart seized. She marveled at what a difference one night could make. Whoever could have imagined the most handsome boy at the dance would desire to search her out—*Lily Posey*? He was tall, dark, and handsome, with the kindest brown eyes she'd ever seen. He was also witty, mannerly, and a divine dancer, as well as being slightly mysterious. As he spun her around the room, she could see the other girls were absolutely pea-green with envy. After all, she was one of those Posey girls, and no one ever danced with one of them.

By the end of the evening, everything had turned magical for Lily. Not only had she spent the entire night on the arms of her Prince Charming, but the most incredible thing of all occurred…he asked if he might see her again—and that was beyond her greatest expectation.

◆ ◆ ◆

It didn't take long for the dark, handsome stranger to set his sight on the prettiest girl in the room. The girl was absolutely magnificent, if a bit too shy and timid. With golden blonde hair, soft curves in all the right places, and long, shapely legs under her muslin gown, she was enough to cause any man's mouth to water. Spending one romantic night with her, under the soft glow of a full moon, he could possibly salvage what was left of a miserable summer. Exiled to his aunt's house for conduct unbecoming a Barker, he had been unfairly sentenced to ten weeks of tedium, spent at hard labor. However, things no longer looked so bleak. After discovering this living, breathing, heart-stopping vision in the flesh, he vowed his luck was going to change. With the help of his good friend, Charlie, he would manage to sweet talk this lovely bit of feminine delight right out of her dainties—or his name wasn't Blackie Barker.

CHAPTER ONE

Kansas 1901

By the time Blackie Barker arrived at the Garden City Community Hall, the dance was in full swing. He and his friend, Charlie Masters, stood just inside the doors, observing all the lovely girls as they glided by in their prettiest party frocks. It was like being a child let loose in a candy store, Blackie mused, as he noticed more than a few sly smiles and coquettish glances directed his way.

Although he wasn't from Garden City originally, he was discovering, much to his delight, this small town was turning out to be surprisingly interesting. The girls were fresh faced, innocent, and quite friendly; and he was like an irresistible magnet drawing them in. It was an obvious advantage to be a stranger from out of town. No one need know of the past offenses, which had made it necessary for him to spend an unspecified amount of time with his aunt. No indeed; that would serve no useful purpose. For now, Blackie was happy to give out with his best and most charismatic smile, going as far as winking at a few of the more charming girls, in spite of receiving scornful glares from their over-protective mamas; warning him to tread lightly. He figured it was all in good fun.

Many of the young ladies, gathered in the huge hall, were quite pretty, but it was one special girl in particular, who caught his attention. She stood completely alone, near the back of the room, with her spine pressed up against a tall column.

Blackie thought she looked as if she wished to be anywhere but where she was, and if she pressed hard enough, she would disappear entirely, through the wall. He could tell she had given up on expecting to have any fun—and that was intriguing.

"Who is that?" Blackie asked his friend, as he nodded toward the girl. "I can hardly believe a girl as beautiful as she, isn't dancing. Do you know if she has a beau? She must have, as she hardly looks the sort to be a wallflower." His eyes darted around the perimeter of the room, taking notice of the too short, too tall, plain-faced women, silently pleading for just one spin around the dance floor.

Charlie snorted derisively. "Oh, her? That's Lily. Don't pay her no mind. Her whole family is one brick shy of a full load. None of us have anything to do with most of them. Bud ain't a bad guy, though."

"Lily, you say? She looks perfectly normal to me—better than perfect, actually. I think you hayseeds must be blind or just plain screwy. I'm gonna ask her to dance."

Before Blackie could take more than two steps in her direction, his friend grabbed hold of his sleeve. "Don't go runnin' off like your tail's on fire. She's from weird folks, I tell you. Who knows what they'll do to you if you get caught up with the likes of them? I hear tell Hank Berger went courting the oldest sister, Forsythia…or something like that. One day, he just up and disappeared, and no one has seen him since. He was kind of a rascal though, so nobody seemed to care too much."

Blackie shrugged off his friend's hand. "Look here, Charlie. I've fought bears, badgers, and my old granny. Nothing scares me. And certainly not a beautiful girl," he muttered softly. "Watch this," he boasted.

Blackie sauntered over toward the golden-haired goddess with the flowers in her hair, and grinned broadly; showing off his perfectly aligned teeth and his irresistible dimples. It was the gleam of her long, cascading hair that first caught his eye, followed closely by the graceful way she kept time to the lively tunes. She was tall and slender, and very appealing to the eye.

Her lush body swayed to the music in perfect measure. Although her full lips were turned up in a slightly sad smile, her large eyes looked to be on the verge of tears, which he found intoxicatingly attractive. This girl's quiet sensuality beckoned to him.

Lily turned her head just in time to see a remarkably handsome man walking her way. Quick to put up her guard, she stuck out her chin and prepared herself for the hurtful assault, which was most assuredly going to occur. As with so many others, this boy would more than likely tease her, or drop an insult and walk away, leaving tears in his wake. However, she swore this time, it would be different. She would not be taken unawares, and she would ignore his insults.

"Excuse me, Miss," the deep, velvety voice said. "I noticed you from across the dance floor and I couldn't resist making your acquaintance. If you're not previously engaged, might I have this dance?" The stranger held out his hand in a most proper manner.

What? Had she heard him correctly? What was it he just said? Lily's eyes nearly popped from her head, as her jaw dropped, trying to make sense of it all. Who was this cocky, albeit adorable stranger, and why on earth was he asking her, of all people, to dance? She was all too aware of what the townspeople said about her and her family. Therefore, there could be only one plausible explanation for his polite invitation—he must be from out of town. She suddenly found herself quite speechless, and feeling almost sorry for his error.

"Miss? Did you hear me?" Blackie frowned. Perhaps she was deaf and that was the real reason she wasn't dancing. Charlie was probably having a damn good laugh right about now; sending him off to talk to a deaf girl, but he'd get even with him. Before morning, he'd make certain his friend paid dearly for embarrassing him this way.

"I'm SOR-RY," he shouted distinctly, loud enough for the entire room to hear. "No one told me you were hard of hearing." He pointed to his ear. "I a-po-lo-gize." Looking chagrinned, as if he had been responsible for a tasteless joke that had gone awry, Blackie gave a sheepish nod of his head and quickly withdrew his hand, preparing to back away.

"Please, stop!"

Blackie spun around on his heels. "Did you say something?"

Lily nodded and put out her hand. "Uh-huh. I—I mean, yes, I did. I simply didn't know how to respond to your unusual request. You caught me off guard. It's not often that I'm asked to dance, you see, but I would love to…that is, if you are still willing." Her large green eyes, so recently swimming in tears, were suddenly filled with the light of happy anticipation. There was a very real possibility she was going to dance.

Blackie had to ask himself how could it be possible that this bit of delightful femininity wasn't often asked to dance? Perhaps the little minx preferred playing it coy. No matter, he had dealt with every type of female, and was wise to all their games. However, he had to admit there was something different about this particular one, and he decided to accept the challenge. With a slightly crooked grin, he strode over to her side. "I'd be truly honored, Miss," Blackie replied, giving a small, polite bow from the hips. She really was breathtaking.

Reaching out, he took her delicate hand in his, and brought his partner to the center of the room. Under the bright overhead lights, she was even more ravishing than he had first thought. As the music began to play, he found there was more to this girl than just a pretty face; she was a surprisingly good dancer, as well. With no thought to their complicated movements, he twirled her effortlessly about the floor and discovered her to be practically weightless in his arms. It was as if she glided on the very air they breathed. Round and round the room they went, lost in the music and the sheer delight of each other's company. Neither one took notice of the disapproving stares from the young women standing along the wall; nor did they hear the harsh whispers as they swirled past the clusters of gossiping old women. For a few, idyllic moments, they were in a world of their own creation; each lost in a perfect daydream. As the last chords of the song began to dissipate, Blackie leaned over and whispered in Lily's ear, "You are the prettiest flower of them all…a rose of unspeakable beauty."

Immediately, he felt her go stiff in his arms.

Lily gasped and looked up into his face. "I am no such thing!"

So it had been a calculated ruse after all, she grumbled. She had allowed herself to believe this stranger's words were sincere. By lowering her defenses, she had let down her guard and surrendered to his gentle hands, as he expertly guided her around the dance floor. She had believed his smile to be genuine. It was quite evident to her now, however, everything had been a lie; a grand scheme to embarrass her in front of his friends, no doubt. Who knows what he would have done by the end of the evening, or what prank he would have dared carry off? Unaware of the boy's true identity, she could only assume he must have heard tales about her, and had decided to join his comrades in poking fun at the odd girl. It had been exceedingly foolish of her to place her faith in a stranger. As it turned out, he was like all the others, perhaps just a bit more clever than most by taking his time to gain her trust. Oh, why had she let herself hope for something so wonderful and unobtainable?

"That's a very hateful thing to say to me, sir," she snapped, angry at herself for being so easily taken in by a charming smile. "I had hoped you would be different, but I know better now. I am completely aware you were making a fine joke at my expense. But I must admit…you were a great deal smarter than most of your ilk."

Blackie tightened his grip on her arms; suddenly afraid she was going to flee. "*Hateful? Me?* I don't understand. Did I do something to offend you? It's a compliment I gave you, and I meant every word of it. All you have to do is look around us. I'm proud to be dancing with the most beautiful girl in the place, and I just said so."

Refusing to believe his flattering words, Lily shook her

head, while trying to disengage herself from his firm hold. "No. I don't believe that was your intent. You are like all the other boys in town...choosing to believe cruel things about my family and me. I no longer wish to dance, sir. Please take me back," she said, turning her face away.

"Sure...Fine!" he spit. "But first you're gonna tell me what it was I said. You owe me that much. I only spoke from my heart. I paid you no disrespect. Heck, maybe Charlie was right when he said you were all crazy," he grumbled.

"You speak of Charlie Masters, no doubt. Well, he would say such a horrible thing, and I am sorry to learn you are a friend of his. It doesn't speak well for you. I'll tell you this much, whoever you are...I am not a flower, a rose, nor am I a bloom of any kind. I'm not any of those ridiculous comparisons. I'm a woman —not a plant—and I want to go home!"

What had caused the girl to overreact in such an explosive way? Blackie had no idea, but she was acting totally irrational and he had to wonder why? Sadly, the rumors must be true. Perhaps insanity did run through their entire family. "Sure thing. I'll return you to your solitary spot against the column. Every *wallflower*—excuse me—every lonely spinster has one, I suppose. But let me say this one last thing...I really did want to dance with you. Whether you believe it or not, I had no motive other than getting a chance to talk with the prettiest girl here, and feel her in my arms as I led her across the floor. It was nice. If that's a crime, Lily, then arrest me, hang me, and bury me deep."

"You know my name?"

Blackie rolled his big, soulful, brown eyes. "Of course I know your name. What kind of goober do you think I am? Charlie told me who you are. I'm John Barker, by the way; but I prefer to be called Blackie." He held out his hand. "How do?"

Lily didn't know what to say. For the second time, in as many minutes, she was stunned. Had she been wrong about him? Feeling rather silly, and with a hefty portion of guilt thrown in for good measure, she felt her cheeks flush. What must he think of her? Perhaps his interest in her had been genuine after all—but it was too late, now. She had ruined everything by pushing him away and behaving in a most idiotic fashion; thereby validating all the absurd stories he had undoubtedly heard from Charlie, concerning all the Poseys.

Lily timidly held out her hand in response, praying it would be accepted, and placed it in his open palm. She smiled sheepishly. "Thank you, Blackie," she said softly; embarrassed by the way she had overreacted. This handsome stranger was obviously not from around these parts, and that fact filled her with hope. Maybe he had no preconceived ideas about her. "I don't know what came over me just now," she said sweetly, trying to cover her embarrassing faux pas. "I suppose you could say I am a bit oversensitive about my name, and all the jokes I've heard about my family because of it."

He raised an eyebrow. "Just a bit."

Lily bristled slightly. "You must believe me when I say my folks are the most wonderful people you can imagine; and yet people take great pleasure in ridiculing them and poking fun at us. They simply don't understand, and it makes our lives practically intolerable."

Blackie gently squeezed Lily's hand and led her over to a blanket-covered bale of straw. He sat, enthralled by her blushing beauty. "Sit down and tell me all about your amazing family, Lily. I'd like to try to understand, if I may," he said convincingly.

Lily's lovely face suddenly lit up, with her greens eyes sparkling with joy, and her pink cheeks glowing with sheer happiness. This was new, unexplored territory for her. No one had ever asked her to explain her lovable—if very eccentric—family. For most of her life, she had had to endure the snickers and cruel barbs aimed at her mother and father. People whispered behind her back and laughed outright, to her face. She and her siblings were never invited to parties, nor were any of them included in social gatherings. The unkind remarks had caused her oldest sister, Amaryllis, to run away in shame. Only a few months later, her second sister, Hyacinth, had chosen to leave town, as well.

"Well...where do I begin?" she giggled. "What would you like to know?"

"How about you start by introducing all of them to me. I don't even know your last name."

Lily dropped her gaze. Very quietly, suddenly feeling unsure of herself, she mumbled, "Posey."

"*Posey*, you say? That's not so bad. I was expecting something much worse," he chuckled. It was kind of a sissy name, but certainly nothing to cry about. Lots of good folks had funny surnames.

"I'm *Lily Posey*," she clarified. "See the problem?" The corners of her mouth drew down, creating a slight frown. "Now do you understand?"

Quite honestly, he did not. "Okay...well, I suppose being a man and all, I'd much prefer a common name like Smith or Jones, but Posey is no reason to hang one's head in shame."

Lily's heart sank further. If only that were true. "I'm afraid the name, Posey, is only the beginning of my humiliation," she grumbled, as she attempted to explain. "You see...my father's name is Forrest. I guess his parents were the first in the family to possess a quirky sense of humor. Later on, even the fates seemed to conspire against us, setting the stage to make us all a laughing stock. My father met the woman of his dreams and her name just happened to be Fern. Can you believe it? What are the chances of that? *Forrest and Fern Posey?* To make matters much, much worse, my father bought a little place on the edge of town...142 Orchard Lane."

Lily waited to see the first glimmer of absurdity appear across Blackie's face, but instead she saw just the slightest hint of a gentle and understanding smile. He looked as if he was finding her unfortunate plight only pleasantly amusing.

"You mustn't forget, Lily, they also live in *Garden City*," he snickered good-naturedly. "The Poseys live on Orchard Lane...in Garden City. I'd say that was too impossible to be a mere coincidence. I couldn't have dreamed of a more preposterous situation for you to find yourself in. Even you have to admit that's rich," he grinned.

"Don't be mistaken, Blackie. I adore my mother and father very much. No two better people have ever walked this earth, but they have a wicked sense of humor and their children have paid a harsh price for it. Perhaps things were different in their day, but this is a new century. In 1900, one is expected to fit in...not stand out from the rest of society. Unfortunately, we Poseys stand out in every way."

As she continued to explain, Blackie ceased to listen, content to watch her luscious lips form the words she spoke. Her eyes sparkled with keen intelligence, and the workings of her slender throat were captivating. It would be quite impossible for Lily not to stand out in a crowd, he thought. This exquisite flower of womanly charms would never be able to blend in with the ordinary peasants of Garden City. They were noxious weeds, compared to her. He continued to sit mesmerized, happily watching her speak.

"I have quite a few siblings—*a bumper crop*, my father would say. Perhaps if I list them for you, you will better understand our true dilemma. The firstborn is my sister, Amaryllis, soon followed by my sister, Hyacinth. Then the twins, Holly and Ivy were born...no Christmas jokes, please. We've heard them all. My father finally had his son and named him Forrest Ash Jr., naturally. We call him Bud. I eventually was added to this lovable bouquet of huckleberries."

Blackie feigned shock, falling back slightly and slapping his hand over his heart. "Easy there, Miss Posey. I do believe you just made a joke about your esteemed lineage."

Lily grinned. "Yes, I guess I did. It does sound rather funny when I put it all into words."

"So, you're the baby?" And what a beautiful baby she was, too, he thought to himself. Her hair shown like burnished gold and her eyes were as clear and as green as bottled glass. Now that she was no longer angry, her cheeks had softened to a pale shade of pink, set against a flawless porcelain complexion. Dimples bracketed each side of her mouth, so succulent; just perfect for kissing. He imagined he could stare at her for hours.

"Me, the baby? Oh, good gracious, no!" she chirped. "There's Poppy and Jasmine. Jas is the last...we hope. I feel it only proper to warn you, however; although my little sisters are small for their age, you must never underestimate their ability to create mischief. Trouble is their middle name. So as you can see, we Poseys are an incredibly fertile bunch of coconuts."

Blackie laughed. "Again with the jokes. Let it be perfectly clear, Miss Posey, that you said that...not I. But coconuts, you say? Mmmm, I do love it finely shredded and sprinkled on top of pie."

Lily giggled in spite of herself. She had spoken more words to this stranger, than she had to any other boy in her entire life, and she found she was actually having fun. He was amusing, and he didn't seem to judge her too harshly.

"That's quite a list, Lily. But I still don't see why people say you're—" *Oh, no.* Blackie closed his eyes and let out a long sigh. Why had he brought up the cruel rumors, when things were going so well? This young slip of a girl was sure to take offense at his unintentional blunder.

"Nuts?" she retorted. "Odd? Crazy? One egg short of a full dozen?"

"Yeah, something like that," he mumbled, feeling like a heel.

"That's not news to me; I told you from the very beginning. It comes as no surprise to any of us children, although I am not certain my parents are aware of the unkind things said about them. My siblings and I know very well what people say behind our backs. I try to give our accusers the courtesy of thinking they are simply ignorant and know no better. People oftentimes ridicule those whom they do not understand and are perhaps above them in intellect. However, intentional or not, their hurtful remarks cut deep. It is for that reason Amy and Cynthia left town. I miss them so much," she said sadly.

"Amy and Cynthia?" he asked. "Are they two more sisters?"

She shook her head. "No, I am sorry," she said. "I forget you do not know us. Amaryllis and Hyacinth are their given names, but we all prefer our pet names over the floral labels. Hence…Amy and Cynthia."

"I prefer pet names, too," he chuckled. "What do they call you? Lee Lee?"

"Very funny," she scoffed. "Much to my dismay, I'm just plain old Lily. It's not such a terrible name, I suppose. I could have been stuck with Daffodil, Petunia, or some such nonsense. My father's sister is Rosebriar. Can you imagine? Of course, a particular favorite of his is Narcissus. I only pray if there is another child, it is a boy."

Blackie smiled. By any name, this girl was truly wonderful and absolutely mouth-watering—definitely worth his time and effort to get to know and gain her trust. He wondered if she tasted of strawberries or peaches? "I think Lily is a rather nice name, and it fits you perfectly. Lilies are a lovely flower—tall, with slender stems, and move most graceful in the slightest breeze." He ran a finger across her wrist. "And so very delicate to the touch," he murmured.

Oh, my. Lily lowered her eyes and tried to silence her pounding heart. She was at a loss as to how to respond to Blackie's compliments, or the sensuous caress of her wrist. She had not received many kind words from those outside her own family—and certainly never from a boy—but here, on this night, she had been told she was pretty and had a lovely name, as well. And he had said she felt soft beneath his thumb.

"Thank you," she whispered, feeling her cheeks glow brightly beneath his intense gaze.

Blackie grinned, as he continued to hold her hand, making small, intimate circles with his thumb. It was an elegant hand, with long, tapered fingers as soft as anything he had ever held. He was suddenly overcome with the urge to press her palms to his mouth and lay hot kisses up and down her hands; but that would only cause her to run off screaming. Clearing his throat, he did his best to ignore the yearnings of his heart, and the subtle ache that was beginning to grow most noticeably to full measure, in the front of his trousers.

"Tell me about your parents, Lily," he said, trying to disregard the pulsing heat of his John Henry. "I know they must have an acute sense of humor to name all their children after plants, but what are they like every day? What does your father do, for instance?"

"My father is a very educated man…a horticulturist," she announced proudly. "That's a scientist of sorts, and he takes his research quite seriously. My dear mother paints lovely miniatures…but only of plants and animals…never human beings. I don't know why that is. She is quite accomplished in her own right. Many important people own her creations."

"I'd like to see them sometime," he hinted.

When no invitation was offered, Blackie took fate into his own hands. "Would it be acceptable to you and your family if I dropped by tomorrow…after church, of course?"

"Wh-what? You actually *want* to come to *my* house?" Lily squeaked.

Blackie chuckled. "Yeah. Is that so unusual?"

Lily couldn't believe her ears. "Well, as a matter of fact, it's extremely unusual. However, I see no reason why you cannot stop by…after church, naturally. Perhaps you would like to stay for Sunday dinner?"

"Heck, yeah! Er…I mean, thank you. I'm very grateful for the invitation, Lily." Blackie stood up carefully, allowing his jacket to conceal the obvious bulge in the front of his trousers, and bowed courteously, from the waist. His mother had taught him well. From out of the corner of his eye, he saw Charlie waving his hand, trying desperately to gain his notice.

"Don't look now, Blackie, but I believe your friend is trying to get your attention," Lily murmured. "I suppose I have kept you to myself, long enough. He probably wants to warn you away from me."

"Aw, don't be suspicious, Lily. Charlie's an all right sort of guy. He probably just wants to go home. He's not one for dancing, and it is getting pretty late."

Lily narrowed her gaze at Blackie's friend and stared pointedly, watching as he started to squirm under her intense glare. "Yes, I guess that must be it—he's tired of dancing." It was common knowledge that Charlie Masters was a bore. He couldn't dance and he couldn't make polite conversation. If there was anyone in town with a worse reputation than the Posey family, it would be Charlie Masters. Feeling charitable, she dropped her gaze and allowed the poor chap to relax.

Blackie started to back away. "I'll see you tomorrow afternoon. It's been real nice talking to you, Lily. Meeting you tonight may make this whole summer actually tolerable for me." He smiled his most engaging smile and gave her a flirtatious wink before turning and striding away.

Lily felt her heart leap in her chest, as she struggled to catch her breath. No boy had ever winked at her before. She could be wrong, but Blackie seemed to really like her...and she was convinced she really, really liked him.

After a few moments of silence, when it was obvious that Blackie was not going to offer up any information, Charlie spoke up. "Well? Tell me! Wasn't she exactly what I said she was? A real odd duck, ain't she? When she looks at me, I feel as if she's picking my brain."

"That would be slim pickins'," Blackie sneered. "Hardly worth her effort."

"Well, she gives me the willies, just the same."

Blackie frowned, showing his displeasure with his friend's comments. "You're a damn fool, Charlie. Lily is a nice girl, and I plan to see a lot more of her in the coming weeks. In fact, I've been invited to her house tomorrow, to share in her Sunday meal. I'm looking forward to meeting the whole family. Until tonight, I was wondering what I was going to do this summer, being stuck here, in this one horse town, with only the likes of you for company. But fate has smiled on me, brother. I believe I may have just stumbled upon the perfect bit of entertainment. She's beautiful and lonely for attention. With a bit of flattery, and a few well-chosen words; it'll be like taking candy from a baby."

Charlie grabbed his friend by the lapels, keeping his disbelieving gaze steady. "You're joshing," he exclaimed, as he waited for a sudden burst of laughter that never came. "My God, man...you're serious! You can't actually eat with them. Don't risk it, I tell ya. You'll never be the same if you start seein' those folks. Mr. Posey talks to plants, for gosh sakes, and Mrs. Posey sings to herself all day. They're all a little touched in the head, if you ask me."

"Enough!" Blackie growled. "I didn't ask you for your opinion. Besides, Lily isn't like that. I like her well enough. In fact, I wouldn't mind getting to know her a whole lot better. Did it ever occur to you that maybe the entire family is simply misunderstood?" More than a few families had a reputation for being a little odd—his own was no exception—and this girl didn't deserve being judged along with her peculiar family. "I'll not stand to hear you cast another disparaging remark against her or her folks. You read me, Charlie? If our friendship means anything to you, you'll shut your mouth about the Poseys. As I said, I believe Lily has been real lonely...and I have a cure for that." He smirked slightly, feeling uncomfortable in his trousers. "She will be mighty grateful to a guy who spouts pretty words in her ear. Get my meaning? Don't go and ruin everything by causing trouble."

Charlie saw the intense look in his friend's dark eyes and knew there was nothing more for him to say. Charlie snorted and relaxed his grip. "I see your mind is set. Go ahead, run off and have your fun, but don't say I didn't warn you," he said cryptically, just before he stomped away, grumbling to himself. After all this was over, how was he going to explain it to Blackie's parents?

CHAPTER TWO

Blackie strained to get comfortable, as he sat on the short bench just inside his aunt's entryway. He watched as the brass hands on the tall clock move torturously slow around its smiling face, mocking his wretchedness. His queasy stomach continued to churn violently; while his head pounded against his skull loud enough to cause his eyes to water…and he blamed his good old friend, Charlie Masters, for all his misery.

After leaving the dance, Blackie's friend had suggested the two of them stop by Marty Veneman's house for some real fun. It was an obvious attempt to make up for their earlier disagreement. Blackie didn't care one way or the other, as his thoughts were still on the lovely Lily, but it seemed important to Charlie; so he agreed to go along. He didn't know Marty very well, but Charlie was adamant they would have a good time.

Marty Veneman had no mother, and his father worked nights at the railroad yard. That left plenty of time for Marty to get into all sorts of trouble. And who knew Mr. Veneman made his own hooch in the basement? At any rate, it took no time at all for the three young men to find their way down to the cellar. Popping the cork to more than a few jugs, it wasn't long before everyone concerned had lost the ability to stand up straight or speak coherently. Minutes evolved into hours, and the dark indigo sky of midnight lightened to a pale shade of pink dawn. Had it not been for Mr. Veneman physically tossing the boys out the back door, who knows what time they would have returned home?

Blackie couldn't remember the long walk back to his Aunt Winona's house, but thankfully, his feet knew the way. Once he stumbled upon his room, and located his plump, soft bed, he gave into the blissful unconsciousness of the overly inebriated; making it absolutely impossible for his aunt to rouse him for church a few hours later. She had no choice but to accept her nephew's abject grunts and groans as a sign of serious illness, and allowed him to sleep.

Hearing the big clock chime eleven, Blackie realized if he were to see Lily this day, he had to force himself to crawl out of bed and prepare to go to the Posey house. Unfortunately, to his sheer dismay, he discovered the simple act of keeping his head erect was a herculean feat, and straightening his spine was utterly impossible. His eyes were bleary and his tongue felt like an old woolen sock. Holding his stomach tightly, he moaned in great agony. Why had he let Charlie talk him into drinking himself into a drunken stupor—and on the night before he was to dine with Lily's family? Of all the stupid, lame-brained... Now there was nothing he could do but wait for church to let out and hopefully, make his way to 142 Orchard Lane and have lunch with Lily. By God, he would do it, too—even if it should prove to be the very last thing he did in his lifetime; for it was surely going to be the death of him.

"Dear God," Blackie shivered. How was he ever going to manage to keep food down, when the mere thought of it had him running for the toilet? In a vain attempt to appear sober, he ran his fingers through his wet hair and down over his face. A quick shower had done little to improve his condition. He cupped his hand over his open mouth and sniffed his breath. Grimacing at the sour odor, he figured it wise to keep his distance from others, in order to avoid offending anyone, and it was imperative he keep this most recent sin a secret from Lily. He could only wonder what she would think if she had seen the man he was when he fell out of bed this morning. A more dissipated, slovenly, poor excuse for a man, there never was. Right then and there, Blackie swore to never imbibe in alcohol again. He would stick to lemonade.

As the clock finally rang out twelve times, he jumped to his feet, but had to pause for several minutes to allow the room to stop its spinning. That was progress, he thought. Not too bad for a night of total debauchery. Standing up straight, Blackie threw back his shoulders and headed toward the door—then quickly spun around on his heels and ran for the water closet. It promised to be a very long day.

It was nearly one o'clock before Blackie found himself standing in front of Miss Lily Posey's house. The warm sun on his face had done much to ease his various ailments, and he found he was actually looking forward to seeing her again. As he stood just outside the white picket fence, gazing across the wide expanse of freshly mown lawn—green as the Emerald Isle—he breathed a sigh of relief. No doubt, it made for an attractive picture, but he discovered he was slightly disappointed, nonetheless. It was not at all what he had expected. It was a nice, rather ordinary looking house, with not a bloom or a blossom in sight. There were no grandiose statues or shiny-mirrored gazing balls dotting the lawn. Only a simple cupid's fountain, spewing a single stream of water high into the air, greeted the rare visitor. A plain white, wicker swing hung invitingly, from the porch rafters. Of course, the house itself, was painted a cheerful blue—robin's egg, to be precise; and it sported pink and white striped awnings above each window—of which there were many. The roof was highly pitched and there was an interesting weathervane fixed atop the corner turret. What it was exactly, he could not discern. He would have to ask Lily about it, later. Taking a deep breath, he opened the gate and walked through.

There was no way that Blackie could have known about the magnificent gardens in the rear of the house. Several acres of carefully tended plants, row upon row, spread out over the fertile ground. There were also, many "fancies", as Mrs. Posey was fond of calling them. Located across the sprawling green were several fishponds and hammocks, strung between low-slung trees; a carved marble folly, looking as if it were designed by Socrates himself, stood in the farthest corner, and a long pergola, so heavily draped in exotic blooms it bent from the weight, extended the full length of the house. Naturally, there was a large greenhouse in the center of the space, filled with the strangest and most remarkable plants. It was here, in this mysterious, humid glasshouse, where Mr. Posey spent most of his time, studying who knows what.

Sensing there would be no unpleasant surprises, Blackie drew a deep breath and began to relax, as he passed beneath a large sycamore. It was then he felt something land in his hair and tumble down the back of his collar. It tickled, as it wheedled its way down the inside of his shirt. Immediately, he was forced to swat at another unseen pest, as it grazed his cheek, only to scatter in the breeze. "What the heck?" he muttered, looking all around him. Hopefully, he hadn't disturbed an invisible spider web, but at this time of year...well one couldn't be too careful. Hating and despising spiders of any kind, he instinctively brushed the front of his jacket and shook out his hair for good measure.

Resisting the urge to run back to the safety of the wide-open street, Blackie rushed up to the front porch. Just as he placed his boot on the first step, he paused to listen...was that giggling he heard? He held his breath and listened for the sound to repeat—but nothing. It must have been his imagination, he thought—or perhaps it was simply the after effects of bad hooch from the night before.

Stiffening his spine, Blackie raised his hand to knock. However, before he could strike one time, the massive oak door flew open, nearly knocking him down.

"There you are—finally!" Lily exclaimed excitedly, as she quickly yanked him inside. "You're late," she whispered. "I had a devil of a time delaying things. You really should be more punctual, you know. Come into the dining room and meet the family. They're all starving. Are you hungry? I certainly hope so. Our cook is a wonder. Do I talk too much? I'm afraid it's a bad habit of mine, but I only do it when I'm extremely nervous—

which is fairly often. Do I?"

"Well, I...er...I mean—"

Lily laughed. "Oh, never mind. But you will have to speak up if you want to say anything around here. My constant, nervous chattering is a quality I share with the rest of my family...all except Father. It's the only way anyone can be heard. If you don't believe me, you'll see for yourself, soon enough. You didn't happen to spy two little scamps out in the front yard, did you? My two youngest sisters are missing. They're always up to some kind of mischief—but nothing to worry about, I suspect. They will most assuredly be in their seats when the food makes its way to the table. I hope you like roast beef. What am I saying? Everyone likes roast beef and gravy. But I don't know about the nasturtiums...oh, well, it's too late now, I suppose." She gave him a little shove, as Blackie was moving too slowly through the foyer to suit her, causing him to stumble slightly. "Go on, Blackie. You've nothing to fear from us. Honest. It's only my family...and they're not going to *eat* you."

Blackie could have said that was plenty of reason to be concerned, but Lily kept on chattering, nonstop—*and why was she doing it so loudly,* he wondered? Had the beautiful girl been so talkative last evening, or was he simply too enamored of her charms to notice? He didn't think so—but still...

Unfortunately, his ears were now beginning to ring, triggering his queasiness—and all this was in addition to a splitting head. If God were truly merciful, this little assemblage would be silent during the meal today; otherwise there was no guarantee he would be able to make it through this ordeal. Blackie closed his eyes in an effort to fortify himself. He hated to admit it, but there might have been a speck of wisdom in Charlie's ominous warnings after all, for this day certainly had all the portents of a monumental mistake.

Finally, Lily stopped under an immense Victorian archway, richly festooned in vines, carved gingerbread, and fringed swags. It opened into an enormous formal dining room with not one, but two, gilded chandeliers suspended over the long table.

Lily stood there beaming, her arm placed possessively through her young gentleman caller's arm. Clearing her throat, she announced, "Everyone! I beg your attention, if you please. I would like for you to meet a new friend of mine...Mr. Blackie Barker. I met him last evening, at the dance. We *actually* danced," she gushed. "He kindly accepted my invitation to share our Sunday dinner. He will be our guest today. I know you will welcome him most graciously."

With her back straight and her head held high, Lily and her beau glided casually, arm in arm, to the far end of the table. Lily's presentation was flawless; it was almost as if she brought a young man home to meet the family, every Sunday.

"You will sit there, Blackie," she instructed, in her most refined voice, "and I will sit across from you. It will make it easier to discuss the events of the day...*and you will be far enough away from my annoying little sisters to actually enjoy your meal*," she whispered aside.

Before Blackie had time to respond, a tall, distinguished looking man entered the room and took his chair at the head of the table. He was meticulous in appearance; with a perfectly trimmed mustache perched on his upper lip, and thick, silver hair combed with precision, he cut quite a figure. Apart from that, there was nothing so very unusual about him. The man could be any ordinary professor or even a prosperous banker, if judged by his attention to dress and demeanor. He didn't appear to be dangerous or overly eccentric. He wasn't twitching, rolling his eyes, or chewing his tongue. Blackie had an old maiden aunt who did that, but she had to be locked away for her own safety. No, there was definitely nothing that would sound an alarm. However, as Blackie would soon learn, appearances can be deceiving.

Never glancing at the people seated around the table, the man declared in a rich baritone, "Two are missing, Mother. Have you an explanation?"

"Oh, well...let me see. I believe I saw them in church, Father," she murmured.

Suddenly, two lively little sprites danced into the dining room, giggling and sprinkling colored leaves all over the rug. They ran one complete circle around the table, in opposite directions, before settling into their own assigned chairs. Oddly enough, no one seemed to think his behavior was the least bit out of the ordinary.

"At long last, we are all here, and can now have our supper," Mr. Posey proclaimed, as he picked up a small silver bell and rang for the food to be brought in. The man still hadn't made eye contact with anyone. His concentration was solely on the fold of his napkin.

"Father," Mrs. Posey said, addressing her husband. "You may have noticed we have a guest for dinner. A friend of Lily's." She turned her head and looked directly at Blackie. He was a very handsome young man, she thought, in spite of his sickly pallor.

"Blackie is a very unusual name," she commented. "I had a kitten named Blackie...or was it Whitey? I can never remember such things. What a bother. Do tell me, whatever were your parents thinking? Are you from around here? But of course you are not; otherwise I would have known, wouldn't I? Where are you from...if you don't mind me asking?"

Blackie cleared his throat. So many questions. "Well—"

Mrs. Posey continued. "Do you like our small town, Blackie? Have you seen all of it? Pretty, isn't it? I fell in love with Garden City at first sight. How did you say you met our daughter? At the dance was it? I wasn't aware she danced. The things a child keeps from her parents. My husband does not dance. Mr. Posey, is a horticulturist, you know. He is a very fine man, but works entirely too hard, and I paint miniatures—flowers, mostly—sometimes birds or cats. Perhaps you have seen some of them? They are quite popular around these parts. We're having roast beef for dinner. I hope you approve. But then what red-blooded boy doesn't like his beef? You don't say much, do you?"

"Well...I—"

"Do you realize you have dandelion blooms on your person, Blackie? One down your collar and one resting on your shoulder, I believe. If I'm not mistaken, there's something in your hair as well. Were you by chance playing with my girls?" she inquired.

The slightest sound of two little girls snickering came from the younger Posey children, as their bright eyes glistened with outright mischief. The one with the carrot colored braids, slyly tucked what was left of a bedraggled dandelion bouquet underneath her bottom, as Blackie hastily ran his fingers over his shoulders and through his hair. The young culprits must have been perched high up in the tree he had been standing beneath. Recognizing their ornery grins as a challenge, he smiled, accepting their unspoken dare. If it took him all summer, he swore he would get even with those two pesky little rascals.

"It is quite a coincidence that you appreciate flowers, Mr. Blackie. Of course, dandelions are considered a weed. We are rather partial to anything that blooms, however, as you probably can ascertain. Oh good! Here's our Flori now," Mrs. Posey exclaimed. "We have a guest, Flori. He likes roast beef."

All eyes shifted from Mrs. Posey to the swinging door separating the kitchen from the dining room—and Blackie took the opportunity to draw in a deep breath. Lily's mother hadn't stopped talking long enough to breathe. How on earth was the woman capable of doing that? Just listening to her had made him breathless. He bet she would be a terrific swimmer, though. She would never have to come up for air.

At first glance, it appeared as if an enormous tray of roast beef floated into the large room all on its own, so tiny was the woman carrying it. She was hardly five feet tall and her weight so slight she could be in danger of being carried off in a stiff wind. Her snow-white hair was caught up on top of her head in a great bun, allowing feathery soft wisps to curl around her pink apple cheeks. Twinkling blue eyes danced in her merry face. Blackie couldn't help but smile.

"It's aboot time you rang the bell, Mr. Posey. Ah dinnae ken the meat will be fit for the eatin'. Ye said ah should serve the dinner at one o'clock, straight up. It's nigh onto two," she scolded, as she plunked the tray down hard on the table, right in front of the master of the house. "Ye can serve it up, yerself. I'll not be takin the blame for it tastin' like an ole leather shoe," she announced, as she spun around and stomped off, returning to her domain.

Blackie waited for the yelling to commence. Surely, this little woman would not be allowed to address Mr. Posey in such a disrespectful manner. His Aunt Winona would have reprimanded her and sent her on her way without a word of recommendation. But as he would soon learn, this was not his aunt's house, nor did the Posey family carry on their daily lives in the usual sense.

"Flori outdid herself today, Father," Mrs. Posey declared. "The beef is cooked superbly, just the way you like it, dear."

He grunted, as he picked up the carving knife. "I can see that for myself, can't I? Floribunda knows her away around the kitchen and never fails to do things properly. Where's the horseradish?" he shouted.

Immediately, the little woman returned, carrying another tray bearing a bowl of hot, buttery mashed potatoes and a platter of green beans with flowers sprinkled over the top. In fact, there were green leaves, flower petals, and other such unusual toppings present on every bowl on the table.

Lily saw Blackie's confusion. She leaned forward and whispered, "Don't worry. They're all edible…and most are delicious. The nasturtiums are particularly nice. Spicy, you know. Go ahead. Eat one," she coaxed.

"Nas-nas—"

"Na-stur-tiums," she stated distinctly, as if he was a small child. "My father is working on a new variety and we are currently seeing a lot of them used in our cooking. It's common for us to consume Father's experiments," she added, as a matter of fact.

"*Experiments?*" he croaked.

"Relax," Lily giggled. "We're not going to poison you; but if we wanted to…well, you'd never see it coming. Colorful blooms, or distinctive leaves, disguise the most lethal poisons. They can appear totally harmless and leave no trace in the bloodstream. It would be the perfect murder."

Suddenly, Blackie didn't feel so well. His head was beginning to spin and his collar was entirely too tight. He felt his upper lip begin to perspire. When the little cook leaned over and whispered in his ear, advising him not to eat the beef, he knew he was going to be sick. Without warning, or a single word of explanation, Blackie pushed back his chair and bolted for the door, keeping his hand held tightly over his mouth. He could hear Lily calling after him, but there was no time to look back. He needed air.

"Blackie?" Lily called out, sounding confused and rejected. What had caused him to run away, she wondered? Was it something she said? Lily looked across the table at her dear family and saw nothing unusual. Suddenly her eyes filled with tears, as the realization of what had just happened dawned on her. It must be true. All the mean and cruel accusations; all the hateful gossip she had had to endure while growing up, being different; it all must be true. She and her family were every bit as strange as everyone claimed them to be. By simply being themselves, they had scared away her first potential beau. *What was wrong with them?* She was too close to the problem to see it.

Jasmine and Poppy continued to giggle, while Mr. Posey remained oblivious to the entire scene that had just played out in his own dining room. The twins, Holly and Ivy, sat looking at one another, commiserating in their odd, wordless language. They knew what it was like to be a Posey, and it was time for Lily to understand that, too.

Only Mrs. Posey reached across the table to comfort her daughter. "There, there, my dear. Don't get yourself overly upset. If he is as nice a young gentleman as you think he is, he'll be back for you. I could see goodness in his eyes. They're such a soft, warm brown. In a way, they remind me very much of our old dog, Samson. Do you remember him, dear? There was no finer dog than he...even if he did piddle in the house on occasion.

He was brave and loyal and willing to lay down his life for you. He fought that snake most admirably. Sadly, it cost him his life… but you were saved in the end. Remember, dear? I could see that same kind of devotion in the eyes of your young man. Give him time to adjust, dear. He's at a vulnerable age."

"Oh, Mother," Lily cried. "I do like him very much, and I want him to like us. Are we really so peculiar?"

Mrs. Posey glanced toward her husband. "Yes and no, Lily. Your father has seen many terrible things in his lifetime. The daily hardships we must endure affect us all differently, I suppose. We Poseys are unlike anyone else in this town…that is for certain, but you can be proud of your family, too. Someday you'll understand. In the meanwhile, you must hold your head high, accept that you are a Posey, and believe yourself to be quite special."

"Yes, Mother," Lily mumbled, still not wholly convinced. "But what was it that made Blackie bolt?"

"Well…" Flori hesitated, as she approached the table. It had been impossible for her not to see the man run from the room, one hand across his mouth and the other held tightly against his belly. "Ah cannae say for sure, but it might be what ah said aboot the beef. Ah told him nae to eat it. How did ah ken he would be so dafty to run away? He may be a braw laddie, but he is nae too brave."

"Oh, Flori, how could you? Why would you caution him about eating the meat? It's perfectly fine!" Lily shouted, as she slid back her chair, jumping to her feet. "He probably thought we were going to poison him! You saw the look on his face when he saw all the flower blossoms. His mind was already questioning the good sense in coming here for dinner. Then you warn him about the roast? What was he to think?"

The old woman stood her ground, placing her fists on her bony hips. "Ah dinnae think he would take me seriously, *Miss Lily*. It was only me way of apologizin' for the overcooked beef. Ah'll nae have him think it was me own fault it be as tough as shoe leather."

"If I don't ever see him again, I don't think I'll be able forgive you, Flori," Lily threatened.

"And ye'll nae be a speakin' to me in that tone of voice, lassie. Ah was there the day ye were laid in yer mother's arms... and a wee, bonnie babe ye was, too. Ah'll nae stand for ye to shout at me, now." The old woman splashed the water pitcher down on the table and stormed off into the kitchen.

Lily's mother looked directly at her daughter, peering through the enormous hydrangea centerpiece she had placed in the center of the long table. "Of course, you realize you will have to apologize to Flori," Mrs. Posey said softly. "I imagine she's in there now, crying over the custard. She meant no harm, dear. It's only her way."

Lily wiped the tears from her cheeks and returned to her seat. "I know...and I will, but she's made such a muddle of everything."

"If you all don't mind...can we eat now? The nasturtiums are beginning to wilt." Mr. Posey bellowed, as he reached for the horseradish sauce. "I assume all the female histrionics have been played out? If I live to be one hundred, I'll never understand the workings of a woman's mind—no, not ever. Women should try to be more like men. Take your brother, Bud, for instance. He hasn't said a word—not one word. A man has better things to do than to cry over a little overdone meat."

"Papa," snickered Poppy, as she twirled a single orange braid over her potatoes. "Bud's not here. He's upstairs with the sniffles."

Mr. Posey looked up for the first time since taking his seat and searched the faces of those present around the table. "I see," he stated, after several moments of thoughtful consideration. "Didn't we have a dinner guest...a friend of Lily's?"

"Oh, Papa," Jasmine said, rolling her eyes dramatically. "He left *hours* ago."

Forrest Posey sat for a moment, looking rather nonplussed by the sudden revelations. After all, he couldn't be bothered with the comings and goings of any stray beau that may find his way to their Sunday dinner table. His wife could very well take care of that nonsense. "Very well. No harm done. Everything's back to normal now," he announced. "Let's proceed with our magnificent roast beef. A calm, quiet atmosphere is good for the digestion…as well as the healthful consumption of nasturtiums. Now eat up, children."

Having lost her appetite, Lily quietly picked up her fork and stared at the juicy, pink meat dangling from it. She'd had such high hopes for the day, but now those hopes were all dashed and discarded as so much useless fantasy. There was nothing to be done about it. She glanced across the table at her two older sisters and sighed. Hadn't Holly or Ivy ever once in their lives yearned to be like everyone else? Didn't they long to know how delicious it felt to be held in the arms of a handsome man as he twirled you across a dance floor? No, they had not. Neither of them saw any reason to leave the security of their home. They had each other and that seemed to be enough for them—but it wasn't enough for her!

Lily placed the meat in her mouth and chewed with determination. As quickly as she swallowed, she refilled her fork. This dinner may not have gone as planned, but she wasn't about to give up on the very best thing that ever happened to her. Blackie was worth fighting for. If she got hurt and knocked down in the process—she would jump up and go back for more. She was Lily Posey, and as everyone knew, lilies, although appearing quite delicate, were known to be an extremely hardy flower. With every bite, she could feel her resolve strengthen. Her plate was soon cleaned and she asked for second helpings. She told herself she was getting ready for battle and would need all her strength.

"What's for dessert?" she shouted.

CHAPTER THREE

"I figure I was lucky to get out of there with my life," Blackie exclaimed, as he shoveled the simple, but delicious tasting stew past his lips. He slathered a thick slice of bread with plenty of sweet, creamy butter and stuffed the entire thing into his mouth. "Poisonous flowers," he repeated, before swallowing. "On everything!"

Charlie sat back with the smug look of satisfaction on his face. "Didn't I tell ya? They're mighty queer folks—them Poseys. Everybody says so. I hear tell their own two daughters up and left without a word to anyone. I'll wager their bodies can be found buried under the cellar floor."

"Don't be ridiculous," Blackie muttered, as he wiped his lips on the back of his sleeve. "They don't murder their own—only strangers, I'm thinking. They have a Scottish cook that has the eye of the devil in her. She pretends to be tiny and helpless; all the while she's conjuring up mouth-watering dishes filled with poisonous flowers. I'm surprised Lily played a part in all of this, though. She tried to convince me the flowers were edible; but I didn't see her eat one. Her two little sisters sat there, all the while giggling and snickering; just waiting for me to take a bite and keel over. I just don't understand it. Lily seemed so sweet and innocent. I thought she truly liked me." He rubbed his distended stomach.

"Guess not," his friend chuckled. "I guess that smile of yours only goes so far with the ladies."

"I don't know...she sure seemed to take to me. And

she's so damn pretty. It almost takes my breath away."

"Sure it ain't the poison?"

Blackie snorted at his friend's lame attempt at a joke. "You can laugh, but I'm telling you there's not another girl in all of Garden City that can come close to her…hell, not even back home. Without Lily Posey, this promises to be a very long and boring summer, my friend," he grumbled.

"There's always fishin' and swimmin' in the river.

Blackie sat back with his jaw hanging open. He couldn't believe what his friend had suggested. To compare swimming and fishing with courting a girl as lovely as Lily, was pure laughable. "Do you have rocks in your head?" he asked in utter disbelief. "I can do that at home."

"Well, there's always the old Windsor Hotel."

Blackie rolled his eyes. "What's so special about that place? It looks as if it's seen better days."

"It's kind of a museum. Buffalo Bill Cody stayed there, once. His entire show came to town. They got some souvenirs he signed, and some other things they left behind when they took off. You can see 'em for yourself."

"And when was that?" Blackie snorted. "Way back in *1880?*"

Charlie's cheeks reddened. "Pertinear. It was around 1883, I think."

Blackie groaned. "Good God. If I'd wanted a history lesson, I would have stayed home."

Charlie shrugged his shoulders. "Well, there's always Marty's father's liquor."

"Yeah, I suppose…but a fuzzy head and a queasy stomach sure seems to be a poor substitute for what I had planned with Lily Posey."

"Give it time. You'll get over her. The Posey's are a lost cause. To understand them, you'd have to be one of 'em."

Blackie's large brown eyes widened. He had an idea. "That's it! I'll pretend to be one of them and learn all their secrets. Meanwhile, if I can just get Lily alone—"

Charlie let out with a huge laugh. "I know what you'll do then, boy," he said admiringly. He had never been with a girl, not in *that* way, but he had heard tales of Blackie's exploits. Back home, Blackie was reported to be a veritable Casanova. "She'll never see you comin', boy. Just promise me you won't eat nothin' while in that house."

Blackie was starting to feel better, as his plan began to take shape. "Food is the last thing I have on my mind, Charlie. This may not be such a lost summer, after all. There's a mystery here, Charlie, and a pretty girl to help me solve it. In fact, I think I'll drop around tomorrow morning and apologize for today's hasty departure. I'll tell them I was sick." It wasn't too far from the truth. "Hopefully, I can convince them I have an interest in those stupid flowers...those...nasty turims, I think they're called."

Charlie rolled his eyes. "That doesn't sound right to me. You'd better ask your aunt. She might know what they're called. You come by afterwards and let me know what you've found out—and don't forget to check the cellar floor!"

The sound of the skylark's comforting melody was beginning to die away, as twilight approached, and birds returned to their nests. Day was coming to a close. Lily had been sitting in the swing on the front porch, ever since stuffing herself at dinner. It was so unlike Lily to carry on this way, filling her face with food; but she had seemed so determined to consume every morsel left on every platter.

"It's time to come inside dear, out of the evening air," Mrs. Posey said softly. She was worried her daughter may be coming down with something. "It's getting much too cool and you forgot your shawl. I shan't call the doctor if you get the sniffles," her mother warned.

"You called him for Bud," Lily grumbled. It wasn't fair that the doctor would not be called for her. But that was immaterial, as she never got the sniffles and she didn't feel the chill. Her blood was boiling, in fact, and her flesh was warm to the touch. Blackie had been just plain rude, she decided. Her family had done nothing but open their home to him and offer him a delicious meal.

"Lily?" her mother repeated.

"Just a minute!" she snapped, a bit too disrespectfully, but she simply needed to be left alone with her thoughts. It was imperative she be allowed to sort out her feelings. There was a battle to be fought. Her heart warred with her head. It tried to convince her she was wrong about him; the boy was not rude, only skittish. She could understand that reaction. Her family were all strangers to him, and her father could be most intimidating. Yet, why had she received no word of explanation or note of regret? The boy had had more than ample time to compose a short letter and have it delivered. No—he was rude and thoughtless and she was better off knowing that now, rather than later.

Her mother quietly went back inside and closed the door.

As Lily stood up to go in, she paused briefly, to gaze out over the porch railing and beyond the wooden gate. Looking down the street toward the sugar beet factory, she watched as the moon rose up behind the feed store, casting its silvery light over the rooftops, just as the first star of evening shone brightly overhead. As twilight gave way to darkness, the resident barn owl greeted the night in his usual way, "Whoo. Who-whoo." Everything seemed as it should; as it had always been; completely unchanged—but not so with Lily. Since looking into his dark eyes, she had been awakened to thoughts of what might be possible, and she knew without a doubt, her life would be forever altered.

As the stars began to fill the night sky, Lily couldn't help asking the man in the moon, "If I'm better off without him…why do I feel so miserable?" Even though she told herself all was not lost, she couldn't help but feel like crying.

"The heart knows what it wants," her father said simply, as he rounded the house with a spade in his hand. "There's no explaining it, daughter. I felt it for your mother and there was nothing to do about it, but wait."

"Wait?" Lily had never before heard her father speak of love, or how he had met her mother and fell in love.

He pushed his hat back from his forehead and rested his weight on the handle of the spade. His eyes seemed to glaze over, as his thoughts drifted back to a time, long ago. "I met your mother during the war. She was a pretty little thing, much like you, and she quite stole my breath away. She was also much younger than I and far too innocent to be exposed to such cruelty and suffering. I worried about that, but she insisted. Throughout the conflict, I kept my eye on her; in part to keep her safe, and in part to rest my weary eyes upon something as lovely as a rose."

"Was it love at first sight, Father?" she asked, as her romantic imagination conjured up the image of her father, a handsome young soldier courting her beautiful young mother.

"It was for me, but I doubt your mother would say the same. I shouted at her quite often; gave her orders and threatened to have her dismissed…on a daily basis, I might add."

"That doesn't sound like you, Father. I've never heard you raise your voice in anger. Besides, I thought you said you loved her from the first moment you laid eyes on her."

"I did. But you'll soon learn a man will say and do many things he doesn't mean, to keep those he loves safe from harm…even if that causes them to despise him. It was a time of war, Lily, and I wanted your mother far removed from the battle scene."

Lily was never told how her parents met. This was all news to her. "Were you a soldier in the war?" she asked. "Did you…did you kill anyone?" The possibility of that was too horrible to contemplate. Father was a pacifist. He even preferred picking off the harmful beetles and caterpillars and transferring them to the meadow, rather than using poisonous dustings.

"Yes, I did," he grumbled, as he picked up the spade. "Now listen to your mother and go inside, child. We can't have you getting sick." He turned and strode quickly to the potting shed. The impromptu conversation was over.

That evening as her mother relaxed in her chair beside the table, with the jar of brushes and tiny pots of paints scattered about it, Lily decided to seek clarification of the earlier conversation she'd had with her father.

She picked up a small brush and dipped it in a pot of bright, periwinkle paint. As she mindlessly began to doodle around the border of a small plate, she subtly began her inquiry. "I was talking with Father this evening. He told me the most interesting story. He told me all about how the two of you met… during the war."

Fern Posey gasped; a look of surprise and shock clearly displayed on her face. Her hand trembled slightly, as she replaced her own brush on the tray and put the tiny bit of porcelain back on the table. "Forrest spoke to you about the war?" She couldn't believe it. Neither of them ever discussed those years—never!

Lily smiled and nodded. "Oh, but he did though. He said it was love at first sight, for him. Tell me, Mother…was he incredibly handsome? Naturally, I have always thought he was, but that is most common among doting daughters. Did you think so, too? Did you fall in love with him instantly?"

Her mother's eyes teared up, as she searched for the proper response. "We…we don't speak of those early years, Lily. It was a bad time."

"Yes, I know all about the war, but—"

Fern turned on her daughter. "You know nothing of war, young lady, and I pray to God you never shall!" She stood up and quickly gathered her things. "I'm going to my room, now. We will not discuss this ever again. Suffice to say I married your father and we have had a wonderful life together. I believe that should satisfy even your inordinate sense of curiosity, young lady." The woman whirled around, leaving her daughter stunned and speechless.

"What happened?" Lily mumbled. Twice in one day, she had been left; abandoned in her own home because of something she apparently had said. It was becoming a disturbing pattern—one that required solving. Just what was it that made her mother react in such a peculiar fashion? Perhaps her father could shed some light on this mystery. But she wouldn't think about it now. Her head was beginning to ache and it was nearly time for bed. Hopefully, she wouldn't dream about Blackie or the blasted Civil War. Neither was very comforting at this moment in time.

As she passed the room her parents shared, she could swear she heard the soft, muffled cries of her mother. Not since her sister Amaryllis left home, had she heard that heart-wrenching sound. Her mother was a cheerful, happy person. A smile was always on her face. However, tonight, and all because of her infernal nosiness, her mother was sobbing in the solitude of her room. Lily had to try to make amends.

"Mama?" she whispered softly, through the door. "May I come in?"

It was several minutes before the door opened. Standing there, with her long braid hanging down her back, Fern tried smiling at her daughter. She was embarrassed by her daughter's concern and dreaded the inevitable questions that were sure to follow.

"Mama, are you all right?" Lily could see the telltale signs of tears, as they had flowed unrestricted down her mother's cheeks. "I didn't mean for my prying to cause you pain. Forgive me, Mama."

"No, my dear girl. You are quite blameless. It is only when I remember back all those years, to the final days of the war, that I find it too painful to withstand. You can't imagine the horrors, Lily. That's why I snapped at you when you said you understood war. The truth is…you don't. And I'm glad for it. There will never be another war as horrible as that one."

Lily stepped up to her mother and placed a kiss on her damp cheek. "You're right, Mama. I don't know anything about war, and I do not wish to be the one responsible for causing you to relive it. I only meant to ask about you and Father."

Fern smiled, a small half-grin. "Could this sudden interest in how we met be because of a certain young gentleman?"

Lily felt her cheeks blush. "I really like Blackie, but I don't know if I'll ever see him again. The way he ran from here..."

"He'll be back, dear. That young man doesn't seem the type to shy away from a stiff challenge. I imagine he goes after what he wants."

"I hope so...and I hope I am the one he wants. Only time will tell, I suppose."

Fern Posey took a deep, cleansing breath. Her histrionics were over and she was feeling her old self, once again. Seeing the hope in her daughter's eyes, set her on a different path. She would have sweet dreams tonight, and then tomorrow she would set out to see what could be done about Lily and Blackie.

"Good night, Daughter," she said. "Don't let the bedbugs bite."

Lily giggled. "We've never had bedbugs, Mama. I'm not sure they even exist."

Fern shivered. "Oh, they exist all right," she said, briskly rubbing her arms. "Good night, Lily."

"Good night, Mama."

By the time Lily made her way down to breakfast, her entire family had already gathered around the table. Upon her entering the room, they immediately ceased their enthusiastic chattering and looked up at her, staring wide-eyed, like statues. No one made a move or uttered a single word.

"What is it?" she asked. Her family was acting very queer—even for them.

The two youngest girls started to giggle, while Ivy and Holly exchanged knowing glances. Bud snickered and avoided looking directly at his sister.

"Is someone going to tell me what is going on? Do I have something on my face?"

"Take your seat, Lily," her mother directed. "Eat a nutritious breakfast and then you and I are going on a little errand."

An errand. At this time of the day? Her mother very seldom ever left the house, and absolutely never departed before noon. Even her father was smiling, as he pressed a particularly lovely blossom in his journal. Something was brewing, and she wasn't at all sure she wanted to find out what it was. There had already been enough drama in her usually, predictable life and there was no need to add more to it.

Lily's stomach tightened with the feeling of impending doom. What had she done? How was she expected to eat a hearty breakfast when the threat of the unknown was hanging over her head? "I...I don't feel very well, Mother," she muttered. "I think I'll return to my room and come down for lunch."

"Nonsense," Fern Posey exclaimed. "You'll be feeling right as rain, once we complete our morning task."

"Show her the note, Mama," Poppy urged, just before Jasmine gave her a kick under the table.

"Ow! Stop that!" she cried. "Mama...Jasmine kicked me."

Her sister's eyes grew enormous with scalding indignation. "But she wasn't s'posed to say anything. You told us not to tell, Mama," Jasmine whined.

Poppy quickly gave her pouting sister a hard pinch on the arm, and was promptly rewarded with a dollop of strawberry preserves in her carrot-colored hair. War had been declared.

"Girls!" their mother scolded. "You will each apologize to the other and then you will remove yourselves from this table. Carry your plates out into the kitchen and finish your breakfast there. You know how squabbling annoys your father. It disturbs his digestion. Go now and apologize."

"Yes, Mama," grumbled Poppy.

"See what you did?" accused Jasmine. "I'm not playing with you for the rest of the day."

"I don't care," whimpered Poppy.

The two little girls continued arguing until they were well out of hearing range and hidden behind the closed kitchen door. Flori would take them in hand and put them to work. It would be almost noon before they would be free to terrorize anyone.

"What did Poppy mean, Mother?" Lily asked. Her sister's intriguing comment only added to the mystery of what they were planning to do. "She mentioned a note."

Her mother blushed, as she wiped a nonexistent crumb from her bosom. "She wasn't supposed to say anything. I didn't want you to learn about it until we were well on our way." She fumbled in her skirt pocket and pulled out a sheet of paper, folded neatly and precisely. She handed it to Bud. "Pass this down, son."

Bud passed it to Ivy, who proceeded to pass it to Holly, who then reached across the table and handed it to Lily. She smiled sweetly. "Don't fret, Lily," she murmured low.

Lily noticed her fingers were trembling as she took the paper in hand. A bold, masculine stroke met her inquisitive eye. She glanced to the bottom of the page and saw that it was signed, *Blackie*. Her heart threatened to burst from her chest, as her eyes suddenly filled with tears. It was a message from him to her...and everyone in the house knew it...everyone except her. She would have to address that matter later, but for now, she couldn't refrain one second longer from reading the words written in his own hand...and meant only for her.

Dear Miss Lily Posey,

I beg you to forgive my rude conduct of yesterday afternoon. Rest assured it was nothing that you or anyone else in your household did that caused me to run out like a scalded cat. I have no excuse, except I'm afraid I was not myself. I believe the unseasonably warm temperatures had their effect, leaving me without the luxury of asking to be excused from your delightful presence. Simply put... I was ill and needed to find some privacy. Surely, you can understand?

If forgiven, I would welcome your presence at my Aunt Winona's house today, at one o'clock, for lunch. I beg you to give me this one chance to redeem myself. Her house is the large yellow monstrosity at the corner of Elm and Maple. I will be waiting, Lily. I pray you do not break my heart.

*In all sincerity,
Blackie*

Lily felt her cheeks burning. This was the most beautiful and heartfelt letter she had ever read, and it was written solely for her. It was obvious he must care a great deal for her and was most eager to see her again. Her stomach did small somersaults at the mere thought of having lunch with him. She could barely conceal her excitement—which only made it more difficult to hide her resentment at being the last one to read his letter.

She turned her glistening eyes toward her mother and addressed her through tightly drawn lips. "This note was meant for me, Mother. How is it I am only now told of its existence? Why did you and Father, and Lord knows who else, read its contents?" She ran her gaze accusingly, over all the familiar faces gathered around the table. "The words written on this sheet of paper are private in nature. Surely, you must have known that. None of you had any right to read it. Blackie couldn't have suspected my entire family would be privy to his private sentiments."

Lily jumped up, preparing to flee from the suddenly too warm room. "I'm furious with all of you," she railed, "and I may never be able to forgive you for this intrusion. It is because of behavior exactly like this, that Amy and Cynthia felt the need to leave home. Must I run away as well?"

Fern gasped and felt her heart miss a beat as she listened to Lily's harsh and inaccurate accusations. She certainly had not expected an attack as vitriolic as this from her daughter, and sat there, dumbfounded. True, she had read the letter...but no one else had read it. She simply insinuated its contents to the rest of the family in an effort to receive their support, and aid her in helping Lily prepare for a wonderful afternoon. She was thrilled the handsome young man had apologized so artfully. She had never meant to anger Lily, or show her the least bit of disrespect by reading its contents. A silver tear gathered at the corner of her eye, as she struggled to find the appropriate words to say.

Rising from her chair, Fern addressed her husband, who was scribbling away in his notepad. "Lily and I need to speak privately, dear. Please continue on without us." If Mr. Posey heard his wife, he made no notice of it. Fern then motioned to Lily. "Let's go into the parlor."

Lily was so angry with her mother, she refused to nod, but followed closely behind her, fists tightly clenched at her sides.

Once she was certain no one could overhear, Fern halted and turned to face her child. "My dear daughter," she began. "Forgive me, but you misunderstand the situation. Your father and your siblings did not read your letter. Only I saw it. I briefly skimmed its contents to make certain it was not hate filled. I figured you had shed enough tears over this young man and there was no need for more. Had it contained wretched, callous words, I would have tossed it into the stove and you would have never been any the wiser. My actions would have saved you from additional heartbreak. However, the very instant I saw his apology, I knew you would be elated and my heart soared with relief and happiness for you. I admit, it was then that I read the entire missive. I was too happy to keep it to myself, so I shared the intent of the letter...but not *his* words. Your family was overjoyed and very eager to lend a hand in making everything perfect. We love you very much, you know."

Lily could feel her anger begin to slip away as her mother's tender words soothed her ruffled feathers. Mrs. Posey could be very convincing, when she felt she was in the right of things.

"Flori is baking the most lovely chocolate torte for you to take with you, and Ivy has graciously offered you the use of her new ivory combs. Naturally, Holly could not be outdone by her twin; she is lending you her coveted moonstone bracelet."

Lily's eyes grew round with surprise. Her sisters had the reputation for being extremely proprietary with their personal items—stingy, the little ones called them—and had never before offered to share anything with her.

"Why, even as we speak, your brother is polishing the wheels on the carriage so you can arrive in style. Your best dress has been pressed and I have loaned you my finest gloves and new silk petticoat. I also believe there is a new bottle of honeysuckle perfume on your dressing table."

"Oh, Mama," Lily exclaimed, surprised to hear her mother would loan her such a personal item of clothing. "I have a perfectly suitable petticoat." It was cotton with blue ribbons adorning the ruffles—perfect for church.

Her mother waved her off. "Nonsense, darling. While yours is perfectly adequate, there is nothing more alluring than the sound of rustling silk under a lady's skirt. You will feel like a princess, and he will never know why." She giggled softly. "As impossible as it may be for you to believe, I wasn't always an old woman. I know a few things about men. I hope you approve, dear. We've done all this for you."

Lily threw her arms around her mother's neck. "Oh, Mama," she cried. "I love you so much. I didn't mean those hurtful things I said earlier. I can be such a brat sometimes."

Fern smiled. "I think I know my children very well, daughter. Of all the precious and beautiful flowers in my garden, I believe the lily is the most endearing. You are one of a kind… lovely, and sweet, and full of grace. I don't think *brat* is applicable in your case. However, I believe it is time for you to finish your breakfast and prepare for a most enjoyable day. Time waits for no one."

CHAPTER FOUR

Blackie nervously paced back and forth in front of the annoying clock in the foyer. The slow, repetitive tick of its pendulum was driving him mad. Impatiently, he yanked his watch from his pocket and stared at its gleaming face, only to discover it was a mere five minutes later than it had been the last time he checked. If Lily didn't arrive soon, he was going to lose his nerve.

What was he going to say to her? How was he supposed to behave in her presence considering his abysmal behavior the day before? Would she forgive him his cowardice? In any event, why did he care so dang much what she thought of him? His concern for her opinion was a complete mystery to him. He liked girls just fine, always had. In fact, it was because of a girl that he was forced to leave home. Being a gentleman, he hadn't argued his innocence, but he silently swore he would never again be willing to go out of his way for any one of them. It was always so easy to coax a starry-eyed girl into falling in love with him. Caring very little for the pain he might inflict, he blithely went from one to another, never stopping long enough to consider how they felt when he up and abandoned them—and that was the crux of his problem; with Lily, he did care. He cared a great deal, in fact.

"Johnnie, would you please sit down," Winona Barker pleaded. "You're wearing a hole in my carpet. I don't understand what has you so anxious. This is just lunch for a friend of yours, if I'm not mistaken. Charlie has visited several times. We're not entertaining royalty."

"It's not Charlie, Auntie Winona. It's a girl," he groaned. He was going to be sick—again—and this time, he was stone cold sober.

Winona was somewhat surprised to hear that bit of information. Johnnie had asked for permission to invite a friend for lunch, but he had conveniently failed to mention it was a young lady who would be calling. Considering her young nephew's scandalous reputation and proclivity for getting into trouble, she could only guess as to the character of this young woman. Hopefully, the neighbors would not notice her arrival, else there would be weeks of outrageous rumor and sensational speculation. She was almost afraid to ask, but felt she must. "Do I know her, dear?"

"Heck if I know," he barked. "But I doubt it, Auntie. I don't think she gets out much. Her family is a mite unusual."

"Oh, dear," Winona muttered to herself, fearing as much. This promised to be worse than she had first thought. The girl was more than likely from across the tracks, or perhaps even worse. "Is she from the right sort of people, John? Your mother will have my head on a platter if I allow you to get into any difficulties this summer. If you remember, it is because of the scandal of last summer that you are now spending the next three months with me."

"You don't need to remind me, Auntie. There is no need for you to worry, however. This girl is different from all the rest —I'm different, too. I've learned my lesson," he declared most earnestly. It had taken ten long months to work off his debt to his father, after he had been forced to reimburse Juliana's father for all the damages incurred to his tool shed. Since then, Mr. Barker had kept his eyes keenly trained on his son, watching his every move, and not allowing him any freedom to get into more trouble. But worst of all, there was not a single father, in his entire hometown, that would allow him to come calling on his daughter. Yes, he'd been forced to learn a hard and brutal lesson…and to Blackie's mind, the punishment had not been quite equal to the crime. It had all been a terrible misunderstanding and much ado about nothing, he reasoned, but Juliana needed to get her revenge.

However, that was ancient history, and things had changed. Since coming to Garden City, he had turned over a new leaf and was eager to prove it. "I promise you'll like her, Aunt Winona. She's a nice girl. Her name is Lily Posey."

Winona sucked in her breath. "She's a *Posey*? Oh, dear Lord," she gasped.

At that moment, a shiny black buggy pulled up in front of the big yellow house, and a graceful young woman stepped down—accompanied by another lovely woman; a slightly older version of the first.

"She's here, Auntie. You be on your best behavior," he warned, as he opened the door and stepped out onto the porch to welcome his guest.

"You've finally arrived," he exclaimed, smiling from ear to ear. "And you've brought your mother. That's grand," he said a little less enthusiastically.

Lily giggled. "Mama is just seeing to my safe arrival. She's not staying for lunch, but she must meet your aunt. Otherwise, it isn't proper."

Blackie let out a long sigh of relief. "I see...well, that's good," he blurted out, before he could censure himself. Immediately, his cheeks flushed with embarrassment. What had he done? "Forgive me, Mrs. Posey. I certainly did not mean anything by that remark. You are naturally most welcome to stay... if you truly wish to."

Lily turned her expressive eyes toward her mother, silently pleading for her not to agree to his hasty invitation.

"Relax, Blackie," Mrs. Posey said, wishing to set the young man at ease. "I am returning home, but it is only fitting for me to see where my daughter will be spending her afternoon. I have not yet made your aunt's acquaintance."

"Oh, of course. You would want to meet her. I'll introduce you," Blackie said, feeling slightly uneasy. He turned around to see his aunt standing in the doorway, her eyes squinting with a look of disapproval. He motioned with his extended hand for her to come forward. "Mrs. Posey, this is my favorite aunt, Miss Winona Barker. Auntie…" he growled softly, letting her know he would tolerate no sign of disrespect, "this is Mrs. Fern Posey and her beautiful daughter, Lily. Lily will be staying for lunch. Come and meet them."

Winona gave a smug smile, but kept her feet planted. "Very well, Nephew. I will see to the arrangements." She spun around and disappeared back inside, letting the door slam firmly behind her.

Fern stood staring up at the closed door. She had not expected to be welcomed into this stranger's home, but she had not expected to be shut out, either. Squaring her shoulders, she returned to her buggy. Retrieving the warm chocolate torte, and the exquisite bouquet of exotic blooms meant for Blackie's aunt, she turned her face toward Lily's young man, and looked deeply into his soulful brown eyes. "You take good care of my daughter, son. If she has any complaints, I will hold you entirely responsible. She is due home by four o'clock…and not one minute past. Mr. Posey is a stickler for punctuality. Enjoy the dessert."

"Yes, ma'am," he replied. "Four o'clock…and the cake smells delicious." He then noticed the flower petals sprinkled liberally across the top.

"It's a torte, dear, and made especially for you." She smiled slightly, and stepped up into the carriage.

Lily approached her mother. "I'm sorry the woman was so rude, Mama. I don't have to stay."

Fern patted her hand. "Nonsense, darling. She just doesn't know us yet. Give her time."

"Yes, Mama…and thank you for everything."

As the driver began to pull away from the curb, Fern and her daughter exchanged nervous glances. One did not want to leave, and the other wasn't sure she wanted to stay. Fern gave a small, reassuring wave, as Blackie took up one of Lily's gloved hands.

"Don't be scared," he whispered. "My aunt won't eat you," he chuckled. "I intend to see that you have a wonderful day."

"But your aunt looks so fierce. I am not entirely sure I am welcome in her home."

"Don't be ridiculous," he snorted. "She's just surprised you're not Charlie."

"Charlie Masters?" she shrieked. "Is he coming for lunch, too?" The enjoyment of the day was quickly evaporating.

"Heck, no. I just forgot to tell her who was coming. I figured it shouldn't make a whole lot of difference to her if you were a girl or a boy."

Understanding was slowly beginning to dawn. Lily recognized Blackie's unwillingness to inform his aunt of her invitation. The woman had no idea a Posey was coming for lunch. Lily narrowed her green eyes, as she prepared to straighten him out on few things.

"Blackie Barker...you should be ashamed of yourself," she hissed. "Not only have you shocked your poor aunt, you have succeeded in embarrassing me. Had you told her I was coming, she would have tried to talk you out of it. I'm not stupid. I saw the look of displeasure on her face when you introduced me. How could you?" Lily tried to hold back the tears that threatened to run down her cheeks. She felt humiliated, but she was too angry to cry.

"But...but Lily," he stammered. "I only wanted to see you again," he blurted out. "Surely there's no harm in that. I made an awful mess of things at your house, and I was only trying to make up for it. I didn't mean to embarrass anyone. My aunt would have made the same irritated face if you had been Charlie, or any of my other friends. Honest, she would, Lily," he tried to explain. "Heck, she doesn't approve of me most of the time; but my father pays her well to keep me here. Come inside, Lily, and have some lunch," he begged. "There's not a single poisonous flower on anything."

Knowing his words were simply a feeble attempt at

being humorous, she crossed her arms and shot him a look of displeasure, daring him to say more.

"Lily, please say you'll stay. We can do our best to ignore my Aunt Winona." Tucking the bouquet under his arm, he took his free hand and pulled on her wrist, trying to coax her up the sidewalk, toward the door; but he could feel her firm resistance.

Seeing Blackie's aunt peering at her through the lacey curtains, with a foreboding scowl firmly planted on her face, Lily quickly lost her nerve. In true Posey fashion, she raised her stubborn chin a few notches and snatched her hand out from his grasp. "I have suddenly lost my appetite, it would seem," she said peevishly. "I wish to go home now, Mr. Barker. You may keep the torte and the flowers. I sincerely hope your aunt enjoys them."

Blackie was beside himself with disappointment. Everything was going all wrong. What could he possibly say or do to make her change her mind? It was absurd. Standing there, his arms loaded down with cake and flowers, the heavenly scent of chocolate filling his nostrils, causing his stomach to rumble loud enough for Lily to hear, he growled with frustration.

She snickered. "Enjoy your torte, Blackie. Flori baked this one especially for you. Curious, though…we were not allowed even one tiny taste of the creamy batter." Keeping her face serious, determined not to giggle, Lily kept her eyes trained on his. "It must be one of a kind," she purred. "Flori was very upset with you, you know. How strange it is, she was willing to bake you a treat." She smiled slyly. "You may take me home, now—if you are still willing."

Blackie practically dropped the cake on the ground. Special indeed, he thought. He could already feel his stomach begin to seize with deadly spasms. What was it with her family's desire to poison him? Were they all crazy?

He carefully placed the torte on the porch railing and tossed the flowers on the lawn. If his aunt wanted a bouquet, she could pick them up for herself. As far as the torte…well, maybe she'd find it very tasty and consume the whole darn thing. That would end some of his problems…but no…what was he thinking? He couldn't let his own aunt be poisoned, even if the cantankerous woman was proving to be a pain in his neck. It was just wishful thinking. In a quick decision, he reached out and gave the chocolaty smelling concoction a little nudge, sending it crashing to the ground.

Splat!

Lily's eyes grew enormous with disbelief, as she watched the heavenly torte tumble top down, into the dirt. Flori had worked very hard to create it for them. There was love in every spoonful, and this ungrateful brute had just destroyed it; filling her with a degree of rage, never before experienced. What would she say to dear Flori when asked how they liked it? And her father's contribution fared no better. The rare and delicate flowers he'd chosen, and cut from his own greenhouse, were now trod into the mud—broken and bent beyond salvage. She stomped her foot and wiped the scalding tears from her face.

"You're a mean and despicable person, Blackie Barker! I do believe I hate you! Do you hear me? I hate you! Never call on me again. Don't dare send me another note, either. I'll sick the dog on you, if you ever darken our door again."

He rolled his eyes and snorted. "I'm not afraid of any dog, and furthermore, I've got more sense than to come around your house again. I don't like getting poisoned every day, Miss Posey. I don't know why, but your cook is trying to kill me. Rest assured, the last place I'll ever go to is your crazy house."

"Flori did what? Tried to kill you? Are you insane, as well as bad-mannered?" she countered.

He folded his arms across his chest and stood defiant. "I know all your secrets, Miss Posey, and Charlie is right…you're all wacky. Come on, I'll see you home—one last time."

Lily snatched her arm away. "Oh, no you won't, Mr. Barker. I wouldn't let you escort me across the street. Do you have a telephone?"

"Of course. My aunt had it put in last winter."

"Only last winter? We were the first on our street to have one installed. We're very progressive, you know," she boasted. Never mind that her mother refused to use it, saying it was unnatural for a person to speak into a box and be heard clear across town. Something so unexplainable had to be unhealthy.

Not to be outdone, Blackie replied, "I suppose you have only one."

Lily's jaw dropped and her eyes narrowed with skepticism. "Are you saying you have *two*? Nobody has two telephones, Mr. Barker."

Blackie shrugged his shoulders and grinned playfully. "Just askin'. Who do you want to call?"

"I want to ring up my brother, Bud. I'll have him come fetch me."

"Absolutely not," he argued. "I told you I will take you home, and I intend to do just that. I won't have your father accusing me of bad manners. Now quit fighting me, Lily!"

"Let go of my sleeve," she screamed, as she snatched her arm back and made straight for the gate. "Stay away from me!"

"Dammit, Lily!" he cursed. "You're behaving like a child and the neighbors are looking. I insist on being a gentleman. I'll not let you get away from me!" Blackie lunged for Lily, just as she reached the sidewalk.

She screamed and pulled away most forcefully, causing her to lose her footing on the curb and tumble into the street, turning her ankle and twisting her knee in the process. "Help!" she cried out, as the searing pain ripped through her foot and up her leg.

Blackie was nearly on top of her, red-faced and perspiring heavily, when a deep voice demanded that he step back.

"I said to step away, lad," the man in the black uniform ordered. "What goes on here?" he demanded to know, as he looked down at the lovely young lady lying disheveled in the street. He noticed her sleeve was torn and tears streaked her pretty face. "Has this young man hurt you, Miss?"

The pain was excruciating, making it nearly impossible to speak, but Lily could nod. Blackie had refused to let her go and she had fallen. Everything was entirely his fault.

Suddenly, his Aunt Winona appeared at Blackie's side, looking terribly concerned and crestfallen. She spoke in hushed tones to the police officer. "Is my nephew in trouble again, officer? I cannot say I'm surprised, as he has a penchant for finding it, I'm afraid. His parents, my dear brother and his wife, sent him to me for the summer. This was to be his last chance."

Blackie let out with a groan and closed his eyes, willing his aunt to shut up. She was just making things worse. The last thing he needed was to have this policeman think he was a delinquent and a troublemaker—which was precisely what Officer O' Toole was beginning to consider.

"This young lady needs a doctor, ma'am. Can you inform her parents of her situation, while I take care of the young culprit responsible for her injuries?"

Flustered, and simply mortified that this should occur in front of her house, in full view of her neighbors, Winona frowned at her nephew and nodded. "I suppose I can ring them up," she grumbled. But how was she supposed to explain to a Posey that their daughter was lying in the street, near the gutter, directly in front of her house? Oh, dear, this was bound to grow into a scandal of epic proportions.

"Well, just don't just stand there, woman. See to it," the police officer demanded. He took out his handcuffs and ordered Blackie to turn around.

"What are you doing?" Lily asked, between great hiccupping sobs.

"This lad will not be able to hurt you again, lassie. I'm arrestin' him and cartin' him off to jail. You just relax until your parents arrive to get you."

"But why? Blackie didn't do anything...well, not exactly," she hedged.

"But o' course he did. I asked you if he hurt you, and you nodded your head. As I arrived upon the scene, I saw with my own two eyes he was attackin' you."

"No, you've got it all wrong. We were arguing, yes, but I pulled away and tripped over my new silk petticoat. See?" She lifted the hem of her dress ever so slightly, displaying a large tear in the ruffle of the petticoat. "It belongs to my mother, you see, and it is a little too long for me. I simply got caught up in it and fell, twisting my ankle. She's going to be terribly upset, I'm afraid. It was new and now it is ruined. You can't arrest Blackie for that. You mustn't."

"Humpf!" Officer O' Toole thought for a moment, looking the boy up and down. He was a handsome lad and a bit too cocky to please him. It was evident the boy was in dire need of learning a lesson. "Even his own aunt says he's a troublemaker, Miss. This is not the first time he's been arrested, I'd wager."

Blackie jumped in. "Oh, but you're wrong, sir. I've never been arrested—not actually." He lowered his voice, so that Lily could not hear. "I had some problems with a girl, back home. She got jealous and didn't want me seeing anyone else. Things happened and there was some property damage. What was I to do? I didn't want to ruin her reputation. I made it up to her father, by working off the damages, and he forgave me... eventually."

The policeman smirked, remembering his own younger days and the wild oats he himself had sown. "Is that so? Is this one jealous, too?"

"No. We fought because her family is trying to *kill* me," he shouted distinctly.

"They're what?" the old man replied, not sure he'd heard the boy's words correctly.

"They have a cook in their employ and she doesn't like me, I guess. I don't know why, but on two separate occasions she has tried to poison me with flowers."

"You're a hateful man, Blackie Barker!" Lily shouted, from her place in the street. "Flori would never think of such a thing. She's a kind-hearted woman and a marvelous cook." Then grinning wickedly, she purred, "However, I suppose if she wanted to harm you, she could do just that and it would be too late for you, bucko. She knows nearly as much about flowers as Father."

A broad grin came across Officer O' Toole's round face. "Ah, lassie, is it Florence Brodie you're a speakin' of?"

Lily smiled. "It is indeed. Only, we call her Flori…or Floribunda. My father prefers floral names for everyone. Do you know her, Officer O' Toole?"

"Aye, I do. I was sweet on her once…but that was before she threw me over for a Welshman. How's the girl doin' nowadays?"

It was odd to think of Flori as a girl. "She's right as rain. You should come by and see her, officer. I know she'd enjoy that. We live at 142 Orchard Lane. We're the Posey family."

A light of understanding shown bright in the officer's twinkling blue eyes. He chuckled softly, as he removed the handcuffs. "Ah…the Poseys," he mumbled. "Now, I see." He glanced into Blackie's fearful face and smiled. "Good luck, there, me boy. They're a strange lot, but a fine one, too. Odd as they are, I can guarantee my little Florence isn't tryin' to poison you. She's the best cook in the entire state, and that I know for a fact."

"Oh, no," Blackie groaned, remembering the heavenly scented chocolate torte that lay in crumbled bits upon the ground. The memory of it caused his mouth to water. It probably tasted as delicious as it looked. "But what about all the flowers? Aren't they poisonous?"

The officer snorted. "If they were, I'd be kickin' up me own heels. She's more than likely only humoring Mr. Posey, don't ya know? I hear she cares for that family as if it were her very own. If it makes the old man happy to know she uses his flowers in her cookin', where's the harm? It's healthy enough. You should stop your gripin' and look around you, lad. Miss Lily is a real beauty. You'll not be doin' any better than her, I'm a thinkin'…even if she bein' a Posey and all."

"Ahem." Lily cleared her throat to gain some attention. Her ankle throbbed like the dickens, her dress was completely ruined, her mother's new silk petticoat was torn, and these two dolts were talking about her as if she wasn't even there. "Excuse me," she snapped. "You do realize I'm sitting right here, not more than five feet away, and I can hear every word the two of you are saying. I'll have you know, Officer O' Toole, I have a thing or two to say about all of this. Perhaps I no longer wish to see Mr. Barker. He has ruined our luncheon...twice; and twice he has humiliated me beyond repair. In case you haven't noticed, a rather large crowd of onlookers have gathered around us, and are staring at me, Lily Posey, sprawled in the middle of the street." She threw out her arms to demonstrate. "I expect you to do something about it."

As a matter of fact, the policeman had not noticed the curious bystanders. "Go on with ya, now," he shouted. "There's nothin' to see here. A lovely wee lass has sprained her ankle, and a doctor is on his way. Go on back to your homes now, before I start takin' names." He gave them his most threatening scowl, and the crowd began to immediately disperse.

"That's taken care of now, Miss Lily, and I believe I see two carriages speeding this way. It must be your parents and the doctor, I'll wager. Things will soon be put to rights." He gave Blackie a small nudge. "If I were you, lad, I believe I would make me self scarce. Surely, you've got somewhere else to go?" He winked at the anxious young man.

"Yeah, I do...and thanks," Blackie mouthed silently.

Just before he tore out across the freshly mown lawn, Blackie gave one last look back at the lovely Lily, still squatting in the street, looking woefully tragic. Knowing how she felt about him, and realizing she would more than likely never speak to him again, caused his breath to hitch and his eyes to burn. He really did like her and now everything was ruined. He hadn't even had the chance to tell her how beautiful she looked with her ivory combs holding back her golden hair, and that spectacular blue-gray bracelet worn around her dainty wrist. Oh, what blasted, miserable luck he had. It was always a dog's life for him, and he'd about had enough of it. It was high time for him to change his ways.

Although Lily was unused to the pampering she received upon her unexpected arrival home, she discovered it was rather nice to be waited upon. Her entire family treated her as if she was a fragile, hot-house flower. A bloom of the rarest kind. Although she hated to admit it, after the horrendous afternoon she'd spent in front of Blackie's aunt's house, sprawled in the gutter and covered in grime, it felt well deserved. So relaxed and comfortable was she, she could almost forget her humiliation at the hands of one Mr. Blackie Barker—almost.

Doctor Martin had treated her swollen ankle; declaring it badly sprained, but thankfully not broken. Her knee was wrenched, but would heal in a couple of days. He left precise instructions with her mother and Flori, all to be followed to the letter and carried out in his absence. She was ordered to stay in bed for the next seven days, and he would return in two or three to check up on her. For the next week, it seemed she would have nothing more important to do than to lie back and ponder the mysteries of a certain John Blackie Barker.

Even though he was responsible for much of her pain and humiliation, Lily couldn't help but think of him fondly. The memory of his devilish smile made her insides warm considerably, and caused her pulse to race. She could close her eyes and conjure up the image of his masculine mouth, his lips pressed tightly against hers. Would they be soft and warm, or firm and demanding? Would his breath be sweet and intoxicating? Dwelling on all these things caused her to fidget in her bed and feel too warm under the covers. Had she somehow bumped her head? Why couldn't she get him out of her mind?

When it came to Blackie, she had to start thinking with her head and not so much with her heart. She knew she needed to purge him from her life, but it would be difficult. When she felt stronger, up to the extra exertion it would require, she would fully engage herself in the planning of her revenge. It would have to be spectacular—something unforgettable. However, that was weeks away. For now, she had no choice but to follow doctor's orders and rest; leaving her free to dream of a brown eyed boy with kissable lips and a velvety, deep voice.

"Ah, there be me poor, wee lass," Flori exclaimed, as she waltzed into Lily's room, carrying a tray filled with all sorts of delectable tidbits. "Ah brung ye some soup to build up your strength. In no time a'tall, ye'll be on yer feet again, feelin' like yer old self. Yer sisters, Jasmine and Poppy, baked ye these cookies. Ah watched over them, so Ah reckon they'll be edible," she snickered. "Ye've caused quite a ruckus in this house, this day, dearie. Bud is ready to tear that Blackie boy apart, and yer poor ma is beside herself with worry. Did that lad get his self thrown into the hoosegow?"

Lily giggled at the mere idea of Officer O' Toole physically tossing Blackie into a tiny jail cell. "No, Flori. He is guilty of nothing. We were arguing and I tripped on my petticoat. It's as simple as that. Everything got blown all out of proportion. Officer O' Toole had to let him go."

Flori practically dropped her tray. "O' Toole, did ye say now?"

Lily nodded as she took a bite of a delicious shortbread cookie. "Mmm, not too bad."

"Was he a tall man with a bonny smile?"

"He was tall, I guess."

"Did he have wavy, copper colored hair and a dimple in his chin?"

Lily could barely contain her laughter. She could see by the sincere longing on Flori's face, the man had once meant a great deal to her, and not knowing if this policeman was indeed her old flame, was torture for her. She decided to be kind and tell all.

"Well...let me see," she said, as she tapped a tooth with a finger. "He is tall, and I guess you would say he is braw. But his hair is white, not copper, and I couldn't see his chin for the whiskers covering it."

"Oh," Flori sighed disappointedly. "Then ah guess there's nae to be done about it, now."

"Of course, he did ask about you—" Lily contributed.

"He did, ye say?" the old woman shrieked.

"Yes, he did. He was very interested in learning how you fared. He said he used to be sweet on you, and that you were the best cook in the state. Is that what you wanted to know?"

Flori's bright blue eyes suddenly filled with unshed tears, as she celebrated the moment. So many years had passed; so much time had been wasted. Now here, in Garden City, the love of her life had miraculously turned up and was asking about her. She took out her handkerchief and wiped at her eyes.

"Ach, look at me, now," she said tearfully. "Ah'm such a dafty old woman. He's probably got a wife and nine bairns by now. Perhaps even grandchildren, maybe."

Lily took a spoonful of the delicious chicken soup. "This is very good, Flori. Good enough for company, I imagine. Did I forget to tell you that I invited Officer O' Toole to come for supper? Mother said it was all right."

"Saints preserve us!" Flori blurted out. "When is he comin' for dinner?"

"Oh, you've lots of time to prepare. He's not coming until six o'clock," Lily giggled.

Flori reached for the nearest chair and plopped herself in it. She was afraid to ask. "Nae tonight?"

"Of course, tonight. He is very eager to see you again."

"Land o' Goshen, what am Ah to do?"

Lily drained the last few drops of soup from the bowl and wiped her mouth on her napkin. "You're to take it easy and put on your prettiest dress and fix your hair. Mother and the twins are going to prepare dinner. You don't have to do a thing."

Flori jumped to her feet like a woman half her age. "They're aimin' to fix dinner in *me* own kitchen? For *me* own Mr. O' Toole? Ah do nae think so," she proclaimed vociferously. "He's expectin' me cookin'…and it's me cookin' he'll get."

She gathered up the empty bowl and took away the tray. "You'll not be a seein' me again, this day, lassie," she swore. "Ah've got to turn out a man's supper and run a comb through me hair. It's been a few years and I'll nae disappoint him." She turned and rushed to the door.

"That's my Flori!" Lily called after her. "You go get your man," she mumbled, long after the door had closed and she was once again alone with her thoughts. Even dear, sweet Flori hadn't given up on love; so what did the old woman understand, that she did not?

"Oh, Blackie. What is wrong with us? What's wrong with me?"

Lily took her pillow and bunched it up under her head. If only he would stop by to see her and apologize. Ask how she was fairing. She would forgive him everything and they could start over fresh. If only... "Oh, Blackie," she whispered, as her eyes slowly drifted shut and her dreams gently overtook her.

CHAPTER FIVE

Blackie's Aunt Winona was beside herself with annoyance. Out of the goodness of her heart, she had agreed to take her brother's boy into her own home and attempt to give him a sense of purpose; something his mother had obviously failed to do. In Winona's opinion, the woman had never been quite good enough for her brother, and now their son was showing some of her most undesirable traits.

Blackie sat before her, back stiff, with a torrent of perspiration running into his eyes, stinging them most uncomfortably. He had honestly tried to pay attention, but his mind began to wander. As his aunt continued her rant, pointing out his endless list of faults and shortcomings, he concentrated on more pleasant things. Although he couldn't disagree with the woman, he preferred to spend his time recalling Lily's beautiful face; her guileless gaze—with eyes as sweet and innocent as a new leaf in spring. Her smile bewitched him and her graceful body beckoned him. Lily was different from any girl he'd ever met, and he'd managed to make a real mess of things. He told himself it was nothing so bad that couldn't be undone, if he moved quickly. He just needed to think on it.

"John, are you listening?"

Blackie jumped. "Yeah...I mean yes, Auntie. I agree with everything you say. I'm irresponsible and I need to shape up. Is that what you mean?" He truly hoped she had said something along those lines, as he really hadn't been listening to her ceaseless blathering.

The woman beamed. "That's very good, John. I would hate to have to inform your father of your latest brush with the authorities. I know you can be a good boy, if you'll only try. In order to keep you out of mischief, I have devised a most ingenious plan. You will arise promptly at six A.M. and come down to eat your breakfast by six thirty. Then at—"

Blackie's eyes began to glaze over. His Aunt Winona's voice became a soft buzz in his head, as he started to formulate a plan of his own to win back Lily's admiration.

"Does that meet with your approval?" Winona asked.

He nodded.

Unexpectedly, his aunt approached and placed one hand on each side of his face. "You'll make your father proud yet," she stated, just before she placed a cool kiss on his forehead. "Our new regimen will begin at dawn. Goodnight, John."

"Uh, goodnight, Auntie Winona."

As Winona made her way up the staircase, she couldn't help but be amazed at her young nephew's response to her new rules. She had expected more resistance from him. Perhaps she had misjudged his true character. It could be that he simply needed a stiff hand to keep him in line and show him the acceptable boundaries for a boy his age. She threw her shoulders back and lifted her chin a little higher. Her brother had been wise to send his son to her. Correcting incorrigible boys was something for which she felt well qualified—even if she had no children of her own. How difficult could it be?

The next morning, just before the sun lightened the dark indigo sky to a pale shade of gray, Blackie experienced a rude awakening. Had he been listening to his aunt the previous evening, it is possible he would not have been taken totally unaware. As it was, his drowsy eyes could barely focus on the image standing at the foot of his bed. Was it his aunt or a demon up from the depths of hell striking an enormous brass gong? Whoever it was, the sound being created was nothing less than ear splitting. He put his hands up to deflect the painful assault against his eardrums.

As his aunt raised the mallet to shoulder level, preparing to make another great strike against the brass gong, he shouted, "For God's sake, Auntie! Have a heart, will ya?"

Winona lowered her arm and scowled at her insolent nephew. "Did I hear you take our Lord's name in vain, John Barker?"

Try as he might, there was simply no winning with the woman. Blackie fell back onto the soft, warm mattress and closed his eyes. Gritting his teeth and clenching his jaws tightly, he did not know how he was going to find the strength to get through the day...or the following week...or the grueling months that lay ahead. He was surely in hell.

"I'm sorry, Auntie," he moaned, "but that horrific noise is more than I can bear this early in the morning."

"Very well," she sniffed. "Before rising, you will pray for our Lord's forgiveness and thank Him for this lovely day He has given us. You will then get up and get dressed, as you agreed last night, ready to make a new start. Remember your vow?"

Vow? He remembered no such thing; but she did and that was what was important. "But it's still dark and it's summer," he groaned. "I need more sleep."

"People die in bed, my boy," she retorted. "It's best to get the day started early. Now...up with you and I don't want to hear any more of your grumblings. This is a new day and a new way of living." She walked to the window and threw up the sash, letting the crisp dawn air fill the tiny room. "Just smell that good, clean air, boy. Can you smell the lilacs? Get a whiff of the honeysuckle."

"Oh, God," he mumbled. Lilacs and honeysuckle. Did she have to mention flowers? Weren't lilies blooming this time of year? Hadn't Lily smelled of sweet honeysuckle when she came to visit? He just wanted to cry. Life wasn't worth the living if he had to march to his aunt's drum—or gong, as it were—and be separated from the one girl he couldn't put out of his mind. If by some accident he should live through this summer, he swore he would never forgive his father for sending him here.

Suddenly, the crashing sound of a Turkish gong resonated through his brain, sending a shock wave down every nerve in his body.

"Christ!"

"What?"

"Nothing, Auntie."

It was a picturesque day. Everything was perfect. The sky was a startling shade of blue, and the fluffiest white clouds, in recent memory, sailed along on a soft, warm breeze. The combined fragrance of a variety of aromatic blooms, peonies, lilacs, honeysuckle, and hyacinths, was lifted and carried through the air into the frilly bedroom. Birds sang in the Sycamore tree and her fluffy orange cat lay curled up on the sill. Yes, it was all so very perfect. But if that were true, then why did Lily feel so miserable?

Her family could not have been more attentive. Even her father had spent time in her room, reading the latest horticulture magazine aloud to her; swiftly putting her to sleep. Her mother sat and painted a miniature of Lily lying in bed, with her long golden hair spread out about her like one enormous halo. Is that how her mother actually saw her? Lily had to snicker and roll her eyes. She was not an angel—not even close—nor did she want to be. All she wanted was...

"Oh, dear," she sighed. Lily knew the source of her discontent and his name was Blackie. It infuriated her that she would moon over such a rascal. He was not exactly the kind of boy a proper young lady should encourage, but she couldn't help herself. She was happier arguing with Blackie, than when she was being pampered by her loving family. Even Flori's warm apple-crumb cake could not fill the emptiness inside her.

She had never felt this way before, and certainly not for a boy. She loved all sorts of things; chocolate, cold lemonade on a hot summer's day, swimming in the lake, Christmas, her cat, her family...well, she could think of a hundred things; but nothing gave her that strange sensation she felt in the pit of her stomach, every time Blackie smiled in her direction.

When she closed her eyes, she could picture that smile in perfect clarity. His straight white teeth and dimpled cheeks caused her heart to race. Not to mention the masculine richness of his voice. When he spoke, each word was like velvet to her ears. When he laughed, she couldn't help but laugh with him. It was a sound that originated deep within his chest—a place close to his heart. However, if a man loved to laugh, as did he, how could one explain his quick temper and proclivity to throw insults her way? Lily could not explain it.

"Good morning, Lily-dilly," exclaimed Jasmine, as she skipped across the room, plopping herself down on the fluffy comforter, all the while being very careful not to touch her sister's injured foot. "Wha' cha doin?"

Lily had to smile at her baby sister's sense of cheerfulness. "Now what do you think I'd be doing here, in this bed, with my foot resting on a pillow?"

Jasmine's eyes glanced toward the carefully wrapped appendage. "You could be reading me a story or watching me dance," she replied. "Or I could climb the sycamore and holler at you through your window. Would you like that?"

"You'd do that for me?"

"Uh-huh. I'll holler real loud and you can 'member how I looked in the tree." She quickly climbed down to the floor, always in a great hurry.

"Can you also eat some cookies and milk for me?" Lily asked, good-naturedly.

The child's eyes lit up. "Oh, yes I can. I can eat one for me and one for you. Is that good?"

"Yes, darling. That will make me very happy. Have fun and be careful you don't get stuck in that tree."

"Oh, you don't have to worry, Lily-dilly. Your friend will get me down."

She skipped away and was almost out the open door, when Lily shouted, "Jasmine, stop! What do you mean, my friend will get you down? Who's out there?" She couldn't think of a single soul who would simply be standing out in the lawn, waiting to climb a tree and free her sister if she got stuck.

"Oh, you know," the little girl said impatiently. "That silly boy that came to dinner, but didn't stay to eat—*that* friend."

"You mean, Blackie?" Lily could hardly believe her ears. "Blackie is downstairs?"

Jasmine gave her shoulders a small shrug. "Outside. He's been down there every day. He just stands there, like a sad puppy, looking up at your stupid window."

Lily smiled dreamily. "He does?"

"Yes, Lily-dilly. Now can I go outside and climb the tree for you? You ask too many questions."

Off-handedly, Lily waved the child on. "Have fun, dear," she muttered.

Blackie was here, and it was too good to be true. She began to fuss with her hair, only to realize she was still in her nightgown with her bare toes peeking out from beneath the gauze. How embarrassing, she fretted. What was she to do? Suddenly, Bud passed by her door.

"Bud!" she shouted. "Would you please do me a favor?" She knew he would not refuse her request, as everyone was doting on her every wish.

He stuck his head around the door. "Hey, kid. What do you need? A glass of water? Milk?"

She smiled her sweetest smile. "Oh, no. I'm fine, but I would like for you to go to my chifforobe and bring me my new bed jacket...the yellow one...and my hairbrush and mirror. Don't forget my yellow hair ribbon."

Bud made a peculiar face, raising a quizzical brow; but did as he was asked, nevertheless. It wasn't right, touching his sister's girlie things, but she appeared to be in desperate straits and needed his help. Holding the fussy bed jacket between his finger and thumb, he held it out at arm's length, until he reached the bed and dropped it on the coverlet.

"It's not going to bite you, brother," she remarked.

Ignoring her sarcasm, he replied, "Are you sure this is all I can do for you, *mi' lady*?" He held his breath, praying that was indeed all she would require. He had no idea what had suddenly gotten into his ordinarily commonsense sister, but as long as he wasn't asked to handle more of her delicates, he'd go on his way and try to scrub the memory of it from his brain.

"As a matter of fact...could you cover my foot before you go?"

Bud glanced down and spied her bare toes peeping out from under the bandage. Overcome with the sudden urge to pester his sister, he knew this was a chance too good to resist. "Well, look what we have here," he chuckled. "Five chubby little piggys."

"Oh, no," she cried. "Bud, you wouldn't..."

He laughed. "I would. In fact, I believe this little piggy went to market," he said, as he tweaked her big toe. "And this little piggy stayed home."

Lily began to twitter.

"This little piggy had roast beef—"

The twitter soon became a giggle...then grew into a breathless laugh. "Stop! Don't you go any further," she squealed.

He laughed and moved on.

"Stop it!" she cried, laughing hysterically. Everyone in the family was aware that her feet were unusually ticklish. "I beg of you...I'm going to be sick!"

Ignoring his sister's tearful pleas, Bud continued the torment. "And this little piggy had none."

"Oh, please, I can't—" she gasped, breathlessly. "I can't—" Her ribs hurt dreadfully and she could hardly speak.

He grinned. "Almost done. Now, where was I? I guess I'll just have to start over—"

"No! Have a heart! I'm going to tell Mother," she warned.

Ignoring her threat, her most treacherous brother continued with his tender torture. "Oh, I remember now," he snickered, as he took hold of her smallest toe and gave it a tiny tweak. "And this little piggy went Wee, Wee, Wee...all the way home. Finished," he announced, as he gave her foot a little pat. "Shall I have another go at it? You certainly seem to enjoy it," he laughed.

Gasping for air, with tears streaming down her red, blotchy face, Lily was hardly prepared for what was to happen next.

"Lily! Are you all right? I heard you screaming all the way down to the sidewalk. Oh, my God! Look at you! Did you choke?"

That voice...that beautiful, masculine voice belonged to none other than... "Blackie?" she croaked.

"Yeah, it's me. I'm sorry to intrude, but you scared the wits out of me. What were you doing?" He glanced at her brother, standing by the side of her bed.

"Look, Lily!" Jasmine yelled through the window, from where she had managed to scale to the very heights of the old sycamore tree. "Look at me! I'm at the very tippy top. I can see you. You look awful, Lily. Can you see me? I've never been this high up before, Lily...and I don't think I can get down." Her small voice began to tremble. "I think this is kind of scary."

"Jasmine?" Lily muttered, only now recalling her little sister's intent to climb the tallest tree in their yard. "Heavens to Betsy! Quick, you two," she shouted, glaring at the two men staring each other down, in the center of her room. "Jasmine is stuck in the top of the sycamore. She's bound to fall. Get her down from there this instant. Get her, now!"

Without another word, Bud and Blackie raced down the stairs and out the front door, letting it slam behind them.

Lily could hear them talking amongst themselves, no doubt deciding how they were going to rescue the little girl. One would climb up, while the other would stay on the ground in case one should fall. She could also hear the fear in her sister's cries for help. If the poor little thing fell, she could possibly be killed, or severely injured, and it would be all her fault. Had she had her wits about her, she would have scolded the child for even thinking of doing such a foolish thing. But no, she had her head in the clouds, lost in thought of the handsome rascal standing on her lawn. She was such a wicked, selfish creature and deserved no sympathy from anyone.

"Hold tight, Jasmine, dearest," she shouted from her bed. "Bud is coming for you. You'll be all right." Lily prayed she spoke the truth, for she would not be able to endure anything to the contrary. Both Poppy and Jasmine were allowed to run free, and more than once they had found themselves in harrowing predicaments. Neither one of them knew fear, remembering the time Poppy fell down the well. She and Jasmine were going to give each other rides in the bucket. Maybe now, they would listen to reason and take a few precautions—that is if Jasmine got down in one piece. Lily began to pray in earnest.

Marigold jumped down from the windowsill, obviously displeased at the commotion just outside her window. She plopped her large, furry body on Lily's injured foot.

"Umpff!" she gasped, as the cat settled in for a long nap. At least her bare toes were hidden from view, Lily thought, as she turned her eyes back toward the tree.

Jasmine's frightened eyes had grown as large as saucers, while she waited for her rescue. She gave a valiant attempt to smile at her big sister, but it was all in vain, as she was clearly terrified of falling. "Lily?" she muttered, shakily. "I'm scared. I can't hold on anymore."

"Be brave, darling. You'll be down in a moment and you'll have a great tale to tell Poppy. She'll be so envious."

Jasmine sniffed. "I s'pose she will, but I still don't like it up here."

"Hello, little one. I'm here to escort you to your magical carriage," Blackie said, in a calm, reassuring voice. He set his boot on the limb located just below the window. Somehow, the child had managed to get herself—not to mention him as well—into a fine fix. He could hear the wood groaning and the brittle twigs snapping beneath his weight. They would be fortunate if they both didn't break their necks. "I want you to put your foot here, next to my hand."

"Huh-uh. I can't," she cried, as her grip tightened on the thin branch.

"Yes, you can, Jasmine. You must. Put your left foot on this branch, next to my hand."

"No," she whimpered.

"But I insist. Just do it."

"Jasmine, darling," Lily called out from her bed. "Listen to Blackie, dearest. He will get you down. I would put my foot there, if he asked."

The little girl stared back at her sister. "You would? Honest?"

"Of course. I would do everything he told me. Place your foot where he showed you."

The little girl swallowed and looked down at her rescuer. "Well...all right, but I don't like it."

Blackie chuckled. "I don't like it either, kid, but we have no choice. Come on down," he coaxed.

With a frown firmly affixed to her cherubic face, the child obeyed his every word, and ten minutes later, he was holding her in his arms, with both feet planted firmly on the ground.

"I sure am glad that's over," Bud remarked. "If my mother or father had seen this...well, I hate to think what they would have done. Father would definitely take the tree down. As for Jasmine, she wouldn't be sitting down for a week."

"Oh, please don't tell him, Bud," his sister wailed.

Finally, here was his opportunity to coerce the little hoyden into behaving. "If you promise never to climb higher than the parlor window, then maybe I'll keep this to myself. But if I should ever catch you this high up again, I'll tell Father and Mother and Flori, too. You'll have no dessert for a month of Sundays."

"Oh, no," she cried. "You can't do that, Bud. I give you my word, and Lily's too."

"What has Lily got to do with anything?" her brother inquired.

"It was all her idea. She wanted to see me outside her window."

"She what?" Bud would never have thought his prudent sister would ask the child to do anything so reckless. "That doesn't sound like her. Perhaps you misunderstood."

"I did not. I heard her perfectly well. She was boreded in bed and wanted to see how high I could climb. She even offered me a cookie."

Bribed her with a cookie? Bud took Jasmine from Blackie's arms and set her on the ground. "You run along to your room and stay there. I'm going to have a serious talk with our sister."

Blackie put his hand on Bud's arm in an attempt to hold him back. "Please, if you wouldn't mind. I'd consider it a privilege if you'd allow me to have that conversation with your sister. Both Jasmine and I could have been killed today. Lily needs to be made aware of how careless she was. It's important she know what I think of her."

Bud stared at the young stranger who had willingly risked his life and limb in liberating Jasmine from the tree. "Well...if you're absolutely sure you'll give her a good talking to. She needs to know that she's responsible for all this."

Blackie grinned. "Have no fear. I'll give her a talking to; one she'll never forget, I wager. I have a lot to say on the subject."

"I suppose that would be all right," Bud mumbled. He hadn't really wanted to scold his sister. She had suffered considerable pain in the last couple of days, and was miserable confined to her bed. He didn't want to be the one to make her cry again. "Promise me one thing," he said, as he turned to leave. "Go easy on her, Blackie. She's been through a terrible ordeal. I wouldn't want to see her overly upset."

Blackie nodded. He wasn't sure if Lily's brother knew he was the one responsible for her injuries, but figured it wouldn't do anyone any good to inform him of that fact. "I promise not to make her cry."

"Okay. You know the way to her room. I'll send Poppy

up to keep an eye on the two of you."

"Thanks," Blackie snorted.

Bud chuckled. "You're most welcome."

CHAPTER SIX

Blackie took to the stairs two at a time. There was little time to waste. He remembered Lily's door was first one on the right; having the window open to that blasted tree. Taking no time to catch his breath, he rounded the newel post and found himself standing just outside her door. His hand shook as it grasped the handle. Giving it a twist, he rushed in, closing the door firmly behind him.

"Blackie!" Lily shrieked. "Should you be in here?" It was one thing to run in to see if she was in trouble, and quite another to come in alone, shutting the door behind him. "Does Mother know you're here?" But what did she care, really? Blackie was a hero and deserved a little gratitude. If her mother knew what he had done, she would surely agree.

Lily feasted her hungry eyes with the glorious sight of him. His hair tousled and his shirt collar open, he looked absolutely wonderful. He had returned to her, and that was more than she had hoped for. Seeing the smoldering passion in his eyes, Lily felt her heart pound erratically, as if it was going to beat right out of her chest. Did she look all right, she wondered? She had hastily run a brush through her hair, and had managed to don her yellow bed jacket, but she wondered if that was enough. She had pinched her cheeks and moistened her lips, all in preparation for the moment he would see her perched in her bed; wounded like a fragile dove. She batted her eyes in an effort to gain sympathy.

"No time for that," Blackie gasped, as he quickly approached her bed. "Your sister—"

"Oh, no. What's wrong with my sister? Did she get hurt?" she cried with alarm.

"No...the other one." Blackie tried to suck more air into his starving lungs. "She's...she's coming," he managed to say, pointing at the door.

"I don't understand."

There was nothing to understand. He was going to kiss her and she didn't have anything to say about it. He had suffered as much as any man could be expected to endure, and he had to taste her lips or die—in spite of her sister following fast on his heels.

Grabbing Lily by the shoulders, he held her firmly, as he positioned his face just inches away from hers. Her lips were entrancing. The closer he came, the more they drew him in. Her flowery scent teased his nostrils and caused his head to spin. He could almost taste her sweetness. Yes...yes...

The door squeaked quietly on its hinges. "Oh, Sissy," whined a peckish Poppy. "Bud told me all about it. Why didn't you ask me to climb the tree for you? I wouldn't get stuck like dumb old Jas. You know she's a scaredy cat. Did she really climb up to your window? I bet she was fibbin'. What are you doin' here?" she asked, glaring up at Blackie. "Are you the one who saved her?"

Blackie growled softly. Once again, his plan had been foiled; and by an ornery little imp with orange pigtails, at that. "Yes, I confess. I am the hapless hero and I'm here to check on your sister's health, if you have to know. It has been a most trying day for her." And for me, too, he wanted to add.

"It looked like you was gonna kiss her," she accused. "I'm not a crybaby like Jas. I'm not scared of nothin'."

Lifting a brow, he quietly asked, "You don't say."

"I can climb higher than her, too. You wanna see?"

Blackie had an idea. "Actually, I would like to see that very much. Go outside and climb a tree. I'll watch you from the window."

"Poppy, you will do no such thing!" Lily declared. "There's been quite enough tree climbing this day."

"Oh, pooh," the little girl grumbled. "I won't fall. I can do anything better than little crybaby."

Lily scowled at her sister. "Young lady, you should learn to mind your manners and not say words such as 'pooh'. Not to mention, you know very well your sister's name is Jasmine—a most lovely and unusual flower, grown in the exotic Far East—most definitely not crybaby!"

"Like the Poppy," the child added. "Poppies are pretty and known for smelling good, too. Better than jasmine, I betcha."

"Yeah, and known for a few other things as well," Blackie murmured under his breath.

"Hush," Lily scolded, glaring up at him. "I'm trying to speak to my sister."

"Oh...all right, Lily," Poppy grumbled. "You're no fun. If you're gonna make me, I'll 'pologize. But I can still so climb higher than her." With that said, the child quickly abandoned the room, stomping through the door and leaving it wide open behind her—and leaving Blackie blessedly alone with her sister.

However, before he could react and shut the door, Mrs. Posey entered. He had to wonder if the woman had been loitering in the hall, anxiously awaiting for the most inopportune time to rush in and spoil everything.

"Good afternoon, Blackie. I must say it is a surprise to see you here. Although very thoughtful of you, I am afraid you've come to check on our girl at a most inconvenient time. It is time for her nap. The doctor was adamant about her getting enough rest. Say your goodbyes and I will see you out." She stood there waiting with her arm extended and smiling, as if butter wouldn't melt in her mouth.

It was unfortunate that grown men weren't allowed to cry, because that is exactly what Blackie felt like doing. The girl of his dreams was only an arm's length away, and yet she might as well be in a different town, for all the good it did him. He was cursed; that's what he was. He must have been born under an unlucky star. But he was also tenacious and slow to give up. Like a dog with a bone, he would keep pursuing his dream until there was no other option available.

Reaching out, he took Lily's fragile hand in his and held it tightly against his heart. "May I return, Lily?" he asked, earnestly. "Is there anything I may bring you?"

Lily lowered her gaze and smiled coyly. "No, there is nothing I need that my family cannot provide; and yes, you may come to visit…if it is acceptable to my mother."

Blackie turned his eyes toward a stern looking Mrs. Posey. "With your permission, may I visit Lily, ma'am?"

"I suppose Mr. Posey would approve…as long as this door remains open, young man."

"Of course!" he blurted. "Naturally!"

"Well, that's settled then. We will look forward to your next visit." She held out her hand. "For now, you must come along with me. My daughter is clearly exhausted. She looks as if she's been through quite an ordeal."

"I'm not tired, Mama," Lily argued, refusing to let go of Blackie's hand. "Really, I'm not."

"Nonsense! I can see it in your eyes and in your overly pink cheeks. In fact, I wouldn't be a bit surprised if you were running a fever…of one kind or another," her mother muttered, glancing at the boy slowly backing away.

Well, I'll be damned, Blackie thought to himself. The old gal was onto him. If he were to gain any alone time with Lily, he'd have to be more creative. This mama wasn't about to let her daughter's petals get plucked by a strange boy from out of town.

"Thank you, Mrs. Posey. I'll be on my way now, but I will return tomorrow at the same time. Unfortunately, I have work I must do for my Aunt Winona, before I can stop by," he explained. Work was right. She kept him toiling from just after sunup to just before sundown; allowing him a scant two hours at lunchtime, to rest up. Those two priceless hours, he expected to spend in the company of Lily Posey.

"Yes. Fine. Now, if you don't mind," Mrs. Posey insisted.

Blackie gave Lily's hand a slight squeeze, just before letting it settle back upon the comforter. "I'll see you tomorrow, Lily. Perhaps I can read to you."

"I would like that," she said. "Until tomorrow, then?"

"Yeah…tomorrow. I promise."

It was nearly nine o'clock by the time Blackie finished doing his daily chores. The moon had been up for some time. He hung the yard clippers on the wall of the shed, just above the mower, and stacked the buckets he'd used for cuttings. Pulling out his handkerchief, he swiped the sweat from his brow. His aunt was a firm taskmaster and had comprised a list of more things to do than any man could complete in an entire lifetime. At this rate, he'd be doing his penance until the day he returned home, leaving precious little time for anything else. With the exception of stealing an hour for Lily, this had been a long, arduous day, and he was ready for some well-deserved fun and relaxation.

In another hour, his aunt would give in and go up to bed, finally giving him the opportunity to salvage at least a small part of the day for himself. He'd find some excuse to linger a bit longer downstairs, where he'd secretly wait for Charlie to give him the signal. Together, they planned to make a night of it. Charlie had never been too much in the clever department; but he could always be depended upon to sniff out a good time.

This night would be spent in the cellar of their good friend, Marty Veneman. He had forgiven his friend for encouraging him to let loose and get stumbling drunk. He swore that would never happen again, but the sting of Marty's father's whiskey would help ease some of the frustration Blackie was feeling. A glass or two never hurt anyone.

The first drink was always the worst. It went down like a handful of burning coals, setting the throat and stomach on fire and taking the breath away. However, after the second drink was consumed, a raging heat settled in, dulling the senses. It was after several long swallows, that Blackie began to recount the many trials and tribulations of his day to anyone willing to listen; and it was soon apparent, if only to him, that his words of wisdom would have a most profound impact on the lives of his good friends. It was astonishing for him to hear just how freely his own words flowed from his mouth after only two or three drinks—inspired thoughts and divine revelations of utmost importance were revealed. It was imperative his friends understand what he was trying to impart to them. It would spare them a lifetime of frustration and misery, if only they would just listen. For hours he spoke, insisting on sharing his insightful knowledge with Charlie and Marty Veneman—that is until he became aware of the loud, drunken snoring coming from behind the empty jelly jars.

Charlie had long given up trying to make sense of his friend's exuberant and inebriated meanderings. The more Blackie ranted, the more the room swirled about his head. His eyes no longer focused and his legs failed to do as they should. The last thing he remembered, good old Marty was throwing up in the dustbin, and Blackie was still mumbling incoherently to himself, while tossing back glass after glass of home brew. But that must have been hours ago, as the lamp had long since burned out, and his mouth felt like a an old wool rug.

Without warning, from out of the cool darkness, a bright and excruciatingly painful shaft of light settled across Blackie's swollen, red eyes. He rolled away, trying to gain his bearings—only to have his skull bombarded with an ear-splitting noise? What on earth? Was his Aunt Winona striking that blasted gong again? With the slightest movement of his head, a stabbing pain cut through his brain, causing him to consider tossing the entire contents of his roiling stomach.

"Char...lie?" he whispered in a raspy voice. He felt like hell. The shooting pain through his head was the only thing that told him he was still alive. "Where are we?" He heard a deep moan from across the room.

"Damn, double damn," the voice cursed.

"Is that you, Charlie?"

"I ain't sure. Are you finished talkin' yet?"

Blackie wasn't precisely certain what his friend meant. "Well, I am talking to you. Does that count?"

Charlie tried to stand up, but his feet were unsteady and he tripped over Marty's discarded boots. "Dammit," he shouted, rubbing his injured toe. "Just tell me you ain't still pining over that girl what makes your life so miserable."

Blackie didn't understand. *"That girl?* Are you talking about Lily?"

Charlie stumbled toward his friend, wiping the drool from his chin. "Yeah, that would be her. And frankly, I don't give a damn anymore. I think I'm dyin' and it's mostly your fault. You sure do run on. Damned if my ears don't feel like they're gonna fall off. I'm goin' home and back to bed. You should do the same. I'll talk to you tomorrow or the next day, if I'm not dead."

"No, wait!" Blackie called out. "What is today?"

"What difference does it make? I'm gonna be sick if I don't lie down." Charlie groaned, as he waved his friend aside and hastily made his way to the door.

Blackie refused to allow his friend to retreat. "Lord in heaven, it's Friday," he groaned. "I've got to paint Aunt Winona's fence and arbor today. By the looks of the sun, I'm already late. You've got to help me, Charlie," he declared, grabbing his friend by his sleeve. "I'm begging you. I made a promise to Lily, and it will be impossible to keep that promise if I don't get some help from my friends. With the two of us working together, I just might be able to complete that fence in time to visit her."

"Are you outta your mind?" Charlie countered. "We're both hung over and knockin' on death's door—at least I am. But you don't look too bad...considerin." They had consumed Marty's father's entire stash. Their friend would surely face a beating when his father found out what they had done. If the truth was known, he was still a little drunk, and poor Marty was completely passed out in a pool of vomit. Neither one was in any shape to help Blackie do anything. "Sorry, but I'm just not up to it."

Once again, Blackie could imagine his beautiful Lily sitting up in bed, waiting patiently for his visit; trusting in him to keep his word. And once again, he would break his promise and disappoint her. She was right. He wasn't nearly good enough for her, but he couldn't bring himself to stay away. He had never known a girl with the power to bewitch him so completely. Maybe he could feign an illness and sneak over to Lily's house without his aunt knowing. Surely the woman had someplace to go on such a perfectly, glorious day. He only needed one hour.

"Fine, by thunder!" he shouted to Charlie's back. "See if I ever offer to help you out of a pickle. I thought friends helped friends. Go on, Charlie...walk away," he snorted. "I don't need you, anyhow."

Finally, luck was smiling down on Blackie Barker. He discovered his Aunt Winona had an early church meeting which would more than likely, last all morning. To make things even better, she had failed to discover his bed had not been slept in the previous night. The woman had not the vaguest idea her nephew had spent the night in a drunken stupor, passed out in a friend's dank and smelly cellar.

"Well, you certainly don't look very well," Aunt Winona agreed. She wrinkled her brow with concern, and placed the back of her wrist against Blackie's cheeks and forehead. "I do not detect a fever, my boy, but you never know about such things. Awful diseases, lethal and quite deadly, can hit in such a short time. Before you know it, you're standing before the Pearly Gates, knocking to be let in."

Blackie snickered to himself. Deadly *and* lethal? Imagine the combination.

There were so many fatal diseases one could fall prey to; perhaps it would be wise for her nephew to put off the painting until another day. "I've decided you're not to work today, young man. As of late, you've been most diligent in completing your chores. I believe some rest is in order. Have yourself some breakfast and then go back to bed, John. I'll look in on you when I return."

Blackie smiled most pitifully. "Yes, Auntie...and thank you. You take excellent care of me and I fail to mention it as often as I should. I'm most appreciative." *Small cough...followed by his most charming smile, and flashing deep dimples in her direction.*

Winona's cheeks reddened. "Oh, now go on with you. You're such a rascal. You can save that smile for the pretty young girls. I suppose we have gotten off to a rather rocky start, you and I, but you are still my favorite nephew—I don't mind saying. With my stern guidance and insistence on adhering to the proper values, you will soon find yourself set on a suitable course, appropriate for the rest of your life. Your parents will thank me."

"And I thank you, too, Auntie Winona. If I'm not careful, you'll make a gentleman out of me, yet," he chuckled. *Another small cough, for emphasis.*

She smiled. "Yes, I think I will." Stretching her neck, his aunt placed a light kiss upon her nephew's cheek. "I do believe you feel a little flush. Go on up to bed." Turning away, she made for the door. "Ta-ta," she called out, cheerfully. "Rest comfortably, my boy."

Oh, he would, just as soon as the old bat was out of sight. There was no time to waste. Blackie peered through the curtains and watched as his aunt walked briskly, down the sidewalk, wearing her silly lavender hat with the yellow bird perched proudly on top, bobbing back and forth, as if pecking for seed. As she rounded the corner and stepped out of sight, he ran for the door.

Within minutes he found himself standing before his destination—Lily's front door. Out of breath and perspiring heavily, he suddenly became aware of a rather odiferous scent emanating from his person. Perhaps he should have taken the time to bathe and dress, but there had been such little time to waste. He would simply have to be content with keeping his distance. Simply being in the same room, hearing her soft, feminine voice and gazing upon her gentle beauty would have to sustain him for another day.

He knocked.

The feisty, little cook opened the door, and upon seeing their visitor, she promptly placed her tiny self squarely between him and the object of his affection. "What do we have here?" she asked mockingly. "It cannae be a gentleman caller, as it is nae the proper time for it. No lassie would see a laddie at sooch an hour. Come back later, me boy." She stepped back in and proceeded to close the door; but Blackie was determined and much faster than the old woman. He pushed back.

"Now see here!" she shrieked.

"I apologize, Miss Hollyhock...or Chrysanthemum...or whatever you call yourself, but I must see Miss Lily. She is expecting me."

"Nae, Ah dinnae think so. Today is her first day out of sick bed and the poor thing is in nae condition to be entertainin' visitors. Now, go away with ya!"

"But I promised," he pleaded. "Please?"

Flori looked the young lad up and down, and was terribly displeased by his disheveled appearance. He looked as if he'd been sleeping in his clothes and had forgotten to run a comb through his unruly curls. But she also took note of the sincere longing in his eyes and the sweet curl of his smile. She'd give the boy a chance and put her faith in the young lass, reclining in the parlor, to turn him away.

"All right, then," she sighed. "But next time, ye might consider takin' a bath before callin' on a lass." Flori stepped back and motioned for Blackie to enter.

"Miss Lily," she shouted from the foyer. "Ye have a caller, but he's nae a gentleman."

"Blackie?" a sweet voice called out. "You kept your word. Come in and be quick about it," she laughed.

The sound of her voice was music to his ears and a soothing balm for all that ailed him. Blackie would soon set his eyes on Lily and the world would be set to rights.

Upon entering the front parlor, Blackie spied the object of his affection. She was sitting like a fairytale princess, propped up by a collection of plush pillows and covered by an embroidered blanket, lying across her lap. Her large orange cat, Marigold, had made herself comfortable on the back of the sofa, and was content to reign over the room by keeping a close and critical eye on any unwelcomed intruder. Tall potted ferns stood at each end of the sofa, resembling royal sentries also keeping guard. The scene was like a fortress, protecting the lady fair. It would have been too intimidating had it not been for the lovely vision lying there, stealing his breath away.

Lily's long, blonde hair had been brushed back and left free to flow gently over her shoulders in long, cascading curls. Caught in a single shaft of dazzling sunlight, in an otherwise darkened room, each shimmering strand glistened like a ray of golden sun. She was too lovely for words—his anyway—as he found himself spellbound by her exquisite beauty. Suddenly, he was tongue-tied.

"Don't just stand there, Blackie. Come and sit down beside me. I want you to tell me what you've been doing since I last saw you." She patted the cushion beside her. "You look as if you've been working very hard. For your aunt, I suspect?"

He nodded, trying to moisten his dry lips; but as he slowly approached, he noticed a slight twitch of Lily's nose.

She giggled, delicately pressing a corner of the blanket to her nose. "Oh, my. I do believe it is somewhat stuffy in here. Would you mind opening another window before taking your seat?"

Blackie turned and walked across the room to the enormous bank of windows. He strained to open the last one, grumbling to himself. He was as obedient to her demands as any lap dog and he found that irksome. However, she was correct; it was rather stuffy in the parlor and he prayed for a brisk breeze to lift the curtains and refresh the air; carrying away the foul-smelling aroma that so stubbornly clung to his person—very much like a too-small suit.

"Thank you, Blackie," Lily said sweetly. "I am happy you were able to take time out of your demanding day to visit me. I know you aunt keeps you terribly busy. By the looks of you, she must be having you do something quite disagreeable. Are you sure she isn't taking advantage of your good nature?"

Blackie almost choked. If Lily only knew the truth of it. "She's all right. My aunt is getting up in years and needs a man's strong back. I'm practically finished there. That's enough about me; how are you feeling? I'm surprised to see you downstairs."

"I'm feeling much better, thank you. Father says I can put some weight on my ankle, tomorrow. Within the week, I should be walking again. Isn't that grand?"

"Yeah," he mumbled. What was wrong with him? Where were all the tender words that filled his mind the night before? For hours, he'd imagined just what he would say to her; his words would be poetic and entirely romantic. They would melt her heart, causing it to soar and making her long for his touch. *Where were those words?* Had the alcohol, he'd recently consumed, suddenly dissolve his brain? Maybe so. Maybe he was pickled. His aunt oftentimes said that's what happened to men who imbibed in too much liquor.

"Blackie? Are you feeling all right?"

Lily's soft voice awakened him from his errant wanderings and brought him back to the here and now. "I'm okay," he uttered. He leaned in a bit closer and noticed her move away, but only by a few inches. Trying again, he drew closer...again she pulled back.

"Are you angry with me, Lily?"

Her eyes watered. "Of course not. What makes you ask such a question?"

"You won't allow me to come near you. I promise you I won't bite," he teased.

"Oh, dear," she fretted. She hated to hurt his feelings, but there was just no use in trying to hide her discomfort. "I do not want to say this...and I have no intention of embarrassing you...but... you stink, Blackie. You smell really bad. Whatever has your aunt had you doing for her? Even when Father is in need of more fertilizer, he never smells quite as bad as you do now. Did you have to bury something? Did her cat die?"

Damn Charlie and double damn Marty. Blackie silently swore to never visit Marty's cellar, ever again. He'd never drink homemade hooch again, either, and he'd never allow himself to drink more than he could handle. As it was, the day was ruined. He was just a disgustingly smelly drunk and Lily deserved more from a suitor. If he were to salvage this visit, he would have to think fast and lie.

"Yes...that's it. A cat died," he said grimly. He pulled back and put several feet between them, in an obvious attempt to relieve Lily of suffering his odiferous person. "My aunt's neighbor had an old cat, you see. Unfortunately, it had a disagreement with a rather large dog and lost the fight—naturally. It was the very least I could do for the poor old girl. It was a terrible sight. White fur was everywhere, I tell you. I dug a hole and buried her beneath the roses." He softened his voice and turned his head, pretending to feel deep sorrow for the poor, dead thing. He heard Lily sniff.

"That's the sweetest thing I've ever heard. Thankfully, you were there to help. You've a good heart, Blackie. I always knew you did. I told Mother you were good inside. Do you love animals?" she asked.

"Oh, sure," he replied off-handedly. "I even thought about taking up animal husbandry for a short time. However, my father insists that I follow him in law." That was all true, but Blackie very seldom acknowledged it, even to himself. He didn't want to study law. In fact, he hated the law. All he truly wanted out of life was to find a beautiful woman to marry, and settle down with his own veterinary business. If he was prevented from doing that, then he didn't care much about anything he did. If his family was disappointed in him, or embarrassed by his foolery, then they could just hang. After all, the way he figured it, they held some blame for the way he turned out. By stifling his true interests and forcing him to follow a path in which he had absolutely no interest, they were causing him to be rebellious.

"Somehow I can't see you behind the bench or fighting to put some poor soul away behind bars," Lily said thoughtfully. "When I look into your eyes, I see a special sort of kindness and affection for others. It's like gazing into the lovable face of Bud's old dog, Basil."

"Gee, thanks," Blackie snorted.

"It's a compliment. Once that dog decides to like you, it is unconditional. I see that same loyalty in your eyes, as well. You should stand up to your father and study what makes you happy. I intend to," she declared proudly.

"You're going to college?" he scoffed. "What do you want to do a fool thing like that for? Where would you go? There's nothing around here for a hundred miles…maybe more. It's totally unnecessary for a woman to obtain a degree, you know. It's the responsibility of the man to care for the family. Women belong in the home. Your father will never allow it." The minute those condemning words left his mouth, Blackie knew he had said precisely the wrong thing. As always, he had put his big foot into his even bigger mouth. It was becoming an annoying habit.

"Er, I didn't mean—" he began.

Lily held up her hand to silence him. "I don't want to hear it. You've said more than enough, Mr. Barker. Now I understand what you truly think of women. I suppose you believe we should all get married and have lots of babies. Well, while I'm not totally adverse to getting married and having children, I certainly would like the opportunity to do something for myself. Mother is a painter. My sister, Cynthia, is a novelist…or at least that was her pursuit before she left home. We haven't heard from her for some time; but I'd like to think she is still pursuing her passion, wherever she is."

"I apologize, Lily. Of course women should have the right to choose what they do with their lives. What would the world do without Madame Curie?" Some women were as smart as men, he supposed. But they were exceptions to the norm.

"Who?"

"She's a young Polish scientist…a physicist, I believe. She and her husband have discovered a new element they call Polonium. I wouldn't doubt if she wins a Nobel Prize in the near future. The entire science world is talking about her."

"Wow," Lily mumbled, clearly impressed. "Name some more famous women,"

Blackie grinned. "Okay…well there is Elizabeth Blackwell."

"What did she do?"

"She was the first American woman to be given a medical degree from a medical college. Although she was known to be a good doctor, no school would allow her entrance because she was a woman. So she started a few colleges on her own, just for women. She's changed medicine."

"She's a brave woman. I know about Clara Barton," Lily piped up. "Father met her once, during the war."

"Yes, she was quite courageous, too. Then there is Susan B. Anthony. She's been fighting all her life to get the vote for women."

Lily snorted. "Perhaps, but you and I know that will never happen. Women aren't smart enough to vote."

Blackie couldn't believe his ears. "Are you telling me not one of these amazing women is smart enough to vote for a no account politician who'll go off and make deals under the table? Do you honestly think not a one of them is as intelligent as Arnie Benson? Is that what you truly believe, Lily?" Arnie was infamous for being the one and only town drunk—and yet he voted whenever he got the chance.

"No, I suppose not, but why then can't we vote?"

He groaned. This conversation was getting way too complicated. What he really wanted to do was kiss her sweet, sweet mouth. "It's a way for men to keep you down on the farm…Hell, Lily, I don't know why things are the way they are…

they just are, I guess. Tell me what it is that you'd really like to do with your life. What would make you happy?" Inexplicably, he truly wanted to know. The girl was so desirous, he had only thought of her as a woman; but now he could understand how a girl as smart and as capable as she, just might have a few dreams of her own.

Lily smiled brightly. "I love books. Not the writing of them, but the look of them. I admire their beautiful leather covers and I enjoy reading them from first page to last. Even the smell of the pages tickles my senses. The titles stoke my imagination. If I could have anything in the world, it would be to own a vast array of great books."

Oddly enough, Blackie could understand her passion for books, for he loved them, too. He had often imagined his perfect day would be spent sitting in a large, paneled study, surrounded by his most beloved volumes; a glass of a superb wine in his hand, and a loving wife near his side. Enormous flakes of snow would be falling silently, just outside the floor to ceiling windows, and a roaring blaze would burn brightly, in the fireplace.

"So what are your plans? How do you intend to make your dreams a reality?"

Lily wasted no time in explaining her future plans. No one had ever really shown an interest in what she wanted; but now Blackie was asking just that. He wanted to know. "I've been busy, already. Do you realize Garden City has no real library? A town of this size should have at least one, don't you think? Well, I have taken it upon myself to remedy the situation by establishing the LLA."

"The LLA?"

She giggled, suddenly filled with excitement. "Yes... the Ladies Library Association. We've been collecting all sorts of books suitable for lending. Mr. George Hopkins, at the Palace Drug Store, has been very generous with cash donations. He allowed us to put a glass jar on his counter for contributions, too. Also, the Grand Central Hotel posts a circular of ours, asking for good used books or cash donations for the cause."

"How is it going?" Blackie asked.

"Oh, you know. It could be better, I suppose. The Garfield Elementary School burned down recently, and the city has to find the necessary funds to rebuild it. It must take precedence over a lending library."

"Hmm, I wonder," he mumbled. "Seems to me, both would go hand in hand. With a few thoughtful changes, the plans could be altered to include a public library near the school. When replacing books for the classroom, they could surely procure a few for the lending library."

"I like the way you reason, Blackie. Do you think we could plead our cause to the school board?"

"Better than that," he replied. "I think I'll have a talk with the mayor. I imagine he likes to read. Is he married?"

She frowned. "He certainly is and he has seven daughters. His wife, Prudence, doesn't mix with the rest of us. She looks down her long nose at Mother and Father. She was raised in New York City and believes she is better than everyone else. Why do you ask?"

"That's explains her feelings of superiority over the rest of us. People in New York are just born rude. But never you mind, Lily. Ask her to join the LLA. Tell her that the women of Garden City require her exquisite sense of taste and her expert opinion. If she refuses, promise to hang her name on a plaque near the door. Even a woman from New York City should be flattered by that."

Lily laughed out loud. "I understand what you're saying, Blackie. I'll promise to hang her name above the door in ten-inch letters, if she can help us reach our goal. I'm so happy I could kiss you!" she blurted out.

"There'll be none o' that, lassie," Flori declared, as she waltzed into the parlor. "Your young man is leavin' now. Mrs. Posey has returned from the grocer. He'll have to go."

"But he just got here," Lily protested. "I feel fine. Really, I do, Flori. Why does he have to leave?"

The old woman rolled her eyes. "It's the looks of him, lass. If your mother sees him in his present state, she is sure not to allow him to call again."

Lily took a good honest look at Blackie. Sure, he was wrinkled and a bit smelly, but hadn't he been working for his aunt? It was good honest labor. Her brow wrinkled. "Since when is hard work something to be ashamed of?"

Flori pulled Blackie to his feet and turned him toward the back door. "Ah dinnae want to say, but yer laddie has been drinkin' the whiskey...all night, by the looks of him. Ah smelled him from the first moment he stepped up to the door. Right rank he is, too. Yer mother is no fool, Miss Lily. She'll see him for what he is, and you don't want that."

"And what is that, precisely?" Lily inquired peevishly.

"A drunkard, Miss Lily. Yer laddie is braw, that is for certain; but he's a drunkard, just the same."

Lily stared up at Blackie with tears beginning to form in her eyes. "Is that true, Blackie? Have you been drinking? Is that why you appear as you do?"

Why couldn't the old woman have been quiet and minded her tongue? By her accusation, and her keen sense of smell, she had made things nearly impossible to ignore; but he didn't dare confess his transgressions to Lily. She might not understand. Unfortunately, he found he didn't have much choice—not when she looked up at him with those wide, green eyes of hers. He hung his head in shame. "I'd like time to explain, Lily."

"Nae!" Flori exclaimed. "There is nae time fer talkin'. Write her a letter, me boy. Now, off with ye." She put all her weight behind her, and pushed Blackie toward the door—pushing him right into the arms of a very surprised Fern Posey.

"Whoa!" she shrieked. "Where are you going in such a hurry...and why do you smell of alcohol?"

Blackie didn't know what to say, as the woman's sharp eyes spoke volumes— none of which were good. He could plainly hear the condemnation in her voice. Lily's mother definitely knew what he'd been up to, in the early hours of the morning. There was no time to apologize. Blackie turned his red face away, in an effort to hide his guilt, and rushed past the woman standing between him and freedom.

"I'll write, Lily," he shouted over his shoulder. "I'll write every day until you agree to see me again. Don't you dare give up on me."

Furious, and more than a little disappointed, Lily began to sob. He had led her believe he was smelly because of honest, hard work. There probably wasn't even a dead cat. Again, the bounder had lied. "Don't bother," she retorted, feeling like three kinds of fool. She had gone against the advice of her parents, and what did it prove? Time and time again, Blackie had disappointed her. He always seemed to be sincere in his desire to be with her; always had a logical excuse for his actions. He had a way with words, too—the gift of Blarney, Flori would say—but he never failed to get caught up in a lie or some disreputable scheme. Perhaps dear Flori was right. Perhaps Blackie was bad news and she should forget all about him. For now, it was out of her hands. She had no choice but to try.

CHAPTER SEVEN

Winona was well satisfied with the outcome of the weekly committee meeting. Lydia Brewer had almost completed the embroidery on the new altar cloth and it was decided that Anna Northrup would call on the Posey household. No one had volunteered, so they had been forced to choose straws. Anna had lost.

It was well known in the town of Garden City, that Mr. Posey cultivated the very best flowers to be had anywhere, and when coaxed nicely, he could, on occasion, be persuaded to part with them for a good cause. What better cause was there but to decorate the house of the Lord, they all asked? Vivica Allen was elected to write a note to be given to Mr. Posey, with all the particulars clearly detailed. Each Sunday, for twenty-six weeks, he was asked to provide the most glorious centerpiece to be placed on the new altar cloth. Surely, he would not refuse the church.

By the time Winona returned home, she was quite beyond exhausted. Her friends had that ability over her. Always smiling, while constantly judging, they managed to suck all the vitality out of her. It would be a nice respite to sit down to a quiet luncheon with her nephew and discuss what they would do for the rest of the day.

"John?" she called out from the foyer. "Are you still in bed?"

She waited and listened for his response. There was none. "The poor boy must still be sleeping," she muttered to herself. She would not disturb him, just now. After she warmed herself a bit of leftover soup, she would carry a tray up to his room.

Balancing the tray with one hand was proving rather difficult, as Winona struggled with the door handle. "John," she spoke through the closed door. "I'm afraid I need your assistance. I can't get the door and carry your tray, all at the same time."

Silence was all that greeted her. Puzzled, Winona looked around and placed the tray on a nearby chair seat. Her heart was beginning to race, as she imagined all sorts of distressing scenarios. Was the boy's illness far more serious than she had first thought? Had she run off and left him at home, desperately in need of her care? She rushed back to the door and threw it wide open.

The bed was empty.

"Johnnie?" she called out, knowing it was of no use. After her initial relief at not finding him dead in his bed, a slight niggle of frustration began to build. If the boy was not here, sick in his bed, where was he?

She searched everywhere inside the immense house, growing more and more irritated with each empty room. After her exhaustive search inside turned up nothing, she traipsed out into the yard, and hunted around every tree and bush. Not a stone was left unturned, as she searched the garden shed, the tool shed, and the pump house...but there was no sign of Blackie. She paused, gazing at the unfinished fence, and let out a long troubled sigh. Something felt amiss. It wasn't like him to leave his work undone. Recently, he had been most diligent in tackling his chores, knowing that when they were completed, his sentence would be over and he would once again have the freedom to go off with his young friends—assuming there were no further infractions of the rules.

"Oh, my dear boy," Winona lamented. "What on earth are you up to now?"

Upon entering the kitchen, Winona heard firm knocking at the front door. "Johnnie? Is that you? Why are you knocking?" she called out, as she hurried to let him in.

"Oh!" she gasped, startled to see a woman standing at her door. "I'm sorry, but I assumed you were my nephew. You're Mrs. Posey, if I'm not mistaken."

Fern stood tall and proud, with her back ramrod straight and her head held high. Her mouth was set in a thin, grim line. All in all, she looked quite intimidating, and her countenance allowed no affront. "May I come in?" she asked pointedly.

Winona stepped back, holding the door open. "Of course. Follow me. I'll serve us some tea and we can talk."

"I have no need for tea, ma'am. This is not a social call. I've come to discuss your nephew, Blackie Barker."

Winona suddenly felt a cold chill run up her spine. Her Johnnie had obviously done something quite ungentlemanly, and she didn't know if she had the courage to defend his actions to this woman. Whatever he had done, it was quite serious. Folding her hands in her lap, Winona stuck out her chin and prepared for battle. She was determined to meet this lady head on, and she would stand up for her nephew—if only to protect the family name.

"Yes, Blackie...that is...John is indeed my nephew. What has he done now?" She motioned to a comfortable chair. "It looks as though this may take some time. Please have a seat."

Fern nodded graciously. "Thank you. Your nephew has been visiting our household in an effort to spend time with my daughter, Lily. I believe you have already met her?"

Winona felt her cheeks blush. "I remember the occasion, Mrs. Posey. It was most unfortunate for all of us." Now she realized why the woman was here. She had taken offense at the way she had snubbed her daughter. One would think she would be used to that. Winona assumed it was an everyday occurrence; they were the Posey family, after all.

Fern remembered the incident, as well, and this woman's careless disregard for the welfare of her lovely daughter caused her blood to boil. There was no excuse for Miss

Barker's bad manners—but that was another matter entirely. Not one for today. On this particular occasion, she was here to discuss that rapscallion, Blackie Barker.

Fern sat quietly, composing herself, preparing each word in advance, as she had a tendency to ramble. The last thing she wanted to do was confirm this woman's suspicions about the instability of the Posey family by blathering on and on, in some incoherent rant. The town had enough to talk about without adding additional fodder to their gossip.

Winona sat frozen, waiting for her unexpected guest to speak and throw accusations at her and her nephew. She began nervously tearing at the lace edging on her best handkerchief, knotted up in her lap. What was the blasted woman waiting for? *Perhaps their family really was insane?* But surely, she was in no danger of being attacked by this deranged woman. Or was she? *Oh, dear God, where was Blackie when she needed him?*

Fern cleared her throat and gazed up, directly into Winona's unsettled eyes. "Your nephew came to my home this morning. He was suffering the lingering effects of too much whiskey, from the night before. In other words, ma'am...your nephew was drunk!"

"Drunk?" Winona shrieked.

"Pickled! Smashed! In his cups! Whatever you prefer. The boy was snockered!"

"But that's impossible! He doesn't drink. He does foolish things...boyish pranks, but he does not drink! Where would he get it?"

"Men have their ways. I am not concerned with the whys and wherefores...I am only concerned that he refrains from seeing my daughter. The poor child has imagined herself quite taken with him. At this very moment, she is at home, crying into her pillow. My husband and I believe she can do much better than an inebriated delinquent—handsome though he may be," she added. That was the one thing upon which she and her daughter could agree. Blackie Barker was a most unusually handsome young fellow.

Warm tears began to gather in Winona's eyes. "I am truly sorry and ashamed, Mrs. Posey, but I have tried. I promised my dear brother that I would take his eldest son into my home with the hope of reforming his wild and wicked ways. He has been in trouble with the police and with his teachers ever since he learned the power of a beguiling smile. He can be such a dear, but his neighbors have withstood all they can tolerate, I'm afraid; his parents are nearly at their wit's end. Whatever will become of the boy?"

Fern noticed the woman's frail hands trembling, as she wiped the tears from her cheeks. There was goodness in the woman, even if she was a gossip and a bit too persnickety; and it was obvious she cared deeply for her nephew. Fern's heart began to soften toward the woman. "Is he here, now? May I speak with him?"

Winona shook her head. "I don't know where he is. I was looking for him when you arrived at my door. I have been out for the morning…a church committee meeting. Before I departed, he had managed to convince me he was ill. I expected to return home and find him in his bed, fast asleep."

"Very well," Fern sniffed. She stood and looked down on the woman weeping softly. "You need to have him tell you where he procured his whiskey. It will only go badly for him if he continues to imbibe. Force him to give up his friends, as they are more than likely the real culprits. I condemn the owner of the liquor more so than the silly young men who drink it. You must find the source and destroy it. I will leave you, now. Hopefully, there will be no further reason for me to return to your home." She started to move away.

"Wait!" Winona exclaimed, her voice hoarse and raspy. "Please…I have a confession to make and I would like for you to hear me out. I could never tell a friend or neighbor; not even my pastor would understand…but you…I can tell you. We're not friends or relation. Would you allow me to unburden myself to you?"

This was a complete surprise. Fern had expected to

leave with nothing more being said. She certainly couldn't imagine what the woman had to confess. However, by the stricken expression on her face, it was clear Miss Barker was terribly upset about something...something of utmost importance. How could she walk away and leave the poor woman so distraught? The answer was—she couldn't. Fern retook her seat and smiled kindly.

"If it eases your conscience, then feel free to unburden yourself. What you say to me, will stay forever in this room."

Winona believed her. There was something in the sound of this woman's voice, and the sincerity she saw in her compassionate eyes that set her nerves at ease. At last, she could tell someone her story—why she lived as she did and why she had given up on ever finding true happiness.

"Please hear me out before condemning me," she pleaded. "I will tell you everything. The good and the bad. But I fear you may not approve."

"It is not my place to approve or disapprove, dear. I am just here to listen. You have nothing to fear from me."

"Somehow I believe you." Giving her eyes one last wipe of the handkerchief, Winona Barker began her story.

"I may be the source of my nephew's downfall. I fear he may have discovered what I keep hidden in a locked room, in the cellar. You see...I distill my own whiskey."

Fern gasped, in spite of her vow to listen without judgment.

"I know what you must be thinking. However, it is for myself only, and I never...ever...get inebriated. My father made the smoothest whiskey in the entire county, and he taught me the trade. He learned it from his pappy, way back in the hills of Kentucky. That's where I'm from, originally. I have a small glass, now and then, to help me forget.

"You see, I wasn't always the lonely spinster you see before you. In my day, I was thought of as being rather fetching, but I never had a serious beau—not until I met Jacob. We were divinely happy and perfectly suited for one another. We planned to marry that summer...but the war broke out and changed everything.

"Kentucky was one of those border states. We had slaves, but decided to remain loyal to the Union. Jacob signed up to defend the country against the rebel invaders. He survived several skirmishes and even managed to stop by our home for a short visit. It wasn't until he left for Tennessee, that he saw more serious battles.

"Have you ever heard of Murfreesboro, Mrs. Posey?" she asked, her eyes bright with the horrors of war reflected in them.

Fern did not like the turn this conversation was taking. Distilling her own whiskey was shocking, but returning to the sights and sounds of war was agonizing. She nodded, feeling as if she was on the precipice of a dark and dangerous pit. She knew she should find some excuse to get up and walk away, while still able to do so.

Winona shrugged her shoulders. "I suppose most people have read about the battle. It was particularly gruesome...and my Jacob was there." Her breath caught, causing her voice to hitch. Suddenly, she wasn't at all certain she could continue. It was too painful.

"Go on, dear," Fern struggled to say; even though it was the last thing she wanted to hear. If speaking out would help this poor woman unburden herself—well, Mr. Posey had taught her to face her own demons, no matter how frightening they were, and not to run away. It was sometimes the only way to survive the terrors brought on by war. "You can do this," she prompted.

"Are you certain I can't get you that cup of tea?" Winona asked, praying to have something else to do but divulge her innermost pain to a complete stranger.

"Perhaps later," Fern said, kindly. If she were forced to drink anything at this moment, she would surely choke. "Your Jacob was in Murfreesboro? So was Mr. Posey," she contributed.

That revelation took Winona slightly aback. "I had no idea he fought in the war," she declared. "Maybe he knew my

Jacob?"

"Perhaps, but it is doubtful. They were all very busy, as you can well imagine. He tried not to get to know the men on a personal level. It was too hurtful to know them, only to see them fall."

"It sounds as if your husband might have been an officer. My Jacob wasn't anyone important. He rose to the rank of corporal, and for that he was mighty proud, but he was just a common soldier, you see. He was important only to me."

"I'm sure he did his part."

Winona sighed. "Yes, he did. He fell there, at Murfreesboro. I have prayed to find someone who could tell me of his last days. What were his final words? I've often wondered if they were of me."

Fern felt the familiar, painful lump begin to form at the base of her throat. Her heart was racing and she felt as though she couldn't catch her breath. Anxiety, her husband called it. It could make the room spin and cause her to swoon; and it always manifested itself with her thoughts of war—the war that had almost claimed her own life. Again, she would heed her husband's wise words and face her nightmare, straight on.

"I understand your loss, Winona," Fern said sympathetically.

"With all due respect, I don't believe you do. You can't possibly know the pain I've suffered over the years. His death is as fresh to me now, as it was the day I read his name on a list of casualties. I'm afraid you know nothing of war. You have a fine, strong husband and a home full of healthy children to fill your days."

Fern struggled with herself. Did she dare dredge up memories so painful it took her years to put them behind her? Could she risk the return of the terrible nightmares that had haunted her dreams, night and day? Was she strong enough to overcome the recollections of the horrors she had witnessed, first hand? The sights and sounds of war were forever branded into her mind. But it was the smells that threatened her sanity. The odor of blood and severed limbs rotting in the heat of the sun had filled her nostrils on a daily basis. The scent of gangrene permeated the stale air in the medical tents: and there was always the stench of death hanging over the camp. Lastly, would her own confession bring closure to this poor, wretched woman? She took a deep breath.

"You say your Jacob died at Murfreesboro. I was there… as well as Mr. Posey, and I remember it vividly. I will never forget it."

Winona's jaw dropped, as her eyes grew wide with surprise. "How could you have been there? Surely, you're mistaken, or you are making a jest. How heartless of you. I thought we were becoming friends."

Ignoring the woman's accusations, believing them to be the product of years of grief, Fern chose to forge ahead. "I am quite serious, I assure you. What was your corporal's full name?"

Winona clutched her folded hands close to her heart and prayed that at long last, her prayers would be answered. "His name was Jacob Gooding, and he had the warmest brown eyes I'd ever seen, and a smile to light up the room. He was from a small town in Kentucky…Baileys Switch. I doubt you've ever heard of it. He said it was—"

"Just a wide spot in the mud," Fern interjected. "I know."

"Oh, my Lord," Winona gasped, as breath left her lungs. "You really did know my Jacob?"

Fern closed her eyes in concentration, conjuring up the image of a young soldier with a beautiful smile. "I recall he had the loveliest blonde curls."

Happy tears were now streaming down Winona's cheeks. "Yes, he did. I would tease him about having hair as lovely as any girl's. He would laugh and say all our daughters would inherit his curls. We spent many hours dreaming of our lives together; never once thinking that a war would tear us apart."

Remembering it all in vivid detail, Fern continued. "I

spent many hours sitting by his side. We formed a bond, he and I. And when he drew his last breath, I was there to hold his hand and help him across." As always, these precious recollections brought a great deal of emotional pain to Fern's tender heart, and her own tears began to form in her weary eyes.

Winona went to kneel in front of her visitor. Taking hold of her hands, she looked up expectantly, as if she was a small child looking to a parent for all the answers. "I must know…did…did he suffer a great deal?"

Fern nodded. "I'm afraid so, dear. Most of the men were in much pain—too much pain. The doctors did all they could to relieve it, but medicines were in short supply. It was then, that I began lending a hand whenever I could, wherever needed. Although my heart was in the right place, and I genuinely wanted to help, I proved to be weak. I was too young, I suppose. Just shy of fifteen."

"Oh, my dear. You were just a child."

Fern nodded. "During times of great hardship, childhood ends early. Try as I might, there eventually came a time when I was incapable of facing the day to day tortures of war, and it's deathly decree. It was then I discovered my talent for painting miniatures. I had always sketched pictures of home, my pet cat, and the horses and such. It became a grand passion and allowed me to escape reality, if only for a few hours. You may have seen a few of my paintings around town."

Winona sat silently, but reached for her throat, her hand shaking noticeably.

"It allowed me to spend time with the wounded and provide them a service outside the constant ugliness of the surgical tent. They seemed to enjoy posing for my small portraits and were grateful for the opportunity to leave something behind. With the help of a few officers, every miniature I painted was dispatched to their loved ones. I was assured that each and every one would be delivered.

"Private Jeremy Dalton was my first," she continued. "He was scarcely older than me, just a boy. I sketched his sweet likeness for his mother, and it somehow lessened his suffering knowing he would be leaving his smiling image behind. That's also how I met your corporal. Jacob spoke lovingly of *'his girl'*." Fern paused and grinned at the woman sitting at her feet.

"I knew it," Winona murmured.

"He spoke of you many times, in fact. But of all the nice things he had to say about you—and there were many—he told me it was the sound of your laughter that he missed most. He said he would carry the memory of your tinkling laughter with him to the Pearly Gates of heaven, if need be, and there he would stop and wait for you."

Winona began to sob. To know he'd said those loving things about her was more than she had imagined. Her heart was breaking and soaring at the same time. Her dear, dear Jacob had loved her to the very end.

Winona moved her hands to the back of her neck and unclasped a gold chain. "I never remove this. It is my most cherished possession. It is a remarkable likeness of my dear Jacob... and I believe you painted it." She held it out for Fern to see.

Fern was surprised to see her own hands shake slightly, as she received the precious portrait in her fingers. "It has my mark, and I remember him in great detail. He was a kind and good man, a true gentleman in a time of sheer madness. If I remember correctly, his superior officer commended his service to his country."

Everything Fern said was true. The face was indeed familiar to her—and so very dear. The subject's eyes were bright and sparkling, glowing with good health. His smile was infectious, and his youthful innocence was evident—except this picture was a lie, a slight exaggeration. That's what their loved ones wanted to see. Hidden from view was the terrible suffering; gone were the haunted expressions in their eyes, and the fear etched deeply across their young faces. Jacob had been shot in the jaw and had great difficulty speaking. The bullet had exited through his opposite eye socket. These were the truthful images. These were the pictures of Fern's reality.

"Corporal Jacob Gooding was a very handsome man, Miss Barker, and you were a very fortunate woman to have been his chosen lady. However, you are quite mistaken about one thing. He died a hero, Winona. Corporal Gooding was not just a simple soldier. He saved the lives of three of his fellow men. His last thoughts were of you, and he died well."

"I knew he would," Winona said proudly. "He was that kind of man, and the only man for me. Thank you, Mrs. Posey. If I live to be one hundred, I will never be able to repay the kindness you showed him in his final hours…or for this." She lifted the miniature from Fern's hand, gave it a small kiss, and placed it, once again, in its rightful place around her neck. You've changed my life and lifted a burden so heavy there were days I thought I could not carry on. Bless you, Fern Posey…my new and dearest friend. Bless you."

When Fern stood to leave, she discovered her knees were quivering and her head felt as if it might burst. She was most gratified that she had been able to bring comfort to this woman, but she knew it would come at a great cost to her. Forrest would have to medicate her for several weeks. He would scold her for dredging up memories better left undisturbed. But then he would kiss her and hold her quaking body in his arms until it subsided; all the while telling her how brave and courageous he thought she was. All in all, retelling the horrors of which she had witnessed firsthand, had been worth the pain.

"Goodnight, Winona," she said a bit shakily.

"Please let me fetch my buggy to take you home, Mrs. Posey. It is the very least I can do. I can tell this has taken a great toll on you."

Fern nodded. "Perhaps that would be wise. Thank you."

At that exact moment, Blackie burst into the parlor. Seeing his aunt with her arms extended to Lily's mother, he didn't know what to think. "What goes on here?" he bellowed. "I guess my goose is cooked." After all, what other explanation could there be? These two women hardly knew each other and they were in no way friendly toward one another. They had to be conspiring against him.

"As a matter of fact," Winona said, "you can hitch up the surrey and see that Mrs. Posey gets home safely. I'll not have my friend riding the trolley. She's not feeling well. See her to the door and then return promptly. You and I must have a very long talk, my boy. Our lives have taken a turn, and one for the better, I hope. Now, jump to!"

Blackie didn't know what to say. This wasn't like his aunt, but who was he to argue? "Yes, ma'am. I'll only be a minute. You ladies rest for a moment and I'll come get you."

"He's truly a good boy," Winona said, after Blackie disappeared. "I'll explain a few things to him. I believe we'll all see a great change in him."

Fern grinned. "I trust your judgment, Winona. My Lily will be most happy with the outcome. I'm afraid he has stolen her heart."

"And she has his," Blackie's aunt responded. "I have a feeling everything will work out fine."

CHAPTER EIGHT

The night had given way to an extraordinary new day. It was as if the very angels in heaven greeted Lily as she made her way across the yard and down the sidewalk, on her way to Sunday church services. For two long weeks, she had been confined to the house with nothing more exciting to do than stare out her window at the empty robin's nest, or read in the paper about some rich society girl marrying an equally rich gentleman in Kansas City. Her father had a subscription to the Star newspaper, and it was only a week old by the time it was delivered to Garden City. However, today was different. In another time, another era, it could be said today was her true "coming out" day. The air smelled unusually sweet, and the birds twittered lovely melodies from high up in the trees. The chiming of the bells in the church steeple rang out across the rolling land, and there were smiles on the faces of all the people she passed. Lily felt close to bursting out in song. This promised to be a nearly perfect day...well, almost perfect.

As the Posey family passed under the tall white columns, at the front of the red brick church, Lily could hear the usual whispers. All eyes seemed to be on them. The townspeople's snide looks threatened to dampen Lily's spirit, but today was special. Taking in a deep breath of the fresh, invigorating air, she threw back her shoulders and faced them with courage. Instead of ducking her head and quietly taking a seat as quickly as possible, Lily responded to their glances with a dazzling smile. "Good morning," she said cheerfully, hoping they could not see the quaking of her knees beneath her skirts. Surprisingly, some folks returned her friendly greeting with an appropriate response of their own.

"Good mornin', Miss Posey," some said. "Nice to see you," others muttered. "Lookin' well."

Feeling unstoppable, Lily followed her family into church and gracefully took her seat.

Pastor Littlejohn led the singing of the first hymn. Afterward, he gave a cordial welcome to all newcomers and made announcements pertinent to the congregation. So and so had a new baby...mother and son were doing fine. The new father was reported to be recovering. Everyone laughed. Old Lady Meadows sadly passed away on Wednesday night. Services were held on Friday. To close, the pastor walked away from his usual stance at the lectern and gazed out over his obedient flock. He was searching faces for someone in particular.

"There you are, Mrs. Posey. Would you please rise? And Miss Barker...would you also rise?"

Both women stood up; each looking slightly embarrassed to be pointed out in front of everyone.

He raised his arms to the congregation, addressing them one and all. "It has come to my attention that these two fine ladies have just made each other's acquaintance. Although a joyous occasion, it is a sad state of affairs when two lovely, decent women, each living in this town for more than twenty years and separated by less than four city blocks, are just now becoming friends. How many of us are guilty of this oversight? We owe it to ourselves, and to our fellow man, to get out and meet our neighbors. These women found they were united by a single event. They have been forever changed...and I believe all for the better. Each has found a new and fast friend. That is the subject of today's sermon—Friendship. You may take your seats, ladies."

Fern and Winona made eye contact and smiled broadly. The pastor was right. They were friends, today and forevermore.

Lily couldn't believe her eyes or ears. Had the world gone topsy-turvy while she was laid up in bed? When had her mother gotten to know Blackie's stern and foreboding aunt? What could they possibly have in common? While trying to sort it all out in her head, Lily failed to notice a late arrival.

"Excuse me, sir," a male voice softly whispered. "Pardon me, ma'am," he said, as he climbed over Mr. and Mrs. Applebaum.

"Ouch! My bunion."

"Sorry," he blurted out. "So sorry about your toe, ma'am."

"Blackie?" Lily muttered in disbelief. This was certainly turning out to be a red-letter day. Blackie had come to church without being forced. Not to mention, he was dressed most splendidly. He could have been on the cover of Men's Quarterly. The world had indeed flipped on its axis.

"May I sit here?" he asked Lily, pointing to an extremely small empty space beside her.

Inside, her stomach began doing flip-flops; but outside, she tried to adopt a casual and slightly blasé demeanor. It was important for a girl to seem nonchalant and not appear too anxious to see a boy again; else he would quickly gain the upper hand. "It is a free country. I suppose you may sit here...if you wish," she said quietly, trying her best to avoid his entrancing smile.

Unfortunately, a quick glance from out of the corner of her eye, was her undoing. As always, his manly good looks managed to steal her breath away and cause her to go slightly weak in the knees. The inspiring words of the pastor were lost on her, as she could only imagine Blackie's delicious lips touching hers, and his strong hands holding her tightly against his body. She could imagine him saying romantic things to her, whispering tender words of love into her ear, as she melted into his loving embrace, eager to do his bidding. Lily's eyes closed, conjuring the scene of desire in explicit detail.

"A-hem." Blackie cleared his throat and leaned his head toward Lily's. She was behaving most oddly, and a few people were beginning to stare. "Lily," he whispered. "Wake up."

Her eyes remained closed. "I am not asleep. Leave me alone," she entreated.

"People are watching."

Lily's eyes popped wide open. "Oh, dear," she gasped. "Whatever do you think they are thinking?"

Blackie chuckled. He knew what he was thinking and it fired his blood. "Well, you could always rub your ankle. They might figure you're still recuperating from your injury and feel sorry for your pain."

"That's a very good idea." Lily promptly lifted the hem of her skirt and stuck her foot out into the aisle. Moaning quietly, she stroked and massaged her ankle. Occasionally, she would groan softly for emphasis.

"How am I doing?" she asked discreetly, from the corner of her mouth.

Blackie chuckled. "You're doing great, sweetheart. Half the men in church are now staring at your leg."

Immediately dropping her skirt, Lily glared up at the young man sitting too closely beside her, with a big, dopey grin plastered across his arrogant face. "Do you enjoy making a fool of me? Why are you here? I know it is certainly not for the sermon."

"I've come because it's Sunday...and I knew you'd be here. I've changed, Lily, and—"

"Shush, children," Lily's mother quietly admonished. "You may talk after the service. Invite your young man home to dinner, Lily."

"Yes, Mother," Lily answered obediently. She turned toward Blackie and placed a single finger over her lips.

He nodded. Hadn't he just endured two excruciatingly long weeks without seeing or talking to Lily? Another hour shouldn't be too difficult to withstand, as he could now, at the very least, allow his starving eyes to gaze upon her perfect profile and linger on her luscious lower lip. He could now breathe the same air as she, and he could bask in the warmth of her golden radiance. Yes, he could survive for one more hour—but just.

    Blackie wasn't the only one having a degree of difficulty concentrating on the pastor's message. Lily was exceedingly aware of Blackie's presence at her side. The warmth of his body consumed her, heating her blood and stimulating every nerve in her body. It was impossible not to fidget while sitting in the pew. She tingled in the most unusual places. She noticed her breathing was shallow and rapid, causing her to feel slightly lightheaded. What if she was to faint in church? Would Blackie catch her? Would the pastor even notice? She felt the strength of Blackie's thigh, as it rested against her leg. A man's body was so different from that of a woman's, she mused. Where she was soft and smooth, a man was all hard, sculpted muscle, covered in coarse hair. She could see the dark stubble on Blackie's chin. It would be so exciting to watch him shave. Watching him take easy strokes across his cheeks and down his firm jaw, all the while breathing in the manly smell of his soap and after-cologne, was a persistent desire she felt every morning.

    "Mmmm," she moaned softly, as she longed to reach out and stroke that smooth face. Her mouth began to water.

    "What was that, dear?" her mother inquired. "Aren't you feeling well? Your face looks a mite flushed. I hope we didn't rush things in allowing you to come out today."

    Lily couldn't find her voice. Still overcome with desire for the man pressed up against her, she could only try to force her eyes forward and away from her mother's look of alarm.

    "She's fine, my dear," Forrest whispered to his overly concerned wife. "Let them be."

    It was a fact that sometimes his family underestimated his powers of observation; in reality, there was very little that actually transpired in the Posey household that Forrest Posey did not notice. This particular scenario had been building for the last several weeks. It was only a matter of time before this young man would come to him, hat in hand, and ask to court his lovely daughter. A blind man could see they were in love, and he had absolutely no intention of coming between them. After all, he remembered what it was like to be a man saved by the love of a beautiful female.

By the time the final "Amen" was said, the Posey family was headed for the doors. It had been a lovely sermon, and it was quite nice to gather as a family in the House of the Lord, but this day was simply too delightful to waste. Everyone wanted to be gay, and enjoy the good weather and each other's company.

Bud caught up with his parents, slightly out of breath. "I've been invited to Victoria's for Sunday dinner. I told her I would speak with you first, but I was pretty confident you'd have no objections." He'd been seeing Victoria Spencer for several months, and found her to be perfect in almost every way. Unlike most girls, he'd known, she had yet to put his teeth on edge.

"Well, we were to dine with Lily's beau…I don't know," his mother hedged.

"You go and have a good time, Bud," his father exclaimed. "But next week, you must invite Miss Spencer to our home for dinner. It's high time we met this young woman of yours…and she needs to meet us." He grinned at his son, giving him a sly wink. He knew what everyone in town thought of the Poseys. *They were a strange lot. Beware. Stay clear of them.* What a load of rubbish. Forrest Posey refused to allow a lot of idle gossip keep his children from enjoying life. It was high time they put more effort in joining with the townsfolk. Hadn't he readily agreed to supply flowers for the church altar, not for half the year, but for the entire twelve months? It was true; they would probably never totally blend in, but they would no longer be objects of ridicule, either. He and his wife owed that much to Poppy and Jasmine. The older children had forged their own way; some succeeding better than others, but the little ones deserved an easier time of it.

"Thank you, Father. I'll be home early." Having gained permission, Bud ran off in the opposite direction, soon to be lost in the crowd.

Taking a glance at Lily, walking hand in hand with the Barker boy, Fern let out a long, audible sigh. "I am afraid our babies have all grown up and are leaving us, Husband."

"Oh, I don't know, darlin'. Bud and Lily haven't eloped yet —at least as far as I know—and our two youngest are still climbing trees and skinning their knees. Why, only yesterday, I caught Jasmine in just her drawers, wading in the fountain. When I asked her what she was doing, she replied, 'Fishing!' Can you imagine? In our cupid's fountain, she expected to find a fish. You'll be happy to know she had neatly folded her dress and undergarments, so as not to get them wet, before standing nearly naked in our own front lawn." He chuckled, remembering the delightful scene.

"Oh, my goodness. Did the neighbors see?" Fern asked, giggling at the ridiculous story.

"Only the ones she waved and called out to, my dear."

Fern broke out in great peals of laughter. "That little imp! You're absolutely correct, Husband...it will be years before we are able to enjoy the luxury of quiet solitude."

"Years and years, darlin'. And don't forget Holly and Ivy...there will be grandchildren, no doubt."

Fern squeezed his arm, her eyes twinkling with happiness. "We may need a bigger house."

Blackie and Lily sat quietly, side by side, slowly swinging back and forth on the white porch swing. There was no need for conversation, as it was enough to simply be alone and bask in the glow of each other's company. There were no complaints about the dinner, as it had been most excellent, and the company could not have been more cordial. Lily was relieved that no one said or did anything to embarrass Blackie; even dear old Flori had curbed her sharp tongue and had smiled in his direction. The blossoms were kept to a minimum, as Mr. Posey was currently studying the effects of certain roots.

As for Blackie, he could have been chewing stewed shoe leather and not notice; so content was he in gazing across the table at the most beautiful girl he'd ever seen. Occasionally, she would grace him with one of her smiles and send his heart reeling. It terrified him to remember how close he had come to losing her. She was the kind of girl that would have found it impossible to love a man whom she did not admire. His reckless behavior had almost cost him the love of his life.

Lily smoothed the fabric across her lap, creating perfect pleats in the skirt. She was very pleased with the yellow daisies embroidered around her waist and hem.

"New dress?" Blackie inquired. He could never be sure, because Lily looked perfect in everything she wore. She didn't need some fancy frippery to get his attention.

"Yes," she answered, smiling very prettily. "I chose it myself. Do you like it?"

He nodded. "It shows off your neck."

Lily laughed. "I suppose that's a compliment, but I was expecting something along the line of, 'it enhances your eyes,' or 'it does wonders for your complexion'."

"Well, it does both of those things. But honestly, Lily, you don't need a new dress to do that. You're perfect the way you are."

She blushed. "I could kiss you for that."

"I wouldn't stop you."

"Say something else," she urged. "Did you have a nice time, tonight?"

"I do believe that chicken was the best I ever ate," he said.

"That's nice. I'll be sure to tell Flori."

"The mashed potatoes were excellent, too. You should tell her that as well."

Lily grinned. Was it possible Blackie was still afraid of their little Scottish cook? "The pansies didn't bother you?"

"Ah, heck no. I can get used to a few flowers. They're kind of pretty, and if you like them...well who am I to argue?" He smiled his most charming smile.

"Am I to believe you will give deference to me in all things?"

Blackie's eyes grew enormous. *"Did I say that?"* he

shrieked. "You certainly don't expect me not to have any say at all. That's not the order of things. I'm still a man, and a man is the head of his family. Just ask your father. A man's word is to be taken seriously. A woman...well, a woman is...well, she is...aw, Lily, you know how important a woman is. I shouldn't have to spell it out for you. But a man is important too, you know."

Lily giggled. "Yes, Blackie. I know what you're trying to say, and you say it very eloquently, too. Let me see if I understand your meaning; a man is the head of the family, while the woman is its heart. Is that right, dearest?"

She had called him *dearest*. Then why did he feel as if he'd just been punched in the gut and couldn't catch his breath? His eyes began to water and his pulse became erratic. What was happening to him?

"Blackie? Are you feeling ill? Should I go and fetch Father?"

"No!" he croaked. "Give me a minute to catch my breath, will ya?. I was taken a bit unawares."

"Unawares? Did I miss something?"

Blackie took a deep breath, and reached for her hand,. Gazing deeply into her eyes, he raised her palm slowly to his lips and placed a tender kiss in its center. "You called me, 'dearest'. Is that how you truly feel?"

It was Lily's turn to feel flushed and slightly unwell. Blackie's intense stare smoldered, causing a warm feeling to rush through every inch of her body. She felt so peculiar. Never before had she experienced the heat that now threatened to consume her. Surely, she could not be mistaken about his sentiments. What if he didn't return her feelings? She had been the first to utter those specific words of endearment. Perhaps she'd been too bold. Although a silly and somewhat antiquated opinion, some men insisted on being the one to make all the first moves. True, he had already called her sweetheart and darlin' on more than one occasion, but she always knew it was meant in a flirtatious way. He'd never spoken true words of love and devotion to her. It was still thought unseemly for a woman to address a gentleman in such familiar terms. It may have been wise to wait for Blackie to speak, and now she didn't know how to respond to him. Her mind was a muddled mess. She had to think quickly.

"What was that I said?" she asked, appearing as if she had not a clue. "I say all sorts of silly things, without realizing what it is I'm saying. You know me...I rattle on and on, never saying anything of any real importance. I guess I got that from my mother. Do you remember the first time you came to Sunday dinner? She talked and talked—I guess I did too. That's the way our family is. So what was it you think I said?"

Blackie sat listening to Lily's nervous ramblings. He loved that about her. She'd start to talk and say the funniest things. Her eyes would sparkle as her brain rushed to keep up with her mouth. At the same time, her delicate hands would gesticulate her every word. She was totally delightful to watch, and all he could think to do was silence her with a kiss—a good, long kiss.

"You called me, 'dearest'," he said in a deep, velvety voice.

Lily swallowed, trying not to swoon. "I did?" she squeaked.

He nodded. "You know you did. I heard it most distinctly. Did you mean it?"

"Do you want me to mean it?"

"Hmm, I definitely do, and I'll show you just how much. Come here to me, Lily," he said softly.

Now was the time to swoon. She just knew she would. As if held in a mysterious trance, she felt herself slide closer to Blackie and felt her face lift to within mere inches of his. "Like this?" she whispered breathlessly.

"Mmm...just like that. I'm going to kiss you now, Lily. I'm going to taste your sweet lips and claim them for myself. I want you to remember this kiss forever."

"Okay," she murmured, as she closed her eyes, preparing for her very first kiss. "I'm ready."

Blackie lifted her chin and stared down into her exquisite face. So innocent and pure; it was hard to believe she found anything deserving in him. He'd always been a hell-raiser, and yet, here she was—his lovely angel, waiting for him to stake his claim over her with a simple kiss. She had placed her faith in him. Undeserving though he was, she had placed her future in his hands, believing him to be a man of honor—a man to whom she could entrust her love.

That was when he knew the truth of it all. For Lily Posey, there would be but one man in her life, and the expectations of him being that one single man for her, was terrifying.

However, Blackie had never been one to shy away from a challenge, nor would he in this instance, as he could not help but continue with his gentle seduction. It was evident to him; Lily was not the only one to be caught up in the unsuspecting snare of romance. If his own good aunt had suddenly appeared on the porch beside them, he would have found it impossible to stop and pull away. A sophisticated man about town, he was just as much a victim to the desires of the heart as any man had ever been, and he was compelled to see it through to its inevitable conclusion. As susceptible as any innocent lad, he found himself firmly entangled in her irresistible web.

As the sweetest nectar calls out to the honeybee, Blackie felt the irresistible pull of Lily's full, pursed lips, beckoning him. At the exact moment their lips touched, Blackie felt his world tilt, and a sudden, overwhelming burst of emotion ran through every square inch of him; feelings so strong, he could barely contain his excitement. Lost in the pure silkiness of her lips and the clean, sweet scent of her breath, his senses were quickly and completely overcome. Then when she parted those entrancing lips, opening her mouth just enough to allow him entrance into its silken depths, he felt his heart nearly burst. What was this insanity he was feeling? It was something quite extraordinary, and all he could to do was forge ahead and claim her for himself.

Time stood still, as the kiss remained unbroken.

Melded, practically fused together, their lips continued to play one with the other, searching for more, and rejoicing in what they had already gained. A soft, deep sound rumbled up from Blackie's throat. His breathing moved unevenly, as he hungered to move forward. No one wanted to sever the connection; that which was the magic of a first kiss, but finally, he felt Lily straighten up, in an effort to do just that.

"Oh, my goodness," she said, in voice so raspy she did not recognize it as her own. "My...oh my," she repeated. She had been the first to open her eyes, and she discovered the expression on Blackie's face was quite unsettling. It was not one of rapture, as she had expected it to be, but a slightly pained expression; even appearing a bit hostile; certainly not what she would have expected to see on the face of a man she had just kissed. Had he not enjoyed it? She held her breath in an effort to hold back the tears that were quickly building. If he rejected her now, she would never survive it. Her chest rose and fell rapidly, in an attempt to calm her pounding heart.

"Blackie? Tell me what's wrong," she pleaded, seeing his intense frown. "Did I do something incorrectly?"

At first her words made no sense. His mind was still reeling with the realization he had fallen head over ears in love with this girl, but now she was acting a mite peculiar—considering what they had just shared. Had *she* not enjoyed the kiss? Perhaps he'd been too aggressive and had frightened her. Lily was very innocent, after all, but thankfully, she was also a quick study. Blackie grinned; he had been well pleased. She had quickly taken control of the kiss and returned as good as she got.

"Huh? Did you say something, Lily?"

Blackie looked as if his mind was somewhere else. Was he thinking of someone else—someone he still had a yearning for? Had he compared her to another and found her lacking? Lily's chin began to quiver. "I asked you to tell me what I did to displease you. It was my first kiss; I know I can do better. Please don't be mad. Give me another chance."

Mad at her? Was the girl insane? Was it possible she

actually had no notion of the devastating effect she had on him? After kissing her, Blackie realized his life would never be the same, and that was a lot for a guy to come to terms with. The fathomless depth of his feelings for her, surprised him. Even now, while he gazed at her, seeing her troubled features, her wrinkled brow and her darling little chin trembling with uncertainty, he could feel the heat of desire building in his loins. Now that he had tasted what she had to offer, it would be almost impossible for him to deny himself of her feminine pleasures. His mind began to work overtime, picturing her slender form without the encumbrance of her undergarments, and imagining the soft, silkiness of her naked flesh. She was incomparable to any other girl he'd ever known, and it would be sheer torture to be near her and not take advantage of her naiveté.

Blackie tried to compose himself. Clearing his throat and looking down at his shaking hands, he said, "Don't be a goose, Lily. It was fine. You were fine...quite what I expected, in fact. It's true you haven't had much experience, but that's the way it should be. I, on the other hand, have not been so sheltered," he smirked. That was putting it mildly. His sins were legendary in some parts, and suddenly, for no reason he could comprehend, Blackie felt the urgent need to take a bath. Instead, he ran his fingers through his hair and tugged on his vest, flicking an invisible piece of lint from its lapel, in an attempt to repair his image.

So he thought her earth-shattering kiss was fine, did he? It was what he expected from her, was it? Lily's temper began a slow simmer. How dare he! How did he expect her to get experience kissing boys, if only the "other type" of girl was allowed to try? Life was not fair. Society had seen to that. Good girls were not allowed to hone their skills by kissing boys. The more she thought about the injustice of it all; the madder she became, and her blood began to boil.

"It's only because you're a man," she sniffed. His callous remark was of course accurate, but it still stung, and was inconsiderate of her feelings. Naturally, she would be inexperienced.

What kind of girl did he think she was?

"Don't get me wrong, Lily. You can't help it. A proper young lady is supposed to be chaste. You know...untouched. I wouldn't want you to know how to kiss any better than you already do." That was the truth. If she were any better, he'd be down on all fours, begging her to toss him a bone. "It is for me to teach you."

Lily rolled her big eyes and scooted to the far end of the swing, putting as much distance between herself and Blackie as possible. "I know what *chaste* means, and I also know the meaning of arrogant, conceited, and pig-headed. I believe you fill that definition, Mr. Barker, quite adequately." She rose from her seat. "I find the hour is growing late. I am certain it must be time for you to run off and do the bidding of your aunt. It has been an enlightening afternoon. Thank you for your well-intentioned lesson. Good day to you," she said stiffly.

Blackie jumped to his feet. "Now, see hear!" he shouted, as he grabbed her by the shoulder. "I don't understand what's gotten into you, Lily, but I'll not stand here, while you call me names or accuse me of something I didn't intend. Just what did I do to anger you?" He looked into her face and smiled his most devilish smile. "Come on, Lily," he coaxed. "I only kissed you. Surely, that's not a crime...and you seemed to like it. Quite a lot, in fact."

The man was infuriating, and she was quickly reaching her limit. Lily gritted her teeth and clenched both her fists. Boy, wouldn't he be surprised if she did what she really wanted to do? She'd show him she was more than some starry eyed, simpering girl. After she was finished with him, he'd walk away with a dandy black eye and more, if he weren't careful—but she was a lady, she reminded herself, and would not stoop to conquer. Fighting to keep her voice steady, she declared, "I found your kiss tolerable, Mr. Barker, but frankly, I don't see what all the fuss is about. It was nice enough, but so is having my hair brushed. I suppose I found it mildly disappointing."

"No, I don't believe you. You liked it. A man can tell

these things, you know. You were like jelly in my arms. I heard your soft moans of pleasure. I could detect the slight fragrance of your desire. Confess Lily…you are lying not only to me, but also to yourself. You found my kiss to be more than you ever dreamed, and you just refuse to admit it." Why was that, he wondered? And what in tarnation were they arguing about? A kiss? A kiss that was a revelation; bone-melting in fact? One that should be recorded in the book of love, listed high above all others? Poets would find it impossible to describe their first kiss.

Refusing to let the day end with harsh words and too many unanswered questions, he drew her closer, held her firmly, and buried his face in her golden curls, breathing in the heavenly essence that was hers alone. "Hush, Lily," he whispered. "There isn't much time, and I don't wish to continue arguing with you… not when I could be kissing you again."

Lily felt her anger begin to slip. She tried to hold on to the resentment she felt, the sting of his insult, but the truth be known, when Blackie took her in his arms and held her tight, she knew it was over. Feeling the rapid tattoo of his heart against her chest, she indeed began to melt into a mound of hopeless jelly. All that he had said was true—painfully so. She was an innocent, and he was not. She had enjoyed the kiss immensely, and he thought it was nice. Against her better judgment, she found she did adore him, and she prayed he liked her half as much. The tears that had been threatening to overflow, suddenly began to run down her cheeks in warm, salty rivulets.

"Oh, Lily, please don't cry, darlin'," he begged. A female's tears had always been his undoing; having the ability to pull at his heartstrings and weaken his resolve. "I honestly don't know what I've done to make you cry. Did I scare you by holding you too close?"

She shook her head.

"Did I bite your lip and cause you pain?"

Lily sniffed, and again, shook her head.

Blackie sighed loudly, determined to get to the bottom of things. "Well, if not that, then I am at a complete loss, Lily

Posey. You have me flummoxed. I don't usually have this much trouble with girls, but since meeting you, it seems something is always going wrong." He recalled two ill-fated dinners and several nights drowning in the bottom of a jug of whiskey.

Although Lily wasn't directly to blame for his alcoholic binges, she was certainly the cause for him to search out other enjoyable past times. In a way, he figured she was partially responsible for his terrible discomfort. Looking down at his blistered palms, he recalled many extra hours of labor spent in service to his aunt, with the hope of salvaging a few precious minutes to spend in Lily's company—minutes when he could have been eating a badly needed meal. Only that morning, he had had to make a new notch in his belt. But he had done it gladly. One glance at Lily's sparkling green eyes and dimpled smile, he had no doubt she was worth all the backbreaking work and sacrifice—at least he had thought so until this moment. It was possible he had misjudged her interest in him. Perhaps he was chasing an unattainable dream.

"Look, Lily...I enjoy your company and I thought you enjoyed mine. I admit I think of you all day long, but I need your help to understand how one moment, I can be in heaven, kissing the two most beautiful lips this side of paradise; and the very next instant, you're scooting away from me as if I have something contagious. You kiss me, and then call me names; now you're practically kicking me off the porch. You're a real paradox, Lily. Tell me...where did I go wrong? Have I misjudged your interest in me? If you don't clear up this confusion, I think I'll go mad," he pleaded.

Lily stepped back, slightly out of Blackie's embrace, and as she looked up into his deep, brown eyes, she placed two fingertips against his mouth, tracing his lips. "Are all kisses like that?" she asked, her voice soft and quivering only slightly.

Suddenly emboldened by the look of wonder on her pretty face, Blackie grinned, still holding onto a small measure of hope. "It all depends on what you mean by *like that*. Did you find it good? Bad? Maybe just adequate?" He smirked, knowing she had found it a great deal more than adequate.

Lily's cheeks took on a decidedly red tinge. "It was wonderful," she stated dreamily, finding his mouth absolutely fascinating.

Well, that was more like it, Blackie thought. "So you *did* like it," he chuckled. "I knew it all along, although you did have me worried for a minute. I thought I'd lost my touch, or something."

"I don't suppose you would want to try it again?" she asked demurely.

Blackie snorted. "Oh, wouldn't I? You don't even have to ask," he replied, as he reached for her. He lowered his face to hers, staring unwaveringly into her eyes, moistening his lips just slightly, he prepared to savor her sweet, luscious mouth, once again.

"Shhh! They'll hear you."
"Will not; but they'll smell you."
"Noisy!"
"Stinky!"
"Am not!"
"Are too. Scoot over!"
"But I can't see nothin'."

Blackie stiffened, and cocked his head to listen to the muffled whispers coming from a place not too far off.

Lily groaned. "It's them," she whispered between clenched teeth. "My two monstrous little sisters. Heaven knows how long they've been spying on us. There is never any privacy in this house."

Blackie chuckled. She was so damn pretty when vexed. Sparks flew from her eyes. Giving her hands a little squeeze for reassurance, he playfully tapped the end of her nose with his finger. "We should have known. We could simply ignore them," he suggested.

"And what good would that do?" she retorted. "They'll just run off and tell Mother and Father what we're doing and you will be quickly sent home with orders never to return. No,

Blackie, we mustn't take the chance," she said determinedly.

"Or...we could play a prank on them." Blackie smiled, filling his face with a look of pure mischief. It was an infectious grin, one which caused Lily to giggle with anticipation. She loved everything about Blackie, even his wild, impulsively ornery nature. He had a plan and it would prove to be most enjoyable—at least for the two of them.

"What you say, we—" His voice suddenly dropped off to a soft, almost silent murmur, as he whispered his idea into Lily's ear.

"Move over. I can't hear," Poppy whined, as she shoved her sister.

Jasmine growled and poked her sister in the ribs. "What are they sayin'?"

Poppy let out a long, protracted sigh. "I think they must'a heard you," she accused.

"Did not! It was you, they heard. You always go and ruin everything," Jasmine complained. She wriggled out from their favorite hiding place beneath the porch, and stood behind the flowering azalea bush. Dusting off her skirts, she proclaimed most vociferously, "I'm not ever playin' with you again!"

Following head first, with her orange braids mixing with the dirt and cobwebs, a very indignant Poppy quickly emerged from the dark recesses of the under-porch area. "You're such a baby!" she declared. "And you talk too much...and you smell so bad, I thought I was gonna gag." She grabbed her neck and stuck out her tongue to demonstrate her point.

"I do not smell bad," Jasmine countered.

Poppy pinched her fingers over her nose. "Do to...like a horse, six days dead."

Jasmine gasped. "Do not," she continued to argue, even as her big eyes began to fill with tears. "Not all the time," she sniffed, as her bottom lip began to tremble. "You're hateful, Poppy."

Blackie, biting his lips to contain his laughter, motioned with his eyes to the two quarrelsome children. "Should I put a stop to this?" he inquired. It was all very entertaining, but Lily was beginning to show some signs of concern. It wouldn't do if the children's bickering brought either Mister or Missus Posey out to investigate.

She nodded and placed her hand on his arm. "Be tactful, Blackie. They are complete hooligans, but they are my little sisters and I do love them dreadfully."

He raised a dark eyebrow. "Never fear, Lily. Even though they brought about a premature ending to our romantic afternoon, I will use restraint. You know, they could very well carry tales to your parents," he warned. That was a very distinct possibility, and one that only now became worrisome. How much did the little demons actually hear?

Blackie walked lightly down the steps, staying close to the bushes, and made his way around to the far end of the porch. He came upon the little girls, just as Poppy gave Jasmine a sharp shove—right into the flowering quince and all its prickly thorns. All thoughts of playing a joke on the two meddlesome youngsters, was immediately forgotten.

A howl of enormous proportions went out from the smallest child, as she struggled to detach herself from the grappling thorns. The painful scratches were already beginning to bleed and puff up. The sight of her distress caught Blackie by surprise, and without thinking, he reeled on the responsible culprit.

Grabbing a wide-eyed, unrepentant Poppy by her delicate shoulders, he swiftly lifted her up off the ground, holding her at face level. He wanted to shake the very life out of her, but seeing how frightened she was, he growled instead. "Grrrr! How cruel you are to your sister!" he barked. "I ought to thrash you within an inch of your life, you little monster!"

Blackie was shaking with rage, as little Jasmine managed to tumble out of the sticker bush, covered from head to toe, in stinging scratches and angry welts. With scalding tears cascading down her dirty little face, as she struggled to catch her breath.

Terrified by the tall, angry, dark man, holding her at arm's length, and the seeing the damage she had done to her sister, Poppy began to scream. She screamed as loud as a girl of ten is capable of screaming. Even through Blackie's futile attempts to silence her, she continued to wail.

"What are you doing, sir? Put her down immediately!"

Blackie spun around to see Mr. Posey standing behind him, with a pair of recently sharpened garden shears glistening in his hands. Without another thought, he loosened his grasp on the nearly hysterical Poppy, dropping her at her father's feet. She crawled away on her hands and knees to her wounded sister, and wrapped her skinny arms around her. The two little girls began to comfort one another, in a most heartwarming way; kissing and soothing away mutual tears from wet, dirty faces.

"Mr. Posey, sir!" Blackie gulped. "It really isn't the way it seems. I...I was only trying to...well...you see, they were fussing and I was going to stop it, but the child with the braids...the one that I was holding—oh, forget it," he conceded. "I can only imagine what you're thinking." He held his hands out in front of him, waiting to be taken to the nearest police station. "Call Officer O'Toole and let him haul me away," he said, resigned to his pitiful fate. It was then he heard the man softly chuckling.

"My girls are quite a handful, Mr. Barker. Always have been. At least twice a year, one of them gets pushed into the quince. It stings, but I have something to make it feel better. They'll be each other's best friend by suppertime, I imagine. After all, they now have a common enemy." He grinned. "Where's my other daughter?" he asked, good humor showing in his eyes. The man had his own ideas of her whereabouts, but decided it was best to keep it to himself for now. "She's feeling all right, I wager?"

Blackie at least had the good graces to blush at the man's veiled inquiry. Mr. Posey wasn't an ignorant man and knew the ways of young love. "Yes, sir. Lily is on the porch, swinging. She was the one who asked me to see to the girls."

Mr. Posey had already lifted his scratched and bleeding

daughter into his arms. Handing the shears off to Blackie, he took up the other child's delicate hand. "Before you go, see that this is returned to the potting shed, Mr. Barker. I'm afraid I must tend to my children's wounds."

Blackie nodded. "Yes, sir—and I am sorry, sir. I did not mean to frighten the child."

As Mr. Posey walked away, he said, over his shoulder, "It was to be expected, young man. I know my lovely bunch of Poseys very well. Good day to you," he called out.

"And you, too, sir," Blackie offered to the man's back; ignoring Poppy's impudent stare and Jasmine's small pink tongue, stuck out in defiance. It was difficult to imagine those two little heathens ever maturing into the lovely woman their older sister had become. Surely, Lily had never behaved in such a manner.

By the time Blackie returned to the porch, Lily had worked herself into quite a state. "I heard the screaming," she said nervously, "and then I heard Father's voice. Was he terribly upset? What has happened? You didn't strike the girls...did you?"

"What do you take me for? *Me* hit a girl? Even the one with orange pigtails doesn't deserve that. It seems one pushed the other into the bush with the thorns. I hate to say it, but the child did suffer a painful injury. Your father is taking care of her now."

"So he didn't blame you?"

Blackie did his best to appear indignant, although he too, had been relieved the man had not found him guilty of assaulting his precious children. "As a matter of fact, your father was quite cordial—right up to the point of handing me these ominous looking shears and telling me, '*good day*'."

"Oh, I see," she said thoughtfully. "That is his way of dismissing you. He must think it is time for you to return home. But I don't want you to go, Blackie...not just yet. Perhaps we could take a walk?"

There was nothing he would rather do than spend another hour romancing this luscious female, he mused, but walking out and finding a private little nook, far away from prying eyes, wasn't going to happen. There was something unspoken between Mr. Posey and himself, and if he was ever to gain the man's permission to continue seeing more of the delectable Lily Posey, then it would be in his best interest to abide by her father's wishes. As difficult as it was, he had to say goodnight.

"Don't pout, Lily," he cajoled. "I must try to convince your father of my worthiness. No doubt, he has his concerns. No father ever thinks any young man is deserving of his beautiful daughter, and I am no exception...perhaps worse than most, I imagine. My aunt has asked me to tend to the roof before the next storm. That should keep me busy for the next several days, but I'll be able to see you Saturday."

"Saturday? That's forever," she cried in dismay. "How am I supposed to go an entire week without seeing you?" The days would seem interminably long without his frequent visits to look forward to.

A corner of Blackie's mouth turned up in a most flirtatious grin. With a finger placed tenderly under her chin, he chided, "Now, don't carry on so, my girl. I'll be working all the day through. I won't even have time to eat. Won't you feel sorry for me?"

She nodded. "Yes, but won't you miss me just a little?"

"More than just a little, darlin'. I'll be thinking of you every minute of the day." And most of the night as well, he thought, but managed to keep to himself. His nights were going to be sleepless and filled with hours of yearning for the touch of her soft, sweet flesh. Even now, he could fill his head with her alluring scent and imagine her panting his name. This promised to be a very long week.

Lily took a deep breath and tried her best to appear slightly detached. "I suppose if you have to work for your aunt, then you must; but don't expect me to wait around the house for your call, Mr. Barker," she warned. "I will most likely be out."

Blackie knew this was all bluster, as none of the Poseys ever ventured out. They had few friends and seemed to be quite satisfied staying home. However, if Lily wished to annoy him with her false threats, then so be it. He could play along. "Where will you be going? Not to practice your kissing, I hope."

Trying to sound as if it were a matter of no real importance, Lily replied, "You can be so tedious. I think I may go to the lake. In fact, I may go for a row on Fulton's Pond."

Blackie hid his smile. "And who is going to row the boat? Surely, not even Lily Posey rows her own canoe."

"Well, of course not. I...well...I probably won't be going boating after all. Instead, I believe I'll go bicycling. Yes, that is what I'll do...on a big, shiny red bicycle; one that is made for two, I think."

This was turning out to be a lot of fun. "For two, you say? Tell me...Poppy or Jasmine? Which one will you choose to go with you?"

"Neither!" Lily snapped, as she spun around to look him square in the eye. "You think you're so smart. I have friends, you know. You're not the only boy that comes by the house." It wasn't a lie. Bud had several friends that visited quite often; they just didn't stop by to see her.

Could that possibly be true, Blackie wondered? Had the blinders suddenly been removed, thereby allowing other boys to see Lily for the magnificent creature she truly was; someone so new to the community he had yet to be prejudiced against the entire Posey clan? The fun was quickly beginning to dissipate from their ridiculous conversation. Even if there was the slightest chance...

"Enough!" he snapped. "You're teasing me, Lily. If not, then name this other boy. Tell me! Who is taking you out? I intend to have a talk with him...right before I nail his scrawny hide to my aunt's shed wall. You're my girl, Lily, and no chiseling, dog-faced boy is gonna take you for a ride on his bicycle, or row you across some damn pond. If I have to, I'll camp out in front of your house, morning, noon, and night. My aunt and your father can go to blazes!"

Lily began to snicker, hearing the jealousy build in his

voice. "I'm sorry, Blackie. I admit I am a wicked creature and have been having a great deal of fun at your expense. There is no other boy." There couldn't have been; it would be an impossibility, as Blackie was everything she had ever dreamed of. "You needn't get yourself upset over nothing. It's just that a girl never wants to be taken for granted...even one that has so little to offer. I'm not especially stupid. I hear the rumors and the jokes made about us. Why, there's not a single girl in this entire town that hasn't dreamed of stepping out with the handsome Blackie Barker. Jealousy is a powerful emotion. I know you have many choices. I simply needed to be reassured." She lowered her eyes and suddenly felt as foolish as her two ill-behaved younger sisters.

Blackie felt his temper slowly begin to cool as his heart softened with tender feelings for Lily. He reached for her and brought her into his arms. Keeping the rest of the world at bay, he pressed sweet, comforting kisses on her face. He didn't understand the feelings she held. The fear of being gossiped about, or being made the brunt of every joke, was foreign to him. People gossiped about his getting into trouble all the time, and it never bothered him. To the contrary, he bore it proudly, as a badge of his defiance. What did he care what people said about him? But this wasn't his community. He would be leaving at the end of summer...and leaving her. Leaving Lily to contend with the idle talk and snide insinuations. *Leaving her behind...*

"Forgive me, Lily," he whispered, breathing softly, against her cheek. "I failed to make myself clear. You must know I only have eyes for you...the loveliest girl in Garden City, and I am deaf to the mean-spirited people of this town. There is nothing they can say that will change my mind...or my heart. Put simply...I love you." He drew her in and settled his mouth on hers; kissing her as if it was to be the last kiss they would ever share. He had never said those words before, never to a living soul. Feeling her heart thumping rapidly against his chest, and felt her sway slightly, in his arms, he knew perfect joy. However, after several exquisite moments of pleasure, tasting her lips and feeling her pliant body mold perfectly to his, he was forced to relinquish his hold.

"My God, but you are beautiful," he sighed. Her eyes were bright and glistening with love; her lips were pink and swollen from his hungry kiss. The sun caught every golden strand of her hair, blinding him to any other. She was most extraordinary, he thought, making it nearly impossible to take his leave.

"I've got to go," he struggled to say, drowning his senses in her subtle, but irresistible fragrance. "You go in now. I'll wait until you're safely inside."

Lily moaned. "I don't want it to end," she argued. "When will I see you again?"

Blackie placed his snappy new straw boater on his head —the same one she had failed to notice. It was the latest style and had cost him more than a week's wage. But as it turned out, a man's hat was insignificant in comparison to a lady's new dress. A trim, floral creation, purchased from a mail order catalogue, it fit her as if it was custom made, and just daring enough to make his mouth water. A man's hat could hardly signify.

"Tuesday and Wednesday, I will be helping the LLA with the book fair," Lily mentioned. "You were right about the mayor's wife. Prudence has taken charge of most everything. It is only natural that she be mentioned on a very large plaque," she said, giggling. "I suppose it is a very small price to pay for everything she has brought about. It looks as if we will get that new library before year's end."

"Good. I'm happy to hear it, Lily." It was good that she was getting out and making new friends. "My aunt's roof will take at least a couple of days to repair. Shall we make plans for Saturday? I'll take you for that boat ride," he added.

Lily practically jumped for joy. "Oh, that would be perfection! I've never actually been in a boat, you know. If we don't drown, I think I'll enjoy it, immensely."

He chuckled at her quick wit. "Then it's settled; Saturday, you and I at Fulton's Pond." Blackie started to back away, raising his arms to shoulder height, and splaying his fingers to ward her off. "Now, keep your distance, woman," he chuckled. "I'm warning you. I'll never be able to leave if you come any closer. Be a good girl now, and head on back toward the house."

Lily flashed a brilliant grin. "Is that what you truly want?" she asked coyly. "Can't you spare one teensy weensy kiss? Just a little something to sweeten my dreams?"

Blackie jumped over the gate, keeping it firmly latched between himself and the charming Miss Posey. "You're a wicked temptress, Lily. I can see I'll have to be on my guard from now on, or you'll try to run roughshod over me. Your kisses are spellbinding. Stay away, or I'm afraid I'll never be able to leave." Blackie was laughing now, but what he said was more truth than fiction. Denying himself the touch of Lily's sweet lips was the hardest thing he had ever done.

Lily halted her forward assault. "Okay, Blackie. I promise to be good…for now. You run along and I'll go inside. Mother and Father are probably wondering where I am. It is getting late. I'll see you Saturday…early. Think of me until then?"

Blackie stood in silence, content to take in the glorious image of her figure standing there with an innocence more desirable than any wanton siren. Lily's innate, sensual grace stole his breath away and lit an all-consuming fire within him, causing his body to react in a most inappropriate, albeit natural way. His body ached with wanting her. He desired her in the way every young man yearns for a woman. Taking a deep breath to calm his raging impulses, the corners of Blackie's mouth turned slightly upward. There was reason to smile. He only had to wait one more week—and then maybe—if luck were with him, he could at last satisfy his more carnal nature.

"Don't be a silly goose, Lily. Of course I'll think of you," he answered blithely. *I'll be thinking and planning of a way to finally have you.* "I can hardly wait for Saturday," he muttered. If everything went according to plan, they would have the rest of the summer to meet privately, hidden away from prying eyes and gossiping tongues. He would teach her all she needed to know about pleasing a man—him, anyway. The thought of tutoring her in the fine art of making love was enough to incite Blackie to howl at the moon. If the guilt of stealing her virtue became too bothersome, he would end the summer romance early and leave for school. Young men did that all the time. Didn't they?

CHAPTER NINE

The house was once again blessedly quiet, but only after Mr. Posey treated his youngest with a healing salve of mint, chamomile, and thyme, for her scrapes and cuts. Lulled by the soothing sound of her mother's voice, as she read a tale of two bunnies, little Jasmine finally cried herself to sleep; accompanied by one very contrite sister, Poppy. It was hard to tell who was the most upset, as both youngsters had carried on for hours. In the morning, however, all would be forgiven and forgotten, with the little girls being the best of friends, and to everyone's peril, dreaded co-conspirators in search of more troubling adventures. At least in these few final minutes before bedtime, the adults could sit back, relax, and ponder over the events of the day.

"He kissed her, you know," Fern said distinctly, while drawing the colorful embroidery thread through the crisp white linen, stretched tightly in the hoop on her lap.

Having received no indication that her husband had heard her, she raised her voice slightly. "On the mouth."

"Brumpfa fubble," he grumbled, while turning the page of the evening paper. Forrest preferred to read undisturbed, and there had already been much too much commotion for his liking.

Fern put down her embroidery. "Did you hear me, Father? That Blackie boy was definitely kissing our girl and I believe she liked it."

Flori entered the parlor just in time to hear Mrs. Posey's startling remarks. "Aye, Ah thought as much; him bein' sooch a brawny lad and all. Ye'll have 'ta keep yer eye on him; there's the touch of the divil in him. 'Tis plain to see. Handsome as all get out, he is, and just the kinda lad that can turn a lassie's head."

"Forrest!" Fern shouted. "Say something. Our girl may be in jeopardy."

He carefully folded the pages, placing them over his lap, and took a sip of his good, Scottish whiskey. One drink of a night always helped him to sleep, and usually lessened the severity of the dreams that came to disturb that slumber. With the stroke of a single finger, he methodically wiped the golden droplets from his mustache and let out a long, tiresome breath. It had been a trying day, and his wife still had something on her mind.

"My darling, wife," he said, sighing loudly. "A blind man could see that our Lily has been kissed and that she enjoyed it immensely. If I'm not mistaken, it was her very first kiss and quite special. Is that not the way of it with young women?" He grinned, knowing full well that he had been the one to give his lovely Fern her first kiss.

His wife's cheeks quickly turned a demure shade of pink. How delightful it was, he thought, that he still had the ability to cause his wife to blush by the mere mention of a kiss. Gazing at her now, her sparkling eyes overflowing with love, and a sweet, tender smile upon her soft lips, she appeared not to have aged a single day since that remarkable kiss. He remembered it clearly—and it was obvious—so did she.

Fern recognized the deep, smoldering look in her husband's eyes and it thrilled her, sending delightful shivers through her body and causing her heart to race wildly. He was a lusty man and she adored him. It was only in his bed, while shutting out the world, that she could find her paradise. He showered her with affection and kept her safe. Only in her husband's arms, could she find true contentment. He was a thoughtful and considerate lover. However, for now, it was his mouth that mesmerized—as she waited for the words she longed to hear him say. *Say it*, she silently commanded. Say it's time for bed.

The clatter of the teapot brought both Mr. and Mrs. Posey out of their erotic trances. "Sorry," Flori apologized. "These old hands aren't as sure as they used to be. Now, drink yer chamomile, Missus. It will help you sleep. Do ye need a wee bit more of the drink, Mister Posey, afore Ah put me feet up?"

"Uh, no…no. In fact, you may go on up to bed now, Floribunda. We…my wife and I will clean up in here," he stammered. "It's been a long, exhausting day for all of us. Missus Posey and I will be retiring soon, as well." He stretched broadly; arching his back and extending his long arms high above his head, in opposite directions, while Fern played her part by yawning noisily, into her hand. Their exaggerated efforts to feign weariness only succeeded in bringing about the old woman's laughter.

"Glory be. After eight wee bairns, the two of you still act like newlyweds. Well, that's how it should be, I imagine." She grunted, as she rose from her chair. Looking around, she saw the clutter on the table. "Oh, well…Ah'll be happy to leave the leavin's for the two of you—proper or not. Ah'm an old woman what needs her sleep. Ah'll be up with the chickens, as it is. Goodnight…and may God watch o'er all those in this house."

"Thank you, Flori, and goodnight," Fern responded kindly, silently thanking their cook for not only her constant and loyal service, but also for being so wonderfully astute. Privacy was a rare commodity in their household, and tonight, she and her handsome husband required theirs. "Let's go up, dear."

"Before we clear away the glasses?" he mocked.

"Well…if you'd rather do dishes…"

"Not on your life, Madam." Forrest Posey jumped to his feet, and taking the four steps to his wife's side, he swooped her up in his arms and rushed for the stairs. The dishes could wait—he could not.

The moment the first warm rays of sunshine crossed her face; Lily threw back the covers and leapt from her bed. This morning was not the day for her to languish in bed. She had to see. She simply must. Her bare feet flew across the room, skidding to a sudden halt in front of the tall dressing mirror. Before glancing at her reflection, she closed her eyes and counted to five, her mind whirling with excitement and a bit of trepidation. How had she changed? Would it show on her face? In her eyes or on her lips?

"Five," she whispered softly, as she slowly opened her eyes. Her fingertips lightly traced the curve of her mouth. Her lips were full and slightly pouty, but they had always been so. Her cheeks were pink, but everyone remarked on her healthy complexion. She leaned forward and stared into her eyes. Were they extraordinarily bright this morning, or was there absolutely nothing unusual about her appearance?

"Oh, pooh," she grumbled. "I still look like me...plain old Lily Posey."

She didn't know what she had expected to see from just one kiss, powerful though it may have been, but she had hoped that *something* of the miraculous way she felt would be reflected upon her face. Inside, she was totally transformed. Nothing was the same as it was the day before—before Blackie Barker took her into his arms and kissed the very breath from her lungs. For the first time in her life, she felt like herself, not simply another flower in a beautiful bouquet...and he was responsible for that. She was now a desirable woman and much admired by a perfectly wonderful man. In spite of her inexperience, however, she wasn't stupid. She knew some boys would have forced themselves on a young, innocent women; but not Blackie. She trusted him completely. Blackie had proven himself to be a gentleman, and had put her fears at ease. His warm, puppy-dog eyes showed his true character; and it was good, through and through. Her love was safe with him.

Lily waltzed slowly back to bed and slid beneath the warmth of the blanket. Her hands slid over her bosom, lightly touching the small, perky mounds. She recalled the tingling sensation she felt, when her breasts were crushed up against Blackie's hard chest. His body was well muscled, and so vastly different from her own. She could feel his heart pounding rapidly beneath his ribs, and felt the incredible strength in his arms, as they struggled to hold her tightly against his trembling body. Where she was soft and pliable, he was hard and unmoving.

Her eyes drifted shut, as her right hand slowly glided down over her flat belly and began making broad circles around the soft, creamy flesh. Remembering the smell and taste of him upon her tongue, Lily's mouth watered. Blackie's breath was clean and fresh, and she had the incredible urge to devour his mouth and ravage his lips. She could have continued kissing him for hours. When he finally did pull away, it was almost painful. It was as if he was tearing apart their delicate connection. A warm, moist feeling started up between her thighs, while her hand continued to explore on its own. Suddenly, there was a soft knock at the door, and the errant hand snatched back, grabbing for the corner of the sheet.

"Come in," she said, her voice strangely husky.

Fern Posey entered. "It's just me, darling. You've overslept and I came to check on you." She walked up to the bed and noticed a slight flush on her daughter's cheeks. Placing a hand on her forehead, she felt for a fever. "Are you feeling ill, dear? Your face has too much color, while your skin is cool. Shall I ask your father for a medicinal?"

So, maybe she had changed a bit, after all, Lily thought gleefully. "What else do you see, Mother?"

Her mother grinned. "I see a very lazy young lady who needs to hurry and dress and get down to breakfast before Flori puts it in the compost. Isn't this the day for your library work?"

"Oh, I'm going to be late!" Lily shrieked, jumping out of bed. She'd completely forgotten the LLA. "It's a very important meeting we're having today. The beet factory is promising to contribute money for new shelves. I haven't time to eat. I've worked too hard to miss this," she exclaimed. Running over to her wardrobe, Lily pulled a delightful green striped muslin off from its hanger, and announced she would hide her messy hair under a hat.

"Lily Posey," her mother snapped. "You will do no such thing. Calm down, dress as you should, and take the time to brush your hair properly, coiling it high on your head. You will then eat something nourishing before you leave this house...or young lady, you will not leave this house at all!"

"But Mother!" Lily whined. "I'm going to be late!"

Fern looked at the clock on her dressing table. "I've heard enough. You'll take the trolley and get there precisely on time. Are we agreeable?"

"Yes," grumbled Lily, as she fought with her shoe buttons. "Never say a Posey was seen in public, inappropriately turned out." She stood up and turned her back to her mother. "Button and lace me, please?"

"Of course, dear. And may I say, you look particularly pretty this morning?"

"I do? You mean that, Mother?"

"Mmm, I most certainly do. I wonder what...or should I say, *whom* is responsible for the roses in your cheeks?" She sighed softly. "I bet I could guess."

Lily's entire face flamed. "You do like him, don't you, Mother? And Father doesn't object to me seeing him...or does he?"

Fern picked up the silver hairbrush and began gently pulling it through her daughter's long, golden hair. Since a small child, Lily had always had the loveliest hair. Spending an evening, sitting in front of a cheery fire and brushing her child's long curls into crackling, snapping tendrils, were cherished memories. Lily had always held a special place in her heart. "We hardly know your young man, dear, but your father and I carry no ill will toward him, although he was off to a rather rocky beginning. As long as he makes you smile, we cannot object to him seeing you. Is that what you wanted to hear, dear?"

"Oh, yes, Mama. Blackie means everything to me. I would just die if I were told I could not see him again."

Fern put away the hairbrush and kneeled down to her daughter's level. Looking her straight in the eyes, she said most solemnly, "We trust you, Lily, and we are giving the boy the benefit of the doubt; but he is older than you and not nearly so innocent." She saw her daughter's face flush slightly, at the candid remark. "He can be very persuasive, if he chooses. A young girl, such as you, will need to rely on her good judgment. You cannot allow your heart to rule your head, my dear. Do you understand what I am saying to you?"

Lily shrugged. "Of course, Mother. I am not a child."

"Well, you're not a fully grown woman, either. You may look like a woman, and have all the desires of a woman, but you must remember you are only sixteen."

"And you were fifteen when you met Father. I'm a whole year older," Lily protested.

"But we were at war, dear. It was a much different time, and don't forget…I didn't marry your father until long after the war's conclusion. I was nearly twenty-one when he asked for my hand, and he was an old man of twenty-six," she snickered. "I can still see him standing there, at the altar, so splendid in his uniform and so very brave. I nearly swooned from happiness. He was quite frightened, you know. After all that he had endured during those violent, unspeakable years, it was inconceivable to me that the very thought of taking a wife and having a family should scare him even more. Terrified, though he was, he knew we could not go on living apart. Our lives were not whole without the other."

Lily had never given much thought to those old days, long gone and forgotten by many, but now gazing up at her mother's glowing face, and listening to her heartfelt words, it wasn't too difficult to imagine what a beautiful bride she must have been. The years seemed to melt way into nothingness, leaving a young woman, totally smitten with the handsome, quaking soldier waiting to claim her as his bride. A lump formed in her throat, making it difficult to speak. "What was it about Papa that caused you to fall in love with him?" She had always known her parents cared deeply for one another, but they always behaved most properly, never giving any indication of possessing a deep physical desire, or an exquisite passion for one another. She had never even seen them kiss—not even on their anniversary.

Fern stiffened slightly, and immediately began fussing with the front of her shirtwaist, fidgeting with the pleats. "I've told you before, Lily...it was in the midst of war, and your father was kept busy treating the injured. I tried to help, in my own small way. Then, after the war, I didn't see him for several years. He went away and I stayed behind. When he finally returned home, he proposed marriage. That's the entire story," she said, now nervously tugging on her sleeves.

Lily was puzzled and a bit saddened by her mother's sudden reaction to her question. It was as if the entire period of their courtship was too painful to recount. Her mother had never spoken forthright about that time in her life. Surely, it could not all have been so cold and calculated. In the beginning, her parents must have felt a degree of hunger for one another, or had experienced tender romance under the stars. It was impossible to think that her dear father had never kissed her mother in the way that Blackie kissed her. It would be too sad to contemplate. As her mother turned away, Lily caught her wrist and turned her back around. "What happened during the war, Mama? I know it's painful for you to recall, but I know you would feel better if you told someone. You never talk about it. Didn't you ever once yearn to have Papa hold you in his arms and cover your face with kisses?"

Fern couldn't believe that Lily would ask such a question. "Never!" She jerked her hand free. "Go talk to your father about what happened. He is the only one that can truly explain, as he saw the horrors and carnage for himself." Her eyes welled with tears, as her voice suddenly grew hoarse with pent-up emotion. "I don't mean to be cruel, darling, but I was affected most dreadfully by the senselessness of war. I am afraid to say, some of the rumors you hear about me, are not just rumors. I do sometimes hum to myself, while walking through town. I occasionally block everything and everyone from of my mind. I suppose I can appear to be a little addled, now and then. My excruciating headaches are a result of what I experienced during the last year of the war; and you are aware I suffer from paralyzing nightmares and frequent bouts of melancholia. Can't you forgive me for not dwelling on the specifics of that time in my life?"

Lily reached out for her mother, noticing how her body trembled, and pulled her close to her heart. "Forgive me, Mama," she begged. "I am not heartless. I just wanted to know if you loved Papa in the same way I think I love Blackie."

"So you love him, do you?"

Lily nodded. "Uh-huh."

Fern took a deep, cleansing breath. "Yes, my pet. I love your father in exactly the same way you love your young gentleman. He still makes my heart race every time he enters the room, and I dream of his warm kisses on my face. He quite literally saved me." She smiled serenely. "Does that answer most of your questions?"

"Oh, yes, Mama!" Lily exclaimed gleefully. She gave her mother's cheek a kiss. "I am so happy for you. Being in love is the most wonderful thing I can imagine. Don't you agree?"

Her mother made her way to the door. "Well, just see you don't carried away with the romance of it. Love is a very serious thing…not all hugs and kisses."

"Of course, Mother. I'll remember."

"Well, we shall see. For now, you had better make haste and run all the way to the library; there's no time to wait for the trolley. Grab an apple to eat on the way. The mayor's wife is not liable to overlook your tardiness. She is taking her new position very seriously, from what I hear."

"Yes, Ma'am," Lily shouted, clicking her heels and giving her mother a perky salute.

◆ ◆ ◆

The sun continued to beat down on Blackie's red face

and neck, broiling his brain, as well as evaporating his last drop of good humor. As he struggled to climb the rickety ladder, balancing heavy shingles thrown over one shoulder, he reasoned it would be a miracle if he didn't fall and break his neck. It was a long way to the ground. If he died repairing his aunt's roof, she'd be sorry—probably would never recover from her guilt, and die brokenhearted—but it was too blasted hot to daydream.

Entirely too warm for this early in the summer, he was grumbling to himself about the weather and cursing his present lot in life, when more misfortune was heaped upon him in the form of one Charlie Masters.

"Hey, Blackie," Charlie called out from the safety of the lawn. "What cha' doin'? Still workin'?"

One look at his cocky smirk, and Blackie wanted nothing more than to plant his sweaty fist in the center of his friend's irritating face. Gritting his teeth, he decided to ignore Charlie's ignorant question. Without giving him another glance, he continued to climb to the peak of the roof.

"Can't you come down for just a minute? I got some news to tell ya."

Blackie let the stack of shingles drop to the roof and pulled a hammer from the waistband of his pants. Grabbing a handful of nails, and tossing a few into his mouth, to be held firmly between his lips, he started pounding away. If he refused to recognize Charlie, then maybe the fool would get a clue and go away. The last thing he needed today, or anytime soon, was to listen to one of Charlie's cock-eyed plans, only to wind up in trouble—again. For Lily's sake, and his own, he had to remain above reproach, especially if he wanted to succeed in her seduction.

"What's wrong with you? You got dirt in your ears? Can't you hear me shouting?" Charlie yelled. "I got me a girl. She ain't the prettiest, but she's very friendly...if you know what I mean. She's visitin' her grandma for another two weeks and I'm in hog heaven!" he crowed. "How about you and Lily? Tell me what you've been doin'. You got lucky, yet? I know she must be a hum-dinger."

Blackie's head spun around so fast he almost lost his balance, teetering back on his heels. Looking up at the scorching sun, he wiped the sweat from his brow with the back of his brown work glove. "Ah, to hell with it," he cursed. He couldn't allow his friend to continue bellowing to the rooftops about Lily. "Keep your pants on, Charlie," he growled. "I'm coming down." Unfortunately, Blackie knew the only way to get Charlie to go away was to lend an ear to his boasting remarks, pat him on the back, tell him what a fine and clever fellow he was, and then walk into the house, leaving him standing on the sidewalk. The fool wouldn't dare follow him inside in aunt's home.

"Phew, it's hotter than Hades on that damn roof," remarked Blackie, as he approached a grinning Charlie. "Now what's this about some girl being dumb enough to go out with the likes of you?" He laughed good-naturedly, but it was mostly for show. He really didn't care.

Charlie's face reddened. "It's true, Blackie. As it turns out, this is my lucky summer. Because you've been so busy workin' for your aunt, and continuin' your daily visits to the Posey house, I was forced to find my own amusement. If Stella had seen you first, she wouldn't have had anything to do with me, but she didn't, and now she's mine," he crowed. "Therefore, this must be my lucky summer. You've been keepin' outta sight and givin' the rest of us boys a fair chance."

"Stella is a pretty name. Am I going to meet her?"

"Ha! Not if I can help it," Charlie quipped. "She's not your type, anyway. I don't suppose she would measure up to your lofty standards. But at least she ain't crazy."

"Watch your mouth, Charlie. Lily's not crazy; neither are her folks. They're just a little different from the rest of us."

"How far have you gotten?" Charlie asked in a sly tone, his eyes twinkling with mischief. "Has she let you *touch* her yet?" He made an obscene gesture with his fingers.

This conversation was going exactly where Blackie was afraid it would go. Charlie was nothing if not predictable, having only two things on his mind these days—girls and hooch. It was nobody's business what he and Lily did or did not do in private. It also wasn't wise to let his friend think nothing at all had happened. That wasn't something a guy could freely admit, and it certainly wouldn't do his reputation any good if the other fellas heard he'd made little progress. Blackie struck a confident pose, cocked one eyebrow, and snorted, "What do you think?"

"I knew it!" Charlie replied. "Well...spit it out. How was she? Did you make her holler?"

Blackie suddenly had the urge to make his friend holler —yell out in pain with a split lip and a blackened eye. How dare he ask such impertinent questions? Never mind that his own intentions ran along those same lines. He had every intention of separating the lovely Miss Posey from her virginity, but it was a personal thing, and he would damn well keep the particulars to himself. Clearing his throat, Blackie lowered his tone and spoke menacingly, "If I wanted you to know the intimate details, I would have invited you to watch. As I didn't...well, you will forgive me if I say nothing on the subject. However, I will say I was not disappointed. Lily is perfect in every detail."

Charlie's tongue was hanging out and he was fairly drooling with the mental picture forming in his head. Blackie was the luckiest of men. He always got the prettiest girls to do whatever he liked, and it all seemed so effortless on his part.

"I've got to get back to work, Charlie," Blackie barked. "Time for you to go. Tell Stella hello, for me."

"Not on your life," his friend retorted. Upon leaving, he called back, "Don't do anything a gentleman wouldn't do."

"Too late," Blackie responded. "I already have."

Well, thank goodness that was over, he thought, and it didn't go too badly. He only wanted to partially murder his best friend. Charlie could be so damn annoying sometimes. Even so, he had been able to save face without compromising Lily. That was important. He had even complimented her. Let his buddy think what he may. In time, it would be the truth anyway.

❖ ❖ ❖

That evening, after having dinner with his aunt, Blackie found himself with nothing to do. He should have been exhausted by his long day up on the sweltering roof, but oddly enough, his pulse was racing and he was filled with renewed energy. His mind was consumed with thoughts of Lily. Although he wasn't expected, he decided to throw caution to the wind and run the few blocks to her house. If she were amenable, he would ask her to take a romantic twilight stroll with him. The heat of the day had diminished quite drastically, leaving behind in its wake a lush, warm, sensual evening—a night perfect for young lovers.

Pausing by the mirrored hall tree in the foyer, Blackie ran his fingers through his jet-black hair. Lily seemed to like it long and slightly unkempt. He checked his teeth, looking for any unsightly broccoli that may be hidden between his incisors. Passing muster, he stepped out onto the porch. "I'm going out for a walk, Auntie," he called over his shoulder. "Don't wait up."

Walking at a very fast clip, it took less than five minutes for him to arrive at the Posey residence. Lights had been lit in every room, it seemed. He strode up to the porch, all the while keeping a wary eye out for two little imps waiting to attack from out of the darkness. Just as he raised his hand to knock, he noticed a sister rocking silently, back and forth.

"Oh, hello there," he said hastily. "You took me by surprise. Holly, is it?"

The woman shook her head, but smiled kindly. "No, I'm Ivy."

"Please forgive me, Miss Ivy. I've never been very good with faces."

She found that to be highly unlikely. If the face was female, and pretty enough, she wagered he would remember everything in great detail. But his feigned modesty was amusing. "You're forgiven, Mr. Barker. Unfortunately, that is the way it always is with twins. Holly is reading. Shall I get her for you?"

"Uh, no...no. I'm actually here for Lily. Is she at home?"

Ivy's brow furrowed, as she thought and thought. She tapped her tooth with a finger. "Mmm, she may be home... but then again...she may have stepped out with another beau. I quite forgot." Her green eyes sparkled. "Was she expecting you?"

Blackie turned away. The last thing he wanted was for the sister to see his keen disappointment. He should have sent a message informing Lily of his planned visit. Now, he would have to return to his aunt's oppressive abode. He had no other recourse but to go off to bed and dream of Lily, imagining her floating naked on the cool water at Fulton's Pond. "No, forget it," he grumbled. "Tell her I stopped by." *Who would she have stepped out with?* "On second thought, don't tell her I was here. It's not important."

Seeing her little joke had played itself out, Ivy jumped to her feet. Laughing, she startled her visitor. "Don't go, Blackie. I was just pulling your leg. Lily's here. I'll run inside and fetch her for you. She'd never forgive me if I let you leave. She's been sitting around all evening, mooning over you. Take her for a walk or something. Getting out of the house will be good for her and the rest of us, too." She motioned to the swing she had recently vacated. "Take a seat and wait until she comes down. I'm sorry for the jest."

Relieved, knowing Lily would be down momentarily; Blackie discovered he felt no bitterness about her sister's little prank. After all, the entire family was slightly loco, and he should have known better than to take anything one of them said as gospel. From now on, he wouldn't give up so easily. Another lesson learned.

Like a breath of cool, fresh air, Lily sailed through the open door, her face flush with excitement. "Blackie!" she exclaimed. "I wasn't expecting you, but this is a wonderful surprise. I understand my sister gave you a difficult time of it. Ivy is the jokester, while Holly is the deep thinker. I apologize if she annoyed you."

"One look at you, and all is forgotten," he gushed. "This promises to be a beautiful night, Lily. We shouldn't waste a minute of it. I thought we could walk out and enjoy the sunset, but unfortunately, we've almost missed it." Already the night sky was taking on a deep, luxurious shade of purple, highlighted by the sparkling jewels of heaven, and a shimmering moon of glowing alabaster.

Lily reached out and took his hand. "I enjoy the dark," she whispered. "No one can see us. I can pretend we're alone and free to do as we please."

Blackie grinned. "I like the way your mind works, Miss Posey. Shall we be on our way?"

She nodded. "As soon as I learned you were here, I asked Mother for permission to walk out with you. I must be home before ten o'clock, however. She still regards me as a child."

Blackie noticed her adorable pout and itched to kiss it away. "Cheer up, Lily. Surely, you realize I think of you quite differently, and I can't wait to show you."

Chills ran up Lily's spine. For her, there was no doubt. Before this night was through, she would find herself in his arms, and he would ravish her mouth most thoroughly, covering her face with hot, wet kisses. Anticipating the touch of his lips to hers, her heart began to pound so loudly, she was confident he could hear.

He chuckled. "You're blushing. I wish I knew what was going through that beautiful head of yours. You wouldn't be thinking of what I'm going to do to you...would you?" Seeing her smile broaden and the lowering of her lashes, he knew that was just what she was imagining. He held out his arm. "Come on, sweetheart. Let's walk."

On past his aunt's house and the Baptist church, they walked hand in hand, discussing everyday things and taking in the warm, humid air. There were several couples with like minds, walking along the same street as they. Occasionally,

Blackie would recognize someone and would be forced to smile a casual greeting. Lily kept her face averted. As they approached the drugstore, a group of girls began twittering and snickering, keeping their eyes glued to Lily and Blackie. Rude snorts and derisive laughter caused Lily to want to run away.

Blackie stalled, and chucked Lily under the chin. "Hey, what's wrong? Surely that bunch of squawkin' magpies don't bother you. Honey, they're not fit to shine your shoes. You need to show them that they mean nothing to you, and even less to me."

"I—I can't. It hurts too much," she sniffed.

"Does this hurt?" He leaned down and placed the sweetest kiss on the very tip of her pink nose.

She shook her head. "No."

"How about this?" His mouth pressed against first one cheek and then the other."

Again, she shook her head; but this time she was smiling. "Huh-uh."

Aware of the stunned silence emanating from the nosy females still standing on the sidewalk, Blackie put his arms around Lily and stared down into her adoring eyes. "Let's give them something to talk about," he murmured softly. Planting his mouth on hers, Blackie gave her a kiss that was guaranteed to melt a woman's bones. Her legs began to tremble, as he continued with the kiss—long and passionate.

It was a full minute before he straightened. Shooting a smug glance directly toward their astonished audience, still standing frozen in place, and with eyes as big as saucers and mouths hanging open, he gave a slight bow, and offered his arm to Lily. "You are one of a kind, sweetheart—a rose among many thorns," he said. They got the point.

"Th-thank you?" she mumbled.

Upon returning to 142 Orchard Lane, Blackie felt the need to explain his earlier actions. The girls had been rude, no one would disagree; but he kissed Lily because he could no longer hold back. Every minute spent in her company was exquisite torture, sublime agony, and he had to kiss her or die—even if it was in front of those irritating females.

"You don't have to explain anything to me, Blackie," she insisted. "I know now, they were mean because they were jealous of me. You have chosen me over all of them. They have only each other for company...poor darlings," she giggled, "while I have you. "It must make matters worse to see you with a crazy Posey."

"You're not crazy," he retorted. "But I'm afraid that kiss might have been a mistake. What if they talk about it later? It could be embarrassing for you."

It was Lily's turn to look shocked. "I would never be embarrassed to be seen kissing you. Besides, we did nothing wrong. I'm fairly confident they won't say anything," she said. "I'm not important enough for them to take the trouble."

"Well, I hope you're right," Blackie sighed. The last thing he wanted was to create more difficulty for her. "Will I see you tomorrow?"

"If you wish."

"I wish. I know where I can get a bicycle for the two of us. We could go and get an ice cream."

"Mmm, I'd like that," Lily said sweetly. "And will you promise to kiss me again?"

Blackie laughed out loud. "What am I going to do with you, little lady? I've told you we need to be careful. I'm only a man and you're a delightful bit of woman. But you needn't worry. I can be fairly certain I will be kissing you again."

"Good! Then I will be ready for you at eleven o'clock."

"I can't wait."

"Lily, is that you, dear?" Mrs. Posey called from inside the house.

"Yes, Mother."

"It's late, daughter. Come inside now."

Blackie gave Lily a slow, flirtatious wink and stepped away. "Dream of me," he whispered softly, as he pressed his fingers to his lips and blew her a kiss from across the porch.

"You know I will," she responded. "Good night," she said, as she returned his airborne kiss with a deep sigh.

CHAPTER TEN

Lily had never gone so breathtakingly fast. She was certain no one ever had. Riding behind Blackie, on the tandem bike, was like flying. The stores and houses seemed to dissolve into vibrant streaks of color. Careening wildly around corners, the wind pelted her eyes, causing them to water, whilst her long hair tumbled from its pins and fell around her shoulders, forever tangled.

"Slow down," she shrieked joyfully, as Blackie continued to pick up speed. "I'm afraid," she finally admitted. Afraid, yes, but she was also deliriously happy and thrilled beyond belief. She knew that at any moment, the shiny red bicycle could go in one direction, while they went another, crashing to the ground in a terrible heap of flailing arms and legs. They would surely be most grievously injured…but Blackie showed no fear, and continued to tempt fate. He was the bravest and most exciting person she had ever known, and her heart nearly burst with love for him. "Pleeeease," she squealed once more, as she held on for dear life.

Laughing, Blackie gave in and coasted to a more reasonable speed, slowing their break-neck pace. "I didn't know I had little Jasmine riding behind me," he teased. Everyone knew the child was afraid of almost everything. Dragging one foot, he soon brought the bike to a complete stop. He turned his head to speak, but was taken aback by what he saw. Perched behind him, was the most beautiful vision he had ever seen. Wild and daring, with pink cheeks glowing from the rush of fear and excitement, and golden hair, windblown and tossed carefree down her back. The image of a disheveled Lily was enough to bring a man to his knees. He had to say something clever, or risk lifting her from the bike and smothering her with kisses. "F-feel better n-now?" he asked lightheartedly, praying she hadn't noticed his stutter. "We have arrived in one piece, just as I promised."

How sweet it was he stammered, Lily mused. The ride was no doubt as thrilling for him as it was for her. She gratefully climbed off and found her legs to be a little less than sturdy. Reaching for the wall to steady herself, she attempted to make some sense of her messy and entangled hair. It was a vane endeavor, however. "I believe a leisurely ride would have been most satisfactory. Whatever was your hurry?" she inquired.

Blackie grinned. "I just wanted the pleasure of hearing you squeal. Honestly, Lily, I didn't mean to frighten you, but you have to admit it was fun. What happened to your hat?"

She laughed, and pointed down the street. "Three blocks back, and it was practically brand new."

"I'll buy you another. You did have fun, didn't you?"

"Oh, yes. I truly did. I have never felt anything like it, but I was also terrified we'd fall and break our foolish necks. It would have been quite painful, I imagine," she stated.

"Yeah, broken necks quite often are," he chuckled.

"I wasn't absolutely truthful when you asked me if I could ride a bicycle," she admitted. "To be perfectly frank, I've never had the nerve to sit on one. They are such ghastly things... much too difficult for me to challenge."

"Those were the old ones. These new bicycles are much easier to ride and far safer. You only have to learn to balance yourself. Sweetheart...when you're with me, you're never in danger. I would never let you fall."

Lily snorted indelicately. "I'm afraid you couldn't have prevented it. What if a cat or a squirrel had run out in front of us? What if you'd hit a hole or some loose sand? You could have sneezed!" she exclaimed. In her mind, that would most assuredly have sent them off some imaginary cliff, endangering their very lives.

Blackie carefully leaned the rented bicycle up against the side of the brick building and took Lily by the waist. Staring deep into her eyes, his gaze growing darker, hungrier; his voice softened, as he whispered huskily, "I would have protected you with my life, Lily. I will never allow you to suffer on account of me." He lowered his face to hers and pressed his mouth lovingly against her cheek. "Lily..."

"A-hem," Prudence Whitney coughed, as she exited the drugstore. "Ex-*cuse* me," she said in her most uppity tone. "I would like to get by, if you will allow. The very idea of some people..."

Lily jumped back, looking as guilty as a child caught with her hand in the cookie jar. "Prudence!" she exclaimed. "What are you...I mean, it's a beautiful day, isn't it?" she blurted nervously. She was never at ease in front of the mayor's insufferable wife, but being caught standing too close to Blackie was most discomforting, and only served to compound her feelings of inferiority.

Without another word, the haughty woman sniffed the air, and giving her skirts a loud swish, she slipped around the two young people as if they were of no consequence, whatsoever.

"Oh, no," Lily groaned. "I'm afraid that wasn't good."

"So that's the mayor's illustrious wife, is it? I don't see what all the fuss is about. The woman looks a little less than average, to me. She can't hold a candle to you, darlin', or even to your mother, for that matter. She's nothing more than a delusional, self-obsessed snob, believing herself to be all-important to this town. I wouldn't give her another thought, sweet cheeks. That fat, she-cow is definitely not worth it."

Lily couldn't help but giggle at Blackie's vivid description of dear Prudence, but as amusing as all this was, it could prove to be very serious. "I'm afraid you don't fully understand. She may be too hoity-toity for her own good, but make no mistake, that woman means a great deal to this town. If she doesn't approve of you...well, a person can be cut off from everything. I hope she doesn't think we were up to no good. We were standing inappropriately close," she said fretfully. Suddenly, a look of sheer panic crossed her face. "What if she tells Mother? Oh, Blackie, I won't be allowed to see you anymore," she cried. "This is awful."

With the most honest of intentions, wanting only to ease her fears, Blackie tilted up her chin and kissed her long and sweet—curling her toes and causing her to moan his name aloud—just loud enough for three young ladies, coming out of the ice cream shop, to hear. Immediately, they began to chatter and giggle amongst themselves.

Embarrassed, Lily's eyes flew open. Expecting to cringe at being the center of attention, she surprisingly discovered she only had eyes for Blackie. All she could see was the look of love on his handsome face. Gone was his usual flirtatious smirk, replaced by a heartbreakingly sincere smile. "Let's go in, my love," he murmured. "I'll buy you a chocolate phosphate."

"Mmmm," she said dreamily. "That would be perfect."

It was indeed perfect. Lily couldn't remember anything tasting so decadently delicious. It was even better than Flori's apple cake. Slurping through the straw, it tickled her nose and filled her mouth with frozen goodness. It was only after the glass was two thirds empty, did she do away with the straw and tip it to her lips. She drank thirstily, quenching her desire for the chocolaty, fizzy drink.

"Hey, look at that," Blackie chuckled, pointing to the area just beneath her nose. He laughed, saying, "You've got quite a mustache there, ma'am, the kind just perfect to tempt a man. May I?"

"What?" she muttered, setting the empty glass down on the counter. Before she knew what was happening, Blackie had swiped his finger across her upper lip and stuck it in his mouth. Pulling his finger back slowly, he moaned with delight. "You taste as sweet as you look, Miss Posey."

Overhearing their private conversation, the druggist's son grunted at the disgusting display, seeing that Barker boy tenderly removing the milk from the girl's mouth—Lily Posey's luscious, plump mouth. She had never given him the time of day, and yet, here she was, letting that big city oaf fawn all over her. Those Poseys always did think they were too good for the likes of most honest people. He knew he would never have had the courage to ask her out anyway, but it would have been nice to have had the opportunity to ignore her.

Lily's face reddened. She loved hearing Blackie's words of flattery, but what if others should hear? "Blackie, you mustn't speak that way...at least not in here," she scolded. "People could misconstrue your statements."

He sat back. "The hell they could," he spat. "I mean what I say, and they can take it any way they darn well wish. Honestly, Lily, you're too concerned with what others may think of you. They don't run my life, nor should they run yours...at least I hope not. I have no intention of changing for the likes of these silly, provincial people. Besides, I'm out of here at the end of summer."

There it was. Reality had come calling and Lily had conveniently forgotten about it. Blackie may claim to like her, but he still intended to leave her, come September. What would she do then? Just when she had discovered how wonderful love could be, he would be gone from her life. Her eyes suddenly filled with tears.

Seeing her tears, he apologized. "I'm sorry, Lily. That was tactless of me, but I cannot stay longer. You've known that all along. I have to go back to school and make my father proud," he grumbled. "I never said I would stay. I haven't lied to you."

It was as if a rope had suddenly coiled tightly around her neck, cutting off her air and making breathing difficult. Her heart already ached with loneliness, for the boy who was to leave at the end of summer; even though he was still sitting there in front of her. How was she to ever survive the loneliness after Blackie's departure? She would be a senior in high school, but there would be no parties or celebrations—not for her. No different from any other year, she would study hard and pass her exams, leaving the dances and school outings for others to enjoy. Perhaps he would return the following summer—perhaps.

"Come on, sweetheart," he coaxed. "It's time I took you home. Your father will be watching for you, and I'd rather not anger him. I'll take it a little slower this time," he said. "I promise."

Feeling as if her whole world had crumbled inside the drug store, Lily got up and silently followed Blackie outside to the tandem bicycle. It had been such an amazing day, and there would surely be more to follow. She knew she was being silly. Her mother always told her, "Worry is trouble borrowed." Well, once again she was right. It was a waste of time to worry about what would occur at summer's end, when there was another six glorious weeks in which to enjoy Blackie's company. She swore to herself, then and there, she would make the most of those few weeks left to them—and the gossips be hanged!

Smiling from ear to ear, Lily shook her head. "No, I don't want you to go slow, Blackie. Let's take Tenth Street instead. It's sure to feel like flying, and I'm certain it will scare the wits out of me."

"Really? Some folks say it's suicide." He couldn't believe his good fortune. Every time he thought he had Lily pegged, she would surprise him and prove him wrong. "What a girl, you are!" he declared. "All right, we'll do this thing...but if you get scared, close your eyes and hold on tight. Okay?"

She nodded enthusiastically.

"I'm going to give you a ride you'll never forget."

"I can't wait," she muttered under her breath.

Unexpectedly, the nerves began to build, causing Lily's mouth to go dry and her palms to sweat. Gulping down the nervous lump that had suddenly formed in her throat, Lily tried to appear calm, all the while feeling as if she might jump out of her skin at the least provocation. Where had this desire to experience new and exciting things in life, come from? She had always been so very levelheaded and reasonable, predictable and responsible; her choices had always proven so sensible. What had caused such a drastic change in her? *Blackie*...that's what. Since meeting the handsome stranger, the night of the dance, her entire world had been turned topsy-turvy, end over end, leaving her with the urge to live life to its fullest. What was a little danger, if you were with the one you loved? If a girl always chose the safe and sane pathway through life, she would surly die of boredom—never knowing the real pleasures there were to be had.

Her mind was made up; she would not be one of those hopeless women. Whatever challenges Blackie presented to her, she would readily accept them—while secretly keeping her fingers crossed for good luck.

The next night brought an adventure of another sort —a night of celestial theatre—stargazing. Unfortunately, for Blackie and Lily, it seemed the entire town had the same intention and had turned out to see the heavenly production. There was to be a total lunar eclipse which, as the skies were crystal clear, promised to be a remarkable showing.

Children ran around wildly, playing at all sorts of noisy games and stumbling over several people lying in the grass. More than once, an irate male voice could be heard shouting at the little heathens to stop, but the scoldings fell on deaf ears. The hour was well past the children's usual bedtime and they were going to make the best of the time given to them. A few fretful babies cried, annoyed at being roused from their soft, cozy beds, but all in all, everyone was in a festive mood and was enjoying the warm, evening air.

Lily didn't mind the crowds, as she only had eyes for her escort. Blackie had thought to bring a soft blanket to lie upon, and offered his arm as a pillow for her head. As she stared up into the infinite darkness, resembling a sprinkling of sparkling diamonds against a background of indigo velvet, she couldn't remember ever being happier or more content. At the moment, the world was at peace. It could get no better than this, she mused, as she watched for a subtle change in the moon, and listened to the strong beating of Blackie's heart.

Unfortunately, he didn't feel quite the same. Blackie had planned to have Lily all to himself this evening, and he wasn't willing to share her with the entire community of Garden City. "I'm sorry, Lily," he said gruffly, as he pulled her to her feet and directed her toward a less crowded area, hidden beneath huge, sprawling cottonwood trees. "I like it over here, better." The entire sky was practically obliterated by the thick foliage, but the view was spectacular, nonetheless—at least to Blackie's way of thinking. Lily had never looked lovelier. All the stars he needed, were in her eyes.

"But we can't see the eclipse from here," she argued.

"True...but perhaps we'll create our own heavenly event." Blackie breathed on the back of Lily's neck. "I love this spot, just below these tiny curls," he murmured, as his mouth roamed over her sensitive skin, sending shivers of delight down Lily's spine. "And this little spot over here," he continued. "I dream of kissing you here," he said, as his lips trailed down the center of her shoulders. Thankfully, the night was warm and her sweet flesh was bared just enough for his enjoyment. As his temperature climbed, his kisses became more demanding, more sensual.

"Blackie," she whispered, not wishing to break the spell, but trying to be practical, all the same. "Someone might see us."

"That's why I dragged you under these infernal branches...to be alone with you, Lily. I had planned to be alone with you tonight, looking up at the stars, discovering heaven for ourselves; but it seems like everyone else has the same idea. I don't know why they all couldn't have stayed home and watched the eclipse from their own back porch," he grumbled petulantly. "It's just the moon, for gosh sake."

Lily giggled, flattered by his obvious frustration at not having her all to himself. "They say it is going to be quite spectacular, and the sky is clear; perfect for stargazing. Even Father and Mother have come out."

Blackie's dark eyes widened with the news. *"They're here?"* he gasped. "Where? Point them out to me," he demanded.

That's all he needed; to have Lily's parents looking over his shoulder, watching his every move as he tried to have his way with their precious daughter; they would spoil everything.

It was time to face facts. He'd never get anywhere with Lily tonight—and he had held such high hopes, too. It was supposed to be a romantic evening, with her lying in repose, entranced by the moon and stars, and lost in the moment; thus allowing him special liberties. All he needed was a sign that she would be amenable to his more ardent advances. So far, his courtship of Lily had been rather frustrating; as he had decided to take his time with her, being far more patient than he had been with any other girl. He truly cared for her, but summer was rapidly slipping away, and a man had needs.

"Calm down, Blackie," Lily laughed. "They're somewhere way over there, I imagine." She pointed to a section of the hill, far to their left. "Even so, it isn't my mother and father that should worry you. Have you forgotten Poppy and Jasmine, my dear, sweet little sisters? I am certain they are looking for you at this very moment, in an effort to torment you...it has become their sole mission in life. I'd be worried, if I was you," she snickered, hiding a broad grin behind her fingers.

"Damn," he swore. "I'd forgotten all about those two little mischief-makers. I don't want to spend our time together, dodging them."

His eyes darted over the heads of the crowd, nearest them. "Maybe we should leave here and go back to your house. It seems no one is at home. We'll have it all to ourselves," he hinted, giving Lily his most beguiling smile.

She laughed. "You forget Flori," she reminded him, "and Officer O'Toole. When I left the house, she was preparing a *wee* basket for the police officer. I don't imagine they would enjoy our intrusion on their private evening under the stars."

Blackie groaned. Well, that was just perfect. Even the old Scottish cook and her crotchety old lawman would be free to explore each other without someone peering from around the corner. The thought of that was enough to make a man grimace.

"What's wrong?" Lily asked, seeing the peculiar look on his face. "You look as if you bit into a lemon. What are you thinking?"

Blackie shook his head to clear away the disturbing mental images that had formed, unbidden, in his mind. "Never mind...I assure you it's nothing you want to hear. Just a very unpleasant thought. Oh, well," he sighed, "I might as well take you back to our place on the hillside. At least you can see the moon from there. This evening is a complete loss, anyway."

"Maybe not a *complete* loss," Lily purred, as she put her arms around his neck and pulled him down for a kiss. She figured if you'd seen one moon, you'd seen them all, but a chance to kiss Blackie Barker was a chance of a lifetime.

It was easy to get carried away by the soft, summer night. With Lily in his arms, Blackie quickly forgot the annoyance of people surrounding them. It was as if suddenly, they were totally alone, and she was offering herself up to him —a golden Moon Goddess, his for the taking. His hand softly caressed her back, as he devoured her luscious mouth. With lips as sweet as nectar, a single taste of her fired his blood and caused his nerves to nearly shatter. Hearing her breathy moan of contentment, he pressed her closer, taking in the floral fragrance of her hair, filling his head with erotic thoughts of lust and desire, to finally be fulfilled under the stars. His entire body was set aflame with the yearning to have Lily beneath him, naked and calling out his name.

He had come to crave her. She was addictive; a heady drug that had consumed his free will, making it impossible for him to stay away. Without Lily, he was all at sea, and adrift without purpose. How could she have done this to him...*Blackie Barker*? He had always held the upper hand, and never lost his head over any pretty girl. Not until now, that is, and it worried him a great deal. The thought of never tasting her luscious lips again filled him with a sense of near panic. How could he leave her at the end of summer?

A groan escaped his throat, in part, because he dreaded

that unavoidable moment when he must say good-bye, but mostly because of the indescribable pleasure she gave him, with the touch of her soft, moist lips pressing against his own, and allowing his tongue the freedom to explore her mouth fully. His body ached to possess her, while his breath grew rapid. It was then, her hand innocently grazed across his erection.

"For God's sake!" he shouted.

Lily's eyes snapped open, as she jumped back, putting an arm's length between them. "What's wrong?" she gasped, having not a clue as to the cause of his unexpected outburst. Anyone within fifty yards could have heard his cursing.

Blackie had to think quickly. Swatting at his leg, he pretended to have been bitten by some unseen insect. Pulling on Lily's hand, he demanded they leave at once. "I've had enough," he exclaimed. "There are bugs everywhere and they've decided to feast on me. Let's go get some lemonade and call this miserable evening over."

Hopefully, his pitiful excuse would be enough to satisfy not only Lily, but also the curious onlookers who were more interested in what was going on between the boy and his girl, under the cottonwood tree, than the spectacular show above their own heads. Grabbing the blanket, holding it close to his body in the hope of hiding his embarrassing condition from the public, they started down the hill. Unfortunately, tongues were already starting to wag.

His body still hard and aching with desire, and his mind clouded with unresolved passion for Lily, Blackie failed to take notice of the four boys sitting just outside the canopy of the cottonwood branches.

"Hey, Blackie," Marty Veneman shouted out. "What'cha got there?" Recognizing Lily Posey, he figured she was fair game. "Damn, if she ain't a little beauty. Don't be stingy with her. Let yer friends have a little taste," he snickered. "She looks willin' enough, and we don't mind seconds."

At the sound of the boy's crude comment, Lily spun around and looked directly at four of the biggest troublemakers in town. "Oh," she cried, as she tried to pull away from Blackie's firm embrace. The blood pounded in her head and she felt sick. "Let me go," she pleaded.

Refusing to relinquish his hold, Blackie's grip tightened, as he spun around to face his friend. "Shut your face, Marty. There isn't anything going on here...but if I hear one word outta' any of you fools...you'll wish you'd kept your mouths shut. Got it?"

Marty snorted. "I can bide my time. Lily will still be here, long after you're gone. She'll be wantin' a real man to take yer place, I figure...won't cha' honey?" he slurred. It was obvious he'd gotten into his father's supply again. If he'd been sober, he would have guarded his tongue more carefully. "Onc't you've had a little taste—"

Within less time than it takes to bat your eye, Blackie lunged at the offending boy, grabbing him by his collar, and tossing him to the ground.

"Don't, Blackie!" Lily screamed, as she saw him pull back his fist—but it was too late. There would be no stopping this train. She watched, horror-stricken, as his closed fist smashed into the boy's mouth, causing blood to spurt through the air. Marty's strangled cries fell on deaf ears, as Blackie continued to pummel him with terrific force. There was no help from his friends, as they, too, stood back helplessly, watching their friend absorb the bone-breaking blows.

It was as if Blackie had fallen under some dark spell, compelled to right every wrong Lily had ever suffered from these small town bullies. Taking out punishment on this witless, intoxicated individual, was a first step in receiving some sort of justice for her. It wasn't until two men grabbed him by the shoulders, pulled him back, and secured his flying elbows, that Blackie finally stopped his assault, realizing what he had done.

Breathing hard, a menacing, feral glint shining brightly in his eyes, Blackie tried to calm his tremendous rage. He still saw red and yearned to spill more blood, but he needed to control the beast within. Back home, he'd been in trouble for just this very thing.

After a quick perusal of his injuries, one of the men said to Marty, "It looks worse than it is. You were mighty lucky, son. Go on home now, and have your mother take care of that face. I expect you'll look much worse in the mornin', but I reckon you'll live. Your nose is intact; that's something. Next time, you might want to avoid insulting ladies."

Marty nodded. "Yeah. Okay," he grumbled. Sadly, he had no mother to dress his wounds, but his father had plenty of hooch to take away the sting. No one cared about him, anyway. Tonight, even his friends had deserted him. More than likely, his pa wouldn't notice his split lip or the loss of a tooth. It was better that way, he figured. Hopefully, he could sneak into his room unnoticed, sleep undisturbed for a few days, and avoid Blackie Barker at all cost. He never wanted to piss that bastard off again. As for Lily Posey, he'd eventually get his due. What could a girl do to him?

After the danger had passed and Blackie's blood had cooled, the stranger released his hold and set him free. "You should be jailed, young man. That boy was in the wrong...of that I am certain; but there is no excuse for the brutality of your attack. Get out of here before I call the police," he warned. Turning his head toward Lily, the man inquired, "And you, young lady...you think about what happened here, this night." He glanced over at an unrepentant Blackie. "Is this the kind of individual you want to spend your time with? I wouldn't allow my daughter to see this boy. What's your name?" he demanded to know.

Giving Blackie a furtive look, she uttered, "Lily, sir. I'm Lily Posey."

"I know your father, Lily," he declared. "Should I speak with him about this incident?"

Her eyes grew wide. "Oh, no, sir. Please don't do that. He would be most upset and disappointed with me; he'd probably confine me to my room for the rest of the summer. I promise to be more careful in the future, sir; and I will give serious thought about all you have said. I'm going straight home now," she avowed. "Please don't tell my father."

After a few long, tenuous moments, the man grudgingly agreed to keep his silence. "Very well, young lady. I won't say anything...this time. I hope I'm not making a mistake. You consider what I said. This young man is not of good character."

"Yes, sir," she muttered, as he turned his back and walked away, leaving her staring blankly at Blackie.

"Well?"

"Well, what?" she retorted.

"Did you mean what you said?"

"What was I supposed to say? If that man told Father about any of this, he would most assuredly ban me from ever seeing you again. You looked as if you wanted to kill Marty."

He knew she was right, but how could he let her think that poorly of him? For some reason, he cared what Lily thought of him; and it distressed him to think she might share that man's sentiments. He had to know for sure where he stood with her. "Are you afraid of me, Lily?" he whispered. "You must believe I would never lift a hand to you."

"I'm not afraid of you, Blackie...not for my sake, but I do worry about your response to Marty's harmless taunts. You could have seriously injured him. My whole life I've had to listen to the jokes about my name and my *odd* family. The words hurt my feelings, and sometimes I cry from loneliness, but I never once think about taking revenge. You overreacted, Blackie."

He couldn't argue with the truth. He had wanted to kill his friend. Perhaps he would have, if not forced to step away. He was like a mad dog with not a lick of sense. But he had done it all for her. Didn't she understand that? Blackie reached out and took Lily by the shoulders. Looking deep into her eyes, he asked, "Is it over, sweetheart? Are you refusing to see me?" He waited with baited breath, as he watched many emotions skirt across her lovely face. She was struggling with her answer, and he prayed she chose correctly. He needed another chance to prove himself worthy.

Melting into his arms, Lily rested her head against his chest. "No, Blackie. I am not ending this. Perhaps I should, but I can't help myself. I love you with all my heart, in spite of what my good sense tells me."

"Oh, my darling," he sighed, his voice low and raspy, suddenly filled with relief. Perhaps things weren't as dire as he thought. "Kiss me."

"There you are!" Poppy shrieked. "Where have you been?"

Blackie closed his eyes. "Oh, dear God...not now," he groaned.

"You missed everything!" echoed an exuberant Jasmine.

"We looked everywhere for you. Were you hidin' from us?"

Jasmine hopped up and down. "Did you see the moon? I'm going to paint a picture of it. What were you doing under that tree?"

Poppy glanced over her shoulder and took note of the dense canopy. "You couldn't see nothin' under that tree." Her eyes narrowed with suspicion. "I think I'm gonna tell Mother," she declared. "She'll want to know what you were doin' under that tree."

Having had his fill of threats for the evening, Blackie stepped in front of Lily, shielding her from view. "You little rascal," Blackie growled. "Get this straight. If you say one word to get your sister in trouble, I'll paddle your backside. I'll watch you day and night, and I'll tattle on you for every little thing you and Jasmine do. This will be the worst summer you've ever had."

Jasmine looked terrified and began to whimper. "I didn't do nothing," she protested. "I wasn't going to tattle. Don't paddle me."

Poppy pinched her sister's arm. "Hush up, you crybaby. He's not gonna do no such thing, and Father is the only one who can paddle us. He's bluffin'."

Blackie growled again. "We'll just see about that."

Poppy grabbed her little sister's hand. "We don't like you...but we love Lily. So we're not gonna tell."

"C-cross our h-hearts," sniffed Jasmine, crossing her tummy with two fingers.

"Tell what?" Mr. Posey asked, as he walked up to join the rest of his family. "We've been looking for you, Lily. It was a magnificent display, was it not?"

She nodded.

Blackie's eyes were threatening, as he glared directly at Poppy. Now was her opportunity to make his life hell.

"Well then, I suppose it's home for us," Mr. Posey announced. "You don't have to see our Lily home, Mr. Barker. Our house is out of your way, and the morning will come quite early. We will wish you goodnight. Come along, girls."

"Goodnight," Poppy snapped.

"Night," a tearful Jasmine muttered, accompanied by a small wave of her hand.

Lily didn't have the heart to say anything to Blackie, as she turned to leave. Afraid her eyes would betray her, she blew him a kiss; that was the best she could do. Her eyes remained dry, but her heart was seized with an overwhelming sadness. Somehow, she knew their special relationship had taken a new form—for better or for worse, she could not say. Had it not been for the immense regret she saw in Blackie's brown eyes, she would have thought all was lost...and yet, there he stood, stalwart as ever, remaining steadfast.

He waited and watched as the Posey family walked single file, turning down Elm, and making their way to Orchard Lane. "What a pisser," he groused. If he were a drinking man, he'd get blind drunk. This night had to have been the biggest disappointment of his life, so far. His relationship with Lily had taken a big step backward. At this rate, he'd be lucky to get a glimpse of her soft, sweet breasts, before he left for college. He began to wonder if she was worth all the misery? No sooner had he asked the question, he knew the answer; of course she was.

Lily was special, and try as he might, he could not put her from his mind—or heart. The little vixen had bewitched him. As certain as he was of the sun rising every morning in the eastern sky, he knew he would willingly endure anything for her—even wait an eternity to claim her for his own, if must be. What the hell was he going to do?

It was Tuesday, and Lily would not be seeing Blackie that morning. His aunt had him doing work for her, and she would be busy with a box of donated books, delivering them to the LLA. It had been a stroke of good luck when she discovered them in a pile of rubbish, placed outside the railway depot. The stationmaster explained someone had shipped the box to Garden City, but had not directed it to any one individual or destination. There was also no return address. Having taken up space in the small mailroom for more than six weeks, he decided it was time to get rid of them. She was able to claim the entire lot, with his blessing. Today, she was going to surprise her fellow LLA members with a few of the classics. They would be delighted with the unexpected donation.

Wolfing down her breakfast, she eagerly asked to be excused from the table.

"But dear, it is still very early," her mother pointed out.

"I know, but I am too excited this morning." Lily looked to her brother. "Would you mind harnessing the buggy for me? I have a box of books to deliver and they're quite heavy."

Bud wiped his mouth, and sneered most unpleasantly. "I don't mind doing you a favor, *dear sister*, but first, I'd like for you to answer one question for me."

A question? What on earth could she tell him he didn't already know? She couldn't imagine. "Certainly. What would you like to know?"

He glanced at his mother, who was busy fussing with Jasmine for not eating her oatmeal. Lowering his voice, he asked, "I've heard a rumor about last night. There was a fight over a girl. Do you know anything about that?"

Oh, dear. The rumors were starting and it wasn't even

eight o'clock. Stealing her resolve to appear uninterested, and ignorant of the rumors, Lily shrugged her shoulders and took another sip of milk. "Huh-uh. Haven't heard a thing. Why do you ask?"

Bud continued to stare at her, not believing a word of her denial. He recognized the stiffening of her spine and the slight jutting of her chin. His sister had never been a very good liar. He knew without a doubt, the ugly rumors held some grains of truth. Blackie had humiliated her in some way, and he was determined to get to the bottom of it. "Fine," he snapped. "But you tell a certain *someone* for me, I won't stand for it. This family has put up with enough, without him compromising your reputation. If it happens again…if there is even a hint of impropriety…he and I will meet."

Lily swallowed. She could not remember ever seeing her brother so threatening; and it was a frightening sight to see. Struggling to find her voice, she whispered too defensively, "I swear it's not what you think. Nothing happened."

"Humpf!" he snorted, as he scooted his chair back, preparing to leave the room. "It's not because of his lack of trying, I'll wager. Forget it," he snapped. "I'll harness the horse and put the box of books in the back of the buggy for you. At least at the LLA, you can't get into any trouble."

"What was that dear?" her mother inquired. "What trouble? Is your brother upset about something?"

Lily shook her head. "No, Mother. He just has something on his mind."

"That's good, dear," her mother said, smiling. "It's much too pretty of a day to bother one's self with disagreeable subjects. Now, you go on and get ready to leave. I know you'll have a lovely day, dear."

Lily heard herself agree, "Yes, Mother." But for some reason, she felt uneasy. The sun had slipped behind the clouds, eerily tinting the sky to a pale, sickening shade of green. She suddenly had a bad feeling about all of this, and knew nothing good was going to come of this day.

Within minutes, Bud returned. "Take your umbrella, Lily. I don't like the way the sky looks. Tie the horse up good and tight, in case of thunder." Old Juniper Berry bolted at loud noises. "Don't dawdle," he added, "and go directly there and back." The tone of his voice left no doubt in Lily's mind, to what he was referring. It wasn't a little rain that concerned him. Under no circumstances was she to go out of her way and stop by to see Blackie Barker.

Wasting no time, it took less than five minutes for her to make her way to the front of the LLA building. Currently, they were being housed in a small ante building, just off from the site of the new Garfield School. Rebuilding had commenced in earnest, and was expected to be completed in time for the next school term. Looking up at the modest elevation, Lily couldn't help but feel proud. All her hard work had paid off, and soon there would be a new lending library for all the citizens of Garden City to enjoy.

She struggled to drag the heavy box from the rear of the buggy. Receiving this wondrous donation was going to delight the other women. Perusing through the titles, Lily had discovered well-loved classics in both poetry and fiction writings. Several biographies had caught her eye, as well. Teetering on the first step, but determined to regain her balance, Lily made her way up to the closed doors. Carefully, she lowered the box and reached for the handle. It was then she saw the notice:

Meeting canceled.
Closed for the day.

"How odd," she muttered to herself. This was their usual day to meet, and no one had notified her of any change in the schedule. Had someone suddenly taken ill? She looked up and down the sidewalk, but saw no one with whom she could get any information. "Prudence," she hissed. Somehow, the mayor's wife had to be responsible for this sudden variation of plans. Not only was it inconsiderate, but terribly inconvenient, as she once again had to grapple with the large box of books. After returning home, she swore to get to the bottom of this mystery.

◆ ◆ ◆

The weather took a sudden, violent turn, which gave Blackie a reprieve from his outdoor work. Needing to find something to fill his leisure hours, his thoughts naturally turned to Lily. However, today she was attending a regularly scheduled meeting with the LLA, and he had to find other things to occupy his time. Reading was a poor substitute for her delightful company, and he had no desire to meet with Charlie Masters. Charlie had made it very clear; he did not agree with Blackie putting Lily first, before him. Until he was ready to give her up, Blackie was not welcome in his previous circle of friends. If Charlie only knew how little weight that threat carried with him, he would have laughed. Lily was the only person who meant a damn thing to him.

Bored stiff, lying across his bed, his eyes soon grew heavy. As usual, his imagination soon conjured up an image of Lily, although not one of which her mama would approve. He liked to picture her naked, draped across his bare chest. Soon, he could almost feel the gentle, but firm strokes of an angel's hand against his flesh, her nubile softness comforted his aching body in ways that made his heart skip a beat. He could imagine the unique smell of her arousal, as the level of her desire increased. Writhing beneath him, panting his name, she became a woman.

Waking up in a sweat, Blackie adjusted his throbbing erection, threw on a clean shirt, and decided to walk over to the LLA. Maybe he'd get lucky and he'd be able to escort Lily home. At the very least, the rain would give him a chance to cool off. He would ask her what she wanted to do the next time he took her out. It would have to be something special. Perhaps he would offer to take her swimming.

Lily walked past the Palace Drug Store and then by the Grand Central Hotel. Making inquiries about the notice posted at the LLA, she learned several of the women had gathered at the hotel for tea, that very morning. The deskman thought he remembered seeing the mayor's wife, the doctor's daughter, and one or two others. They didn't stay long. At the first clap of thunder, they had all scattered. He was sorry he couldn't give her any additional information, but he had gotten too busy to notice more.

Lily thanked him, and quickly left the hotel, brushing angry tears from her cheeks. No one was sick; she had been deliberately excluded. This had been a calculated slight—but *why*? She could not imagine what had brought this on. She was under the impression things were proceeding nicely…well, perhaps not with Prudence Whitney.

CHAPTER ELEVEN

Saturday finally arrived in a hot, muggy blanket of air—perfect for spending the entire day in the cool, clear waters of Fulton's Pond. Blackie was practically giddy with anticipation. Lily had been acting strangely ever since her last LLA meeting. He couldn't imagine what had concerned her so, but he figured it was his duty to dispel any and all problems she might have with the library association, and make her laugh again. Secretly, he couldn't wait to get her into the cold water and run his hands over her smooth, slick curves. After a few kisses, he would make her forget all about her stupid books.

He knocked.

"There you are, Blackie," Mrs. Posey said cheerfully. "It certainly is warm today, isn't it? Makes one think of going swimming. Lily is almost ready. Do come in and wait for her. Or if you prefer, you could sit out here on the porch. It is a bit cooler, I must admit. Sometimes I think it would make more sense to live outside in the summertime. Don't you agree?" She was rambling. It was one of her *vague* days. "But I suppose that would be too amusing to the neighbors, seeing all the Poseys huddled under one tent, on the front lawn. My, my, that would certainly give them something to talk about, wouldn't it? Although, houses can get so stifling, one cannot breathe. Yes, I do believe the water should be lovely in this heat. Won't you come in, Blackie," she asked a second time?

"No thank you, ma'am. The porch swing suits me fine."

She smiled and nodded. "Would you like Flori to bring

you something cool to drink? She puts these lovely yellow petals in the ice. I don't know what they are, but they taste delicious."

Blackie shivered. "No thank you, ma'am. I just finished an entire pitcher of lemonade. My aunt insisted," he grinned, sheepishly. His aunt's lemonade was always exceedingly tart, shriveling his lips and screwing his face into laughable expressions. She believed one only received the benefit of the fruit, if the drink tasted exactly like the lemon from which it was derived. Too much sugar only diluted its healthful properties. So—drink up and enjoy good health. He shivered just thinking about the sour beverage.

"You're a good nephew to humor your aunt, Blackie. I know it means a lot to her. She does her best by you. You sure you don't want something cool to drink? Oh, I think I hear Lily, now," she said, looking over her shoulder. "Yes, I do believe I do. You two enjoy yourselves," she called out, just before she disappeared back inside the house.

"Oh, I intend to, Mrs. Posey…I certainly intend to," he muttered quietly.

"Goin' swimmin'?"

Blackie jumped. "What?" he asked, as he leaned over the porch railing, trying to locate the small voice.

"It's hot. Are you and my sister goin' swimmin' at the pond?" Poppy asked, as she climbed over the bannister. Her knees were scraped and her braids had come undone. She looked as if she had gotten in a tussle with a wildcat and had lost the fight. "Did you know I like swimmin'?"

Oh, no. Here it was…the end to his otherwise perfect day. Blackie knew it would be wise to ignore the child, but she made it impossible, plopping herself down next to him, and tossing one skinny, dirty leg over his trousers.

"Look, I got hurt. I bet the water would make it feel better. Don't you think so?" Her big eyes stared right straight through to his soul. "I don't want it to get 'fected, and Lily wouldn't mind if I came with you." A bead of sweat rolled down her forehead and into her eye. Wiping it away with one muddy little fist, she silently took hold of his heart. "Can I?"

Oh, what the hell. "Sure, kid. I guess I can't stop you from taggin' along," he grumbled. "You could stand a bath, at that." The water would probably make her feel better, too. He only prayed it would cool certain parts of his body, as well. "Just don't make a nuisance of yourself. I'm not a babysitter."

"Don't 'cha worry. I'm not a baby and I don't need sittin'," Poppy declared. "Hooray! I'm goin' swimmin'!" she shouted, as she practically fell off the swing, in her rush to the door. "Don't leave without me. You promise? You gotta swear. I need to get into my swimmin' clothes." She rushed past Lily, without a word.

"Where's Poppy going in such a hurry? Is there chocolate cake on the table?"

Blackie grumbled. "Nah, she's going swimming...with us."

Lily's eyes nearly bugged out of her head. She was aware her little sister had been a constant annoyance to Blackie, and wondered whatever had convinced him to invite her along? "I don't know what she said or did to get on your good side, but that was very sweet of you, Blackie. Frankly, it takes me by surprise. Lately, I have felt you were less than happy to be bothered by my family. Poppy is lonesome and bored, with Jasmine stuck in bed."

He'd forgotten the youngest monster was sick with mumps. Luckily, he'd had them when he was just a boy and was no longer in danger of catching them again. That aside, it was too bad the kid was sick.

"Yeah, that's what I was thinking," he lied. "It's hot, and the poor thing isn't having any fun without her sister. I reckon the pond is big enough for her to go her way and leave us to ourselves."

Lily clucked her tongue. "Mr. Barker, if I didn't know you better, I'd say you have nefarious thoughts concerning me."

He laughed. "Me? Sweetheart, you have no idea what goes on inside my head. Let's go fetch your sister and waste no more time. I want to get you wet."

"Huh?" Lily responded.

Realizing what he had said, Blackie's jaw dropped. Once again, his hasty tongue had proven to be an embarrassment. His words hadn't at all come out the way he'd intended; however, he could not deny it was an accurate statement, nonetheless. "I-I am sooo sorry," he stammered, embarrassed by his ill manners. "You must forgive me, Lily. Sometimes I speak before thinking."

She giggled. "I'm not offended, Blackie. I admit I'm a little curious, myself." Her eyes twinkled with humor.

"Then let's go. Don't want to waste one more minute of this sunshine."

Realizing it would take about thirty minutes to walk to Fulton's Pond, he suddenly got a brilliant idea. "Isn't the pond just over that rise, yonder?" he asked.

Lily looked up. "Well, yes...I suppose it is, if you could fly. Why do you ask?"

"I figure we could save time by cutting across that open ground. We could be swimming in fifteen minutes."

Lily's brow furrowed, as she stood chewing on her bottom lip, gazing out over the pasture. "I guess it would save us some time, but..."

"But what? I don't see a sign telling us to stay out," he argued. Tugging on her hand, he hollered, "What are you waiting for?"

Poppy had stopped skipping up the sidewalk and turned toward her sister and Blackie. She saw they were talking, with him pointing to Mr. Harrison's field, and Lily looking troubled. She skipped back. "What'cha doin? Ain't we goin' swimmin'? It's thisaway," she insisted, pointing up the road.

"Calm down, little one," Blackie said. "We're going to take a shortcut through that field."

Poppy's eyes grew large with alarm. She looked at her sister. "But you can't go there!" she shrieked.

"Oh, nonsense, Poppy," Lily retorted. "I can do anything I please."

Poppy grabbed her sister's free hand and began to pull back toward the street. "No! We can't go that way. I'll tell Papa, if you do," she threatened, her little mouth twisted defiantly.

"Hey, kid!" barked Blackie. "We only let you come with us, to be nice. If you're going to be a brat, you can just run back home." No ten year-old was going to tell him what he could and could not do. No sirree.

"But you don't understand," she pleaded. "Lily shouldn't—"

"That's enough, Poppy!" Lily snapped. "We'll do as Blackie suggests, and everything will be fine, but you must promise not to tell Mother or Father. Is that clear?" She waited. "Promise me."

Tears filled Poppy's eyes, but she grudgingly agreed, nodding her head. "All right," she muttered. "I promise not to tell, but I hope you won't be sorry."

"I'll keep her safe," Blackie boasted, "and you, too, little one. Nothing's going to happen today. The sky is too blue, and I feel too good to worry about anything."

With one arm, Blackie swooped down and scooped Poppy up onto his shoulder. The little girl squealed with delight. Maybe she was too cautious, she thought. Blackie was too tall and handsome for anything bad to happen.

But good fortune was not to smile upon the trio, after all. It was just as Poppy had feared. How was he supposed to know Lily had a severe reaction to bee stings, and the most direct route to the swimming hole was through a beekeeper's field? There were thousands of the little swarming insects. Sure enough, Lily was stung multiple times before they could make their escape, back down the hill.

At first, Blackie tried to laugh away the seriousness of the situation by trying to cajole Lily into ignoring their burning sting. Bees never bothered him much, and he didn't understand all the fuss. He spoke of the time when he was chased by hornets into a river, and he told her about his sweet dog, Honey, who got stung on the end of her black, wet nose, making her look purely comical. But no matter what he said, he could not stop the alarming red welts from spreading, and the swelling from reaching her face. He was even forced to open the dainty buttons on her blouse, to make her breathing easier.

"Bees like you cause you're so sweet, Lily," he joked nervously. "Even little old honeybees would rather have a taste of you than of their own honeycomb."

Poppy was crying, hysterically. "I told you!" she accused. "Now, she's gonna die and it's all your fault!"

"Die?" Blackie gasped. "People don't die from a few little bee stings," he countered.

"Lily will. Papa told us she would. She needs medicine."

One look at Lily's swollen eyes and protruding tongue convinced Blackie the little girl was, for once, telling the truth. "Why didn't you say so earlier? I could have had her practically home, by now. You go and tell your papa that I'm bringing Lily home. Have him ready with whatever she needs. Go! Run, Poppy!" he shouted.

The little girl was scared out of her wits, but she wasn't stupid. She had excellent instincts and was off and running before he'd even finished giving his instructions. Her orange braids were flying, as she ran down across the pasture and through the tall grass at top speed, her skinny legs flying over the ruts and stony ground. Blackie could hear her crying for her father to get the medicine—*"Lily's dyin'!"*

"Good girl," Blackie muttered.

He picked Lily up and held her gingerly in front of him, close to his chest. She weighed not much more than Poppy, he noticed. So frail and delicate—he'd been a stupid fool—and if anything happened to her, he would never be able to forgive himself for his despicable arrogance. He could not protect her from every danger, no matter how much he desired to do so. Obviously, in this instance, he had failed. If she died, he could not go on living.

By the time Blackie saw the pretty blue house with the pink and white striped awnings come into view, his legs felt like rubber bands, and his lungs were on fire. Thankfully, Mr. Posey was standing ready, outside the fence, with a bag in his hand; ready to take over and save his child. Blackie nearly collapsed as he placed an unconscious Lily at her father's feet.

"My God," the man growled, seeing his daughter in great distress. "What have you done, boy?" More than angry, the man was terrified he hadn't gotten to his daughter in time. Since she was a toddler, she had suffered extreme reactions to all manner of stings. Wasps and hornets were the most severe, but multiple honeybee stings could be lethal as well. He noticed the front of her dress had been opened to aid in her breathing. He was grateful for it. "Open my bag and hand me the blue bottle," he shouted.

A small crowd had assembled watching the two men huddled over the girl. They were shocked to see her beautiful face painfully swollen and her breathing so labored; all from a bee sting, they had heard. But why was her blouse undone? Her young man's face was as red as a tomato. Could it be the little girl discovered her sister and this young man's dalliance in the field? Could it be they were hiding in the grass when she was stung? It was something to think about...and be discussed among friends. Naturally, they all hoped she would survive her ordeal.

Blackie ignored the onlookers and asked no questions as he did what he was told to do. Waiting, he watched as Mr. Posey measured out a precise amount of the liquid into a flask, and force it down his daughter's swollen throat. Rivulets ran down her chin, wasting more than was acceptable.

"Take the brown bottle and pour it over a square. Get it good and wet."

Blackie nodded. "Yes, sir." He pulled out the stopper and poured a generous amount on the linen square, before handing it to Lily's father, who immediate took to swabbing the multiple wounds. It was at that moment, he heard a woman weep. Mrs. Posey was standing on the porch, with her arm thrown over Poppy's narrow shoulders, giving her comfort.

"Be brave, dear," she muttered. "Father knows what to do." Her husband was an expert in his field and knew a great deal about remedies. He kept a cool head and never panicked. It was obvious he had great skill as a doctor—a knowledge borne out of necessity.

Relying on Mr. Posey to perform a miracle, Blackie closed his eyes for a moment, and prayed to God that the man truly did know just what to do. If Lily survived this, he promised God he would change his ways, once and for all. The old Blackie Barker would be a shameful thing of the past, replaced by a good son, a truly good man, and one worthy of Lily Posey's love. *Amen.*

After another bit of time had elapsed, Blackie noticed Lily's face wasn't quite as red as before, and her breathing had eased some. Suddenly, just as he started to ask, he heard a great intake of breath, and a deep sound of relief emanated from Mr. Posey.

"She's returned to us, Mother," he declared, wiping his brow. "Our girl is back."

People applauded.

Poppy and her mother both broke down in tears of joy. "Praise the Lord, Forrest. You have saved her," Fern cried. "Bring her inside and we'll make her more comfortable."

"Where's Blackie?" Lily whispered.

"I'm here, Lily. You're going to be all right. Your father healed you."

"Papa?" she asked. "Thank you. I love you," she sighed.

Her father grinned, tenderly. "I love you, too, my pet," he said softly. "I'm going to take you into the house, now. Can you walk?"

She nodded. "But I might need a little help."

"Of course, sweetheart," he said, as he helped his daughter to her feet, all the while keeping a strong arm under her for support. Glancing back at Blackie, he grinned. "This has been a rough day for you, too, son. You did well. Go home now and rest."

How could he rest? Blackie needed to be with Lily. He needed to reassure himself she was going to be fine. But he saw the wisdom in the man's words and would not argue with him. He would never argue with Mr. Posey again. Nodding, he started to walk away.

"Blackie?" Mr. Posey called out, half way up the walk. "Don't go blaming yourself for any of this. You had no way of knowing, and it was your swift thinking to get her home quickly, that saved her life. You have mighty strong legs, son, and the Mrs. and I are in your debt. You come around tomorrow. My girl will be feeling more like her old self by then."

It was as if the weight of the entire world had suddenly lifted from his shoulders. While it did his heart good to hear Lily's father say such kind words, he knew he had been lucky. The outcome could have been tragically different. Although he was to blame for putting Lily's life in danger, her father had forgiven him. Thankfully, she hadn't paid the ultimate price for his stupidity.

"Thank you, sir. I will."

Dinner smelled delicious, and Lily had been ravenous of late; owing to the deliriously happy trance she seemed to constantly find herself in these days. It had been three days since the infamous bee incident, and she was eager to put it all behind her. She was determined to let nothing dampen her spirit. The weather was perfect. Blackie was perfect. Absolutely everything in her life was perfect. She had no complaints. Tonight, she would go downstairs and join her family for one of Flori's special suppers; and tomorrow, she had plans to spend the day with Blackie. Lily was veritably walking on air that evening.

As she entered the dining room, her family stood and applauded. It was good to see her smiling, healthy face once again, over their dinner table.

"Oh, please sit down, everybody," she exclaimed, slightly embarrassed by all the fuss. "You would think Queen Victoria was dining here, tonight." She quickly made her way to her customary chair and plopped herself down.

The family followed Lily's example, as Flori made her way into the large room, hefting a huge tray on her shoulder.

"It smells divine," Fern announced. "We can always count on you for making something special and mouth-watering, Flori."

"Aye, that ya can, madam. But this here turkey is for my wee lassie. It'll put roses in her cheeks."

"Mmm, it smells wonderful," Lily sighed, taking in the exquisite aroma of roast turkey and dressing. "Thank you, Flori."

"Oh, before I forget," Fern blurted out, fishing around in her pocket. Pulling out an envelope, she handed it to her daughter. "This was delivered for you, earlier in the day. You were asleep and I didn't want to bother you. I apologize for not having given it to you as soon as you woke up. I hope it's good news." But she had no way of knowing for sure. After the last letter fiasco, she had made certain the seal remained intact, for Lily's eyes only.

Lily couldn't imagine who would be sending her a letter. Outside of her immediate family, she had no real friends or acquaintances with whom she corresponded. Then a thought came to her; perhaps it was from one of her sisters. She said a silent prayer, hoping it was indeed word from either Amy or Cynthia. She missed them terribly, and was aware of how much her parents worried about their two eldest daughters. She ripped off one side of the envelope and pulled out the crisp letter, meticulously folded into three equal portions. Giving it a quick perusal, it appeared to be short and to the point.

At that exact moment, one and all heard the slamming of the front door, quickly followed by the sound of a pair of heavy feet, hurriedly stomping up the stairs.

"Bud, is that you?" his mother called out. "We were just sitting down to eat...Bud?" It was unlike her son not to answer.

Mr. Posey turned his head and took a deep breath. "Forrest Junior," he bellowed. "You will do your mother the courtesy of answering her. Come down here this instant!"

"I'm not hungry," was the shouted reply.

Removing his napkin from his lap, Mr. Posey pushed his chair back and stood erect. "I don't recall asking if you were hungry, son. You were told to come downstairs...or if you prefer...I will come up." He gave his son time to think over his options, before making a move toward the stairs.

Poppy and Jasmine both gulped, their eyes wide with fright. They had never witnessed their father raising his voice in such a fearsome way; at least, not like this. Jasmine began to whimper. "Is Papa going to kill Bud?" she asked, grabbing for her sister's hand.

Poppy wasn't at all sure he wasn't, but she shook her head in a feeble attempt to keep the family crybaby from squalling like an infant. "Don't be silly, Jas," she scoffed. "Papa just wants to look him in the eye...that's all." She hoped she was right.

"Okay," Jasmine mumbled, pretending to understand.

Holly and Ivy, as usual, said nothing, but never so much as blinked. There was a mystery here, and they loved a good riddle.

The moment Bud appeared, it was obvious to everyone why he had tried to hide from the family. His cheek was bruised and his jaw was beginning to swell. He'd been fighting, and was still feeling the rage.

"Oh, my sweet Lord," his mother gasped, as she flew to his side. She ran her fingers lightly over his battered face, wincing at the deep cut above his brow. "Some ruffian has attacked you?" she asked, never for an instant believing her son could ever have been at fault. "What is this world coming to?"

Bud jerked his head away from his mother's soft and loving touch. "It wasn't anything, Mother. Can I go up and lie down now?"

"Wasn't anything? You and I hardly believe that, son," his father remarked. "You will stand there until you tell us the truth as to what happened. Do I need to call the police and have this man arrested for attacking you?"

"No," Bud grumbled. "I don't want to say anything more," he said, his eyes darting toward his sister, still engrossed in the reading of her letter.

His father understood the subtle hint, and took pause.

"I don't understand," Lily mumbled, as she dropped the letter her mother had given her, watching it flutter to the floor. "This makes no sense at all."

"More bad news, dear?" Mrs. Posey moaned. It seemed Lily had problems of her own. "What on earth has happened to our glorious day?"

"This is a letter from Prudence Whitney, the mayor's wife. I have been asked to resign immediately, from the LLA. She requests that I do not return. She says, under the present unfortunate circumstances, my attendance is no longer desirable. They have standards that must be upheld. What is she saying?" Lily asked, her eyes teaming with tears. "What unfortunate circumstances?" She sat there, bewildered and confused. "I work very hard for the library, and I was certain Pru and I were starting to get along...well, we were learning to abide each other's presence. This is all so puzzling."

Her father glanced back toward his son. If he were a betting man, he'd place his money on Bud being able to answer some of Lily's concerns. "Maybe your brother can clear up this mystery. Tell us why you were fighting, son. However painful, Lily has a right to know."

All eyes were trained on Forrest Junior. The snap of a carrot, which Ivy had decided to savor at that precise moment, resounded like a rifle blast throughout the silent room. Bud's face reddened through the dirt and caked blood, while his scuffed fists tightened into a ball. Looking down at the floor, he began his confession and revealed the source of his anger. Gritting his teeth, he spoke in a low and controlled voice.

"First of all, it's not true...none of it. I told them all they were daffy; but when they insisted it was a fact, I got mad and wanted to make them take back the awful things they were saying. I wasn't about to let them get away with making up lies about Lily."

She sucked in her breath. "You were fighting over *me*?" she asked weakly, refusing to believe her ears.

Bud looked directly at his sister. "I didn't want you to find out, Lily. It will just make you cry, and there's none amongst all of them that is worth a single one of your tears. You could have died three days ago," he stressed. "Now this? You don't deserve it," he snapped. "It's that damn Blackie Barker that deserves their nasty accusations…not you."

"Blackie?" Lily repeated. The room began to spin. What did he have to do with it?

"Yeah. Your white knight has been going around town, bragging to everyone that he has had his way with you. According to him, you've been an apt pupil and he scores you all A's."

"Bud!" his father shouted.

"It's a fact, Father. Everyone in town is talking about the two of them. It's the sole topic of the day."

"Surely, not," his mother shrieked, as she collapsed in her chair, grabbing her chest. Her husband ran to her side. "That can't be true," she mumbled incoherently, looking into his face for confirmation.

Mr. Posey picked up her hand and placed a reassuring kiss in his wife's open palm. "No, dear," he consoled. "I'm certain they are wrong. You know our girl better than that. Lily is a good girl, raised properly, with high moral values; you've seen to that. She would refuse any man's inappropriate advances. Don't get yourself overly upset, dear. You know it isn't good for you. These are simply vicious rumors, and you should pay them no heed. I will get to the bottom of this. If I have to, I will set that boy straight," he growled.

"No, Father," Lily pleaded. "You mustn't think badly of Blackie. He's done nothing wrong. I'm certain of it. We have done nothing to be ashamed of."

"For that boy's sake, daughter, I pray you are telling me the truth," he spit.

Flori walked in, preparing to offer hot, buttered rolls.

However, when she saw the distressed look on young Bud's damaged face, she shook her head and clucked her tongue. "It will be mush for the likes of you, me laddie," she announced. "Ye'll be doin' no chewin' fer a couple o'days…and sooch a pity, too. This gobbler is a pure wonder."

"Aw, Flori," he whined. "You know I hate mush. I bet a taste of your creamy custard would go down just as easy, and it would taste a whole lot better. What do you think?"

The old woman giggled, taking pity on the poor boy. The laddie was a charmer, even with a black eye. "Aye, that it would, me boy. Let yer father treat yer face, and Ah'll take care o' yer stomach. We'll have ye set back to rights, in no time a'tall. By the looks o' ye, ye did a right fine thing, standin' up fer yer sister the way ye did. Ye deserve a proper reward, I'm a figurin'."

Bud tried his best to grin, but it hurt something awful. "Thanks, Flori."

Mr. Posey stood, clearing his throat. "Excuse me, my dear. It's time I went out for a short walk."

"But you never go out for a walk," his wife stated. "You're going to go hunt that boy down, aren't you, Father?"

"Yes, Mother. He has some explaining to do, and it is something I have to hear for myself. I can't let our girl's name be dragged through the mud."

"Well, at least take Bud with you," she begged.

He shook his head and took a knee. "Dearest, you needn't worry. I will not lose my composure. I will not thrash the boy unless there is no other recourse. Our son has done his part, and should go upstairs and lie down. Let him have his custard and sooth his face with a cool poultice. I don't need a chaperone." He kissed his wife's cheek. "As for you, it would please me if you would drink some of your calming tea and take a nap. By the time you wake, the world will look differently to you. I promise."

Accepting his promise, Fern got to her feet and gave her husband a hug around his neck. Taking in the masculine scent of his scrubbed face and glistening hair, she could feel her nerves settle and her fears subside. From the earliest days, Forrest had had the ability to calm her. He was one man in a million, and he was devoted to her. "Be careful, dear," she whispered lovingly.

"Always, my love."

Realizing there was nothing she could do to influence the inevitable, Lily ran from the table. Her father would find Blackie and, more than likely, they would exchange words. She just prayed blows would not be exchanged, as well. Her father was strong and healthy, but he was no match for Blackie's youthful stamina. She didn't want Blackie to hurt her father, but she knew he must defend himself, if set upon. Great sobs tore at her chest, as she raced up the stairs.

Throwing herself across the bed, her emotions came pouring out. For too long, she'd been holding it inside; her fear of losing Blackie at summer's end, her struggles to fit in with the rest of the girls her age, and now the loss of her beloved LLA. It was too much. Added to all this, the real pain came with the knowledge she would never again know true love, and what it was like to share that love with one special man. She had dreamed of lying beside Blackie, each bathed in nothing more than soft moonlight. She had imagined their first time together and longed for that feeling of giving herself to him. Now, nothing would come of those dreams, and she would never give herself to any man. That singular feeling of sharing one's being with another would never be hers.

It was nearly dawn before she drifted off to sleep. She never heard her father come in, nor did she hear the soft weeping of her mother.

CHAPTER TWELVE

Dear John—no, too formal. *My dearest Blackie*—but he wasn't her dearest anymore, was he?

Mr. Barker—perhaps, Lily groaned, but that didn't seem to fit, either. How could she be expected to write him a letter ending their acquaintance, when she couldn't even find the proper words for the salutation? Crushing the inadequate attempt in her fist, and throwing it to the floor, simply to join the other rejects, she exclaimed, "Damn it! Why is this so difficult?" In an attempt to compose the perfect note, she had only succeeded in creating a large pile of paper, and was no closer than she had been when she first sat down.

Jasmine was passing by her mother's day room, when she heard her sister spit out a curse. Lily never said bad words. If Mother heard her, she would have washed her mouth out with green soap; and it tasted awful, making your eyes water and your lips burn for hours. She had to warn Lily, and knocked softly, at the door. "Lily? Can I come in?" she asked, quietly. "Are you mad about something?" Not waiting for an invitation, the little girl entered the room and tip-toed toward the desk. Seeing the crumpled pieces of stationery scattered about the carpet, she figured she might know the answer to her own question.

"Go away, Jas. I'm not fit company for anyone, at the moment." That was quite evident, by the sad, miserable look in her eyes and the red tint to her nose. Lily had been crying and was likely to begin again at any second.

"I heard you say a bad word. Are you still mad at Blackie?" Every bit as stubborn as the rest of the Posey family, Jasmine ignored the request to leave, and stood her ground. Holding the wastepaper basket under her arm, she began to daintily clear away the mess on the floor. She started counting, "one, two, three," as she picked up the litter, making a game of it. Not fully understanding the delicate situation her sister found herself in, she needed to ask, "Why are you writing him all these letters, Lily, and why have you been crying?"

Lily wiped an errant tear from her eye. "You wouldn't understand, cherub, but I have decided not to see Blackie anymore, and I'm writing him to tell him so."

Jasmine looked struck by her sister's unexpected revelation, and dropped the trash basket, spilling its contents. She couldn't believe it. He was the first boy her sister had ever invited to dinner. "You don't like him anymore?" she squeaked.

"Of course, I do…very much in fact."

"Then why don't you want to see him? What did he do?"

"It's complicated, Jas," her sister sighed. "You are too young to understand."

A frown of censure settled on the little girl's face. She may be just a child of nine, but she was old enough to recognize stupidity when she saw it. "That's not fair, Lily. He saved my life, you know. I could have fallen out of that horrible tree and broke my neck. Papa said so. Then when you got all swolled up from them mean old bee stings, he carried you home, running all the way. Papa said you could'a died if he hadn't had such strong legs. And he didn't tattle on Poppy and me when he found us…uh, never mind," she said, covering her mouth with her tiny hands. "He's not a tattle-tail."

In spite of her misery, Lily found herself grinning at her little sister's noble sincerity. The child was completely earnest in her defense of Blackie, and remained quite loyal to her friend. Not to mention—he had obviously caught her and her ornery sister deep in some kind of mischief, and had managed to keep their secret to himself. What she couldn't understand...if he could be so trustworthy and reliable toward two little girls, why hadn't he shown that same honorable truthfulness with her? Why had he told strangers made-up lies about her and their relationship, knowing full well it would ruin her? If he cherished his relationship with her sisters, why hadn't he shown the same amount of devotion to the one he professed to love? She couldn't answer that question, and her head hurt, dreadfully.

"Go away, Jasmine. I must finish this letter and I have no idea how to start it. I can't even decide what to call him. Should I address him as Blackie or Mr. Barker? I have spent an hour trying to get it right."

Jasmine shrugged her shoulders. "I reckon he knows who he is. Why not skip over that part? I would. Just tell him what you want to say and send it to him. He'll know it's for him and he'll figure out it's from you." She let out a long sigh. "I don't know why adults make everything so hard," she grumbled. "My teacher, Miss Taylor, does the very same thing. *'Do it this way,'* she says. *'Memorize it that way, and do your arithmetic the long way.'* It doesn't make much sense to me, if you can skip over all that other stuff and still get the right answer. All us kids figure she's just plain mean. It's prob'ly cause she's so homely. That's what Jeffrey says, anyway."

Once again, Jasmine had succeeded in taking Lily's mind off her present dilemma and brought a smile to her lips. "I doubt that, dearest. There are things in this life that must be learned the hard way. You can't skip over them simply because they are difficult or inconvenient." She took a deep breath and let it out slowly. "But you are correct about one thing...Blackie knows his name; therefore I need not put myself out over the greeting. It is the message that is important. Thank you, darling. I will now be able to write this horrible letter."

"But I still don't know *why* you have to? You love Blackie," the little girl declared. "And so do Poppy and me."

"It's *I. I do too*, dear.."

"That's what I'm saying," she argued, slapping her

hands down to her sides and stomping a foot in frustration. This wasn't a hard thing to understand, but adults could be so thickheaded sometimes. "So...if you love him...then why write the letter? Are you just being mean?"

Lily chose to ignore the hurtful barb. "He has broken my trust, Jasmine. By doing so, he has embarrassed the entire family. I'm afraid he is not worthy of our love or our respect."

Jasmine narrowed her eyes and pursed her lips. "I don't believe it!" she argued. "I love him, and I'm going tell him so. You're just being hateful, Lily! Worse than old Miss Taylor!" she shouted, as she ran from the room, leaving her sister sitting in shock.

The child had no idea what Blackie had done to her—to all of them. He had run around town, telling terrible, hurtful lies about her, lies that could not be ignored regardless of how much she wished otherwise.

Taking pen in hand, Lily reached for a new piece of stationary. The paper was the prettiest her mother possessed, pale lavender with curly green vines climbing up the margins. Taking her sister's sage advice, she began...

Sir,

It has come to my attention that you have been telling falsehoods about us. I cannot understand why you chose to speak to half the town of our relationship, but I will not excuse your traitorous behavior. You have lied about my family and me, causing us great emotional distress. My reputation is in shreds and I have lost my position at the LLA, for which I will never forgive you. I cannot imagine why you betrayed me, but in any case, you are no longer welcome in this house. If we pass each other on the street, I will not take notice, nor will I allow you to speak to me. I have learned a very painful lesson. I loathe a liar and a scoundrel. You are definitely not the man I thought you were.

With many regrets,
Miss Lily Posey

With the back of her hand, Lily wiped away the tears that had suddenly formed behind her eyes, and held the letter up for inspection. It was precise and to the point; conveying exactly what was necessary, but omitting any of the real heart wrenching pain she was truly suffering. He didn't need to know how devastated she was, or how lost and alone she felt. That would give him too much power over her. It was better to suffer in silence.

Finally satisfied, Lily put the letter down. It was hard to believe that only one day ago, her entire world revolved around this wonderful man. Blackie had been so sweet and tender. Exasperating at times, but as lovable as a cherished pet. He needed a little housetraining, but given time, she thought he would be the most splendid man on earth, and the only one for her. She had truly believed they were soul mates, destined to go through life together. From that very first kiss, she knew her life would be forever entwined with his...

Even now, after his deceitful behavior, it would be impossible for her to forget about him; he was a part of her. However, she would have to find a way to go on without him, somehow. Cutting him out of her life would be similar to amputating an arm. Painful, ugly, and maimed beyond repair, it would be a necessary evil, if she was to save herself from additional heartbreak.

Blackie was the kind of boy that would have no trouble finding another girl to kiss under the branches of a cottonwood tree. When he eventually tired of her, he would simply move on, leaving behind a similarly damaged heart, and destroying the dreams of another gullible girl. His life would continue on without too much disruption. That's the way it always was with men. For the first time in her young life, Lily found herself jealous of the opposite sex, and despised them for it. Nothing was fair when it came to love. Deciding she had had enough, she vowed to be forever finished with men.

Carefully folding the piece of paper into equal thirds,

she slipped it in an envelope and sealed it shut. In a fluid script, she wrote, *Mr. John Barker*, and then held it up, admiring her determination. The letters were firm and unwavering. She was pleased. It had been an intense struggle with her heart, but her head eventually won out. It was a good thing. It was over.

◆ ◆ ◆

Blackie glanced at the clock in the foyer. Lily had been at her weekly meeting with the LLA all morning, and would now be returning home. He had given a thought to meeting her outside the library's door, and riding back with her on the trolley. Perhaps she would be interested in sharing another phosphate? But unfortunately, he figured he didn't have sufficient time to wash the grime from his face and hands. Rather than let her see him covered in grit, he decided to surprise her this evening. He would drop by for her after supper, and offer to take her for a stroll—right past the pet shop.

Earlier in the day, he had been walking by the window and spied a terrific pup. Curly, with brown and white patches and a wagging tale, the little guy was begging for attention. Bounding over the other puppies, he made himself irresistible by rolling over on his back and allowing his tiny pink tongue to hang to one side. Before he could stop himself, Blackie went in and plunked down the six dollars needed to bring the little guy home. That's when he got an idea.

"What time do you close?" he asked the proprietor.

The young man scratched his head. "Don't rightly know. Sometimes it's when business is slow and the fish are biting," he snickered. "But tonight, I'll close just before suppertime…around seven, I reckon."

Blackie grinned. "I'd like to gift this little fella to my girl, only it must be a surprise. I think she eats around five. Early to bed, early to rise, you know," he laughed. "Could I bring her by afterwards?"

"Sure thing," the young man answered. "If the door's

locked, just pitch a rock up at my winder, yonder. I'll come down and let you in. I sure hope she likes him. He's a great pup."

Blackie nodded, scratching the dog's whiskers. "He sure is. I have a way with dogs. Could you put a ribbon around his neck...and douse him in some good smelling perfume? Lily deserves only the best."

"I reckon I can do all that, but it might cost you two bits more. I wouldn't charge you nothin', but my ma is a real stickler about doin' things right. Heck, I've seen her refuse to sell to someone she thought unfit...no matter how much they was willin' to spend. My ma is a stickler, all right."

Blackie laughed. "No problem. Your mother will love Lily."

Convinced this was going to be a great night, Blackie discovered himself whistling all the way home. He couldn't remember a happier time and he owed it all to Lily. She was one in a million and made his life better in more ways than he could count. He knew he wanted her with him for the rest of his life, to be the mother of his children and grandchildren, and to stay with him until he was put in his grave. There was no question in his mind that he loved her, and before he left for college, he was going to ask her to marry him.

He waited out in the street until he saw movement behind the lace dining room curtains. It appeared the family dinner was over and the Poseys were getting up to go about their evening distractions. Adrenalin rushed through his veins, as he strode up the sidewalk, anticipating the very moment when Lily would open the door and smile at him with her remarkable mouth and dancing green eyes. She was the prettiest girl he'd ever seen, and she only grew lovelier with time. He rapped on the door and waited.

The corner of a lace panel, covering the glass on each side of the big door, pulled aside and then returned to its original position. The door did not open.

He knocked again, only more forcefully. Who knew what outrageous event was occurring inside? Poppy and Jasmine were capable of creating quite a stir. His knocking was simply not loud enough. Were those voices he heard? It sounded as if several people were having a discussion and were not in total agreement. They were arguing.

Just as he raised his knuckles to knock a third time, the door slowly opened and Mr. Posey stepped outside, his tall form forcing Blackie back, away from the door. A shiver ran down Blackie's spine. All was not well. "Is...is Lily home, sir?" he asked respectfully.

"She is...but she is unavailable to you."

Shaking his head, Blackie tried to make some sense of what he had just heard. "What? Not home to me? I don't understand," he mumbled, feeling his shock rapidly turning into anger.

Mr. Posey motioned to the steps. "Sit down, son, and I will attempt to explain."

Blackie did as instructed, but kept his eye trained on the door, left slightly ajar. "Fine, Mr. Posey. Explain, because I haven't got a clue as to why she refuses to see me...or is it because you won't let her see me?" he seethed.

"Did you know she was told she would no longer be welcome at the LLA?"

He had heard no such thing. "She must be mistaken!" Blackie exclaimed. "What reason did they give?"

"She is thought to be unfit," her father said simply.

"Unfit? That's a load of...well; they don't know what they're saying. It's all because of her that there'll be a library in this one-horse town. She's put her heart and soul into the LLA. Who was it that barred her...Prudence Whitney? I'll have a word with her husband and straighten all this out. After I'm finished with him, she'll—"

"You'll do nothing of the sort, Blackie. You've made things bad enough for Lily. It will be years before she can hold her head up in this town. In fact, her mother and I have suggested she go to Saint Louis and live with cousins."

"But what has she done?" Blackie's mind was whirling

and his stomach roiled. Surely this was a terrible misunderstanding. Any minute now, Lily would rush through the open door and fall into his arms, covering his face with her sweet kisses—well, perhaps not in the presence of her father—and would set the record straight.

"Knowing my daughter, she's done nothing of which to be ashamed. But you, on the other hand…you, Mr. Barker, are totally responsible for her woes," Mr. Posey declared. "I have asked around town and everyone agrees you have carelessly flaunted your relationship with my daughter, caring not one whit for her reputation. One of your friends is a veritable font of information. He brags to anyone who should care to listen about your considerable romantic exploits."

"Charlie," Blackie hissed between clenched teeth.

"I should have you flogged." Mr. Posey's face was as red as a beet, and his voice trembled with quiet outrage. "But that would only cause more distress with the females in my household. Instead, you will write an open letter of apology, refuting your stories and condemning your own behavior. Admit you are a liar and a man of low moral character . You will then leave Garden City. Where you go, I don't give a damn, be it far away from my child. Is that understood, Mr. Barker?"

Blackie felt he was going to pass out. His vision darkened and spots floated across his eyes. However, his ears worked perfectly well, and his knees were steady. He got to his feet. "I want to talk to Lily," he demanded.

"No. I insist you leave without speaking with her. She's been through enough."

Suddenly, all vestiges of Blackie's courage deserted him. He could not breathe, as he grappled with the realization he was never going to see Lily again. "Please, Mr. Posey," he pleaded. "I must see her, if only for one minute. There are things I must say to her."

"It's time for you to leave, young man. I can no longer tolerate the sight of you."

"But…"

"Shall I call Officer O'Toole? At this very moment, he is sitting in our kitchen."

Of course he was. Feeding his face, no doubt. Blackie knew when the odds were stacked against him. He had no choice but to do as he was told. "Very well, sir. I'll leave." He turned, took a step, and then stopped to look back. "Will you give her a message from me, sir?"

Mr. Posey took his time to answer. He had to give the boy credit; he had been respectful and somewhat obedient. According to gossip, he had half expected to have a physical altercation with the cocky little bastard. "What is the message?"

"Will you tell her I never intended to bring her harm? I'd lay down my life for her, sir. Tell her...tell her I meant every word I said. Will you tell her that, sir?"

Chewing on his lip, Mr. Posey was slow to decide. In the end he nodded. "I'll do my best. Go on now, son...and don't ever look back."

Blackie turned away and passed through the open gate. His feet felt mired in quicksand. With every step he took, he could feel the agony of a knife slicing through his heart, twisting and eviscerating the very life out of him. What was he going to do now, without her? Without his "Lily...", he moaned.

For hours Blackie walked as if in a daze. He took no notice of the houses he passed. It didn't matter which street he walked down. People stared at him and talked behind their hands. Some had the nerve to giggle or snicker as he passed by. He was the subject du jour, and it sickened him because he knew that not only were these people talking about him, they were also slandering Lily. As he wandered from one end of town to the other, he tried to put the manner of his sins into context. What had brought about this onslaught of recrimination? Where had he gone wrong?

"Hey, Blackie!" someone shouted from across the street. "Wait up." Charlie Masters ran across the street and came up alongside his friend. "Boy, I didn't think I'd see you for days. Figured you and Lily would be layin' low. The two of you are infamous."

"Yeah, I know," Blackie growled. "But I can't for the life of me understand why?"

"You gotta be kiddin, right?" Charlie stood there with his eyes nearly popping out of their sockets. "You and Lily have been seen all over town...you know...*doin' it*. Everywhere! You're a wonder, Blackie. An example for all us men to follow."

Before thinking, Blackie grabbed his friend by the shirt and nearly lifted him up, clean off his feet. Spitting in his face, he shouted, "Tell me, dammit! What's everybody been saying and who started the rumors? I swear, I'm gonna beat the daylights out of you if you don't speak up. Was it you?"

Charlie squirmed, forcing Blackie to loosen his hold. "Don't know why you're so surprised. Everybody's talkin' about the two of you. That's the truth," he rasped. "I didn't say nothin' you ain't said yourself. Besides, you can't be seen kissin' all over town and not have people talk."

What? Kissing all over town? When had that happened? Sure, he kissed Lily every chance he got, but he hardly made a public display of it. They had been always careful to keep to themselves. But suddenly, the heavens parted and the light of understanding suddenly shown down. What a fool he had been.

"Oh, for the love of God," he muttered, as he set his friend back on his feet. "There were several instances—but they were all innocent. I bet it was those hateful girls..."

Charlie took several steps back, putting plenty of space between himself and Blackie's flying fists. "Yeah, could have been them, but the night of the eclipse was the worst of it."

"What do you mean? Marty said some vulgar things and deserved everything I gave him."

"Did he? There were families who saw you and Lily stepping out from beneath that big cottonwood. You were obviously aroused by something...and it weren't the moon."

Blackie's face reddened. "Yeah, but Lily never knew anything about it. I covered myself with a blanket."

"Maybe so, but she must have done something to cause

such a stump. And then there was the day she almost died from the bee stings. The bees were all over her body…just as if she'd been lying down in the meadow. Mrs. Crenshaw noticed her blouse was undone and her hair hung loose. The uppermost part of her corset was untied, as well. The old biddy couldn't wait to spread the news."

"But she was having trouble breathing. I needed to loosen her garments. And it wasn't a corset. It was her swimming clothes. For crying out loud, I didn't do it to take a peek. How was I to know she would have such a violent reaction to bee stings? We had her little sister with us. We were just taking a shortcut through the field to get to the swimming hole."

"Through a beekeeper's field?"

"Yes."

"I could believe that," Charlie continued to say, "if it wasn't for the display of affection you gave the entire town the day you went for phosphates and a bicycle ride."

"Son of a bitch," Blackie murmured. They had run into Prudence, the mayor's wife, and the president of the LLA. "That damn witch!" he snapped.

"You were seen kissing, and every man in town took notice of her petticoats and stockings, as you sped down Tenth Street hill. They're all saying she's wild. You can deny everything, my friend, but it doesn't look too good for Lily, you have to admit."

"I don't have to admit any such thing. It's all circumstantial. Sure, I wanted a lot more from her, but I couldn't bring myself to ruin her. She's the kind of girl a boy wants to marry." He ran his fingers through his hair. "What do I do now, Charlie? How can I make this right?"

Charlie was undone, seeing Blackie so distraught. He had never imagined his friend could ever feel this deeply about a girl. Maybe Blackie was telling the truth after all, and Lily had been unfairly judged. "I wonder…" he said thoughtfully.

"About what?"

"You need to tell this to Lily. Explain it all."

"Her father won't let me see her. I'm lucky he didn't toss my doggie ass off his property."

"It's not her father that you have to convince. Talk to Lily and convince her that this is all a huge misunderstandin'. There might not be any way to fix it with the folks in this town... maybe not even with her own family, but if you could change her mind, well..."

Blackie's dark eyes brightened. "If I could change her mind, I might be able to persuade her to wait for me. We could write letters and perhaps her father would let me visit a time or two, next summer." He grabbed Charlie by the shoulders and pulled him close, kissing him on the cheek. "Charlie, I never thought I'd be saying this...but you're a genius!"

Charlie struggled to get away. Wiping his face with his dirty hand, he glanced around to see if anyone had seen his friend's unusual outburst. "Hey, what do you think you're doin'?"

"You're the greatest friend a guy could have," Blackie shouted. "I want you to be my best man. I'm going to marry Lily."

"Now?" Charlie shrieked.

Blackie barked out a laugh. "Not now, but in a couple of years she'll be all mine. Yes sir. She'll be Mrs. John Barker. See if she isn't. Thanks, my friend."

"You're welcome...I think."

Charlie stood dumbfounded, as he watched Blackie run down the street toward 142 Orchard Lane. It wasn't at all clear what had just occurred between him and his best friend. Had he just persuaded him to propose marriage? Was the infamous Blackie Barker really off the market?

Suddenly feeling as if there was an entirely new world of opportunity open for him and others guys just like him, Charlie turned and strolled away in the opposite direction, whistling a new tune. Who knew he was such a genius?

THE END

EPILOGUE

Everyone was gathering in Garden City for the long awaited event. The mayor, the Honorable Justin Coolidge, had declared the day a holiday, as his wife, Angela, had begged him to do in honor of her best friend's wedding. The sun was shining and the sky was as blue as a robin's egg. Not a dour face could be seen, except perhaps on that of Prudence Whitney, the former first lady. As of late, she had had precious little to smile about, ever since her husband was practically tarred and feathered for absconding with the city's treasury; forcing him to run off into the night, leaving her behind. It was rumored he was now living someplace in South America. Prudence had moved in above the grocery store.

Blackie stood with his arm firmly placed around his fiancé, as they waited anxiously for the 4:00 train to pull into the station, bringing his entire family. "I can hardly believe this day has finally arrived," he exclaimed happily. "There was a time when I thought I couldn't continue on. If it hadn't been for this," he pulled out a crumpled piece of lavender stationary with green vines curling up the margins, "I would have given into despair."

"Let me see that," Lily gasped, as she reached for the paper. "This is my letter to you. You kept it all this time?" Until this moment, she had not been certain he had ever seen it. She remembered how difficult it was to write. Every word brought more heartache. If it hadn't been for her little sister, Jasmine, she might never have written it in the first place. "Why?" she wanted to know. "Why would you keep this?"

"It reminded me of what I had, and then so foolishly

lost. It kept me focused on what was really important in my life...you, sweetheart. These past two years I've thought of nothing but making you my wife. Before I could do that, however, I needed to earn your respect and admiration. I had to assure your father that I was worthy of his daughter's hand." He grasped her lovely hands in his and looked into her eyes. "Am I, Lily? Am I truly worthy of your love?"

Unshed tears filled her eyes. "More than worthy, my dearest. You make my life complete. From the first moment you asked me to dance, I knew I loved you. You had stolen my heart and I knew there would be no other love for me. That hasn't changed."

"And now you have agreed to marry me. I am the luckiest man alive," Blackie said, smiling.

"And I will soon be Mrs. Lily Barker. Doesn't that sound divine? I love my family with all my heart, but it will be a relief to no longer be considered one bloom in an entire exotic bouquet. A lovely bunch of posies, we were," she laughed, "but not for much longer."

"Yeah, about that..." he mumbled.

"Tell me again where we will be living," Lily interrupted. "Is the house beautiful?"

Given a short reprieve, Blackie jumped at the chance to enlighten his future wife. Because they would be leaving Garden City for Topeka, Kansas, Lily had not had the chance to see their new home. At first glance, he had known it was the place for them to settle down. It was perfect for his veterinary business, and a great place to raise a passel of healthy children.

"The land is lush with rolling hills, and a creek runs through the middle of it. There's pasture and woods...perfect for little boys and little girls to have great adventures. But it was the barn that sold me. There are several corrals and small pens for the livestock. It has a place for examinations and surgery, a paddock and a small office for me to do paperwork. I can start practicing as soon as we arrive. Water is pumped right through to the troughs."

Lily grinned. "Yes, dear. That all sounds wonderful, but you failed to mention anything about our house. Is it nice?"

"Sure it's nice. Have I ever lied to you?" *Had he even seen a house? Dear God, the place had to have a house.* He started to sweat. "Uh...well, um...let me see. Where was I? Oh, I remember now. I was telling you about the animal facilities. It's a perfect place to treat sick critters." He had been so excited over the barn; he hadn't given a thought as to where he was going to bring his bride to live. *When would he ever learn?*

Lily stood back and crossed her arms. "I'm sure it's just perfect, but what about the house, Blackie? It has one, does it not?"

Blackie swallowed, hearing an edge to her voice. He had no choice but to fake it, and pretend he had everything under control. Taking Lily in his arms, he smiled his most tempting smile and kissed her lightly on the tip of her nose. "Lily, my darling...my angel, would I buy us a place without a house on it? Give me some credit. The house is nice, although a bit small." It had to be small for him not to notice it. "It's not much bigger than a cabin and could use a woman's touch; but you'll be able to make it into a fine home for us." That's it—flatter her domestic talents. Women liked that, didn't they? He grinned cheekily, thinking he would make love to Lily every night and twice on Sundays, keeping her so happy, she would never notice the condition of the house—or tent, if need be. He'd make sure she wouldn't notice the rain pouring through the hole in the ceiling, or the chilly wind blowing through the broken window glass.

Lily's eyes sparkled. "It sounds simply divine," she chirped. "I am so lucky. I'm marrying the most wonderful man, and now we will have a beautiful house in which to raise our magnificent children."

"Yeah," he agreed, as he pulled on the collar tightening around his neck like a noose. Lily was bound to be disappointed, and it made him feel like a complete failure, threatening to cast a cloud over their perfect day. Hopefully, he wouldn't have to carry her over the barn's threshold and ask her to share a stall with a sick cow. This was a fine mess he'd gotten them into. He was sure to find himself in the doghouse, now. Blackie could only wonder what else was going to go wrong, before he slipped his ring on her finger.

The sound of the train's whistle echoed through the pass, as it crossed the river. Lily jumped up and down. "It's coming!" she shouted. "Do you think your folks are going to like me?" she asked nervously.

"They're going to love you, sweetheart," he responded. She looked radiant and full of life. What was not to love?

"But do you imagine they will think my family strange because of our peculiar names?" Lily worried her in-laws might feel much the same way about the Poseys as some of the townspeople did, believing them to be too eccentric for their own good, and find her not an appropriate choice for their son.

Blackie could hear the rumble of train as it made its way over the trestle. He was running out of time to tell her. It was now or never. "About that, darling…I need to confess something. Before my family gets off this train, I think you should know our little family secret. It's not too important, but you should know, all the same."

Lily frowned, not liking the sound of this. What information had he withheld from her?

Blackie's cheeks reddened. "My family is not at all typical, dear."

"What do you mean?"

"Your family has ties to the botanical world. Mine prefers canines. It is as simple as that." He turned his head and stretched his neck, peering down the track toward the approaching train. It was done. He had told her.

"I don't understand," Lily commented.

"Well, you see…our last name is *Barker*." He waited for a glint of comprehension to dawn in his love's grassy green eyes. "I'm called *Blackie*."

She failed to understand. "Your name is John. Yes, I know."

He nodded. "Yes, but we prefer our nicknames. The entire family answers to familial names. For instance, my father is also named John, but no one would ever address him as such. His name is Duke."

Lily snickered, thinking that was rather grand. "Go on," she coaxed.

"Well...my mother is Goldie, and my Aunt Winona is Duchess. I have a brother, Rover—"

Lily broke out in a spasm of laughter. "No, you don't!"

"I do," he retorted. "Our story isn't any stranger than your family's adherence to flowers...*Lily*."

Lily wiped her eyes, conceding his argument. "Surely, no one ever calls your brother *Rover*."

"No, he's just Rove to us."

"Are there any others I need to know about?"

Annoyed at her flippant attitude, Blackie wished he had never opened this can of worms. "There are three more to add to the litter."

"*Litter?*" she squealed. This was all too much.

Blackie growled under his breath, wondering if it was too late to call off the wedding "Yes...I said *litter*! You're a damn bouquet!"

Stifling a giggle, Lily nodded. "Touché, darling."

"I have another brother, Champ, and two sisters, Princess and Honey." He snorted loudly. "Now you know the whole family and you won't be surprised."

Lily stood there in shock, her eyes wide and her mouth hanging open. Had her betrothed been serious? Litters? Dogs and puppies? She glanced down at the beautiful little dog resting at her feet. He had been a gift from Blackie, before he left Garden City for college. The pet store owner had delivered the little one the following day, explaining the unusual circumstances of the purchase. He said the gentleman had an uncanny ability to ferret out the best dog in the store. It was almost as if he could communicate with them. "Noooo," she muttered under her breath. It was too fantastic to be believed.

Seeing the distressed look on her face, Blackie began to chuckle. "I'm just joshing you, sweetheart," he said. "Trying to get your mind off meeting the family. I thought it was rather funny, however. Didn't you?"

Lily's head popped up, relieved to hear he was teasing. "That's not exactly how I would describe your little joke; but I guess I should be immune to your unusual sense of humor, by now. Imagine a family naming their children after dogs. And your Aunt Winona is called, Duchess? That's just too preposterous."

"Yeah, I suppose it is, but I thought it was funny, just the same. If I promise to never tease you like that again, will you still agree to marry me?"

"Oh, sweetheart, you know there is nothing that can keep me from being your wife. Look!" Lily shouted, as the train pulled to a stop. "They're here!"

The steam began to clear the tracks and the porter opened the doors. Out stepped an elegant woman dressed in the height of fashion; followed by two equally beautiful daughters. Three men stepped down behind them, and they all made their way toward Blackie.

Chattering like magpies, the women looked happy and excited to have arrived.

Blackie stepped forward, with his hand placed firmly in the center of Lily's back. "Mother, Father...it's grand to see you here. I hope your trip wasn't too uncomfortable."

"Not in the least, dear," his mother exclaimed, as she leaned in for a kiss on the cheek. "Introduce us to your lovely bride."

"Certainly. This is Lily Posey. Lily, this is my mother, Elizabeth, and my father, John Barker."

"Oh, please, dear. This family does not stand on ceremony. Please call me, Goldie; and my husband goes by Duke."

"*Ex-excuse me?*" Lily sputtered.

It took a moment for her brain to sort it all out, but then the light finally went on in Lily's eyes. As Blackie silently prayed for forgiveness, she began to laugh. Now, she finally understood. This was his biggest joke of all; but what was she to do? This was to be her new life, and she would simply have to make peace with it—and happily so. Since the moment their eyes first met across the crowded dance floor, Lily knew her life would be forever entangled with the handsome stranger from out of town.

Lily beamed with happiness. "Blackie has told me all about you. I feel as if we are already family."

His mother put her arms around her soon to be daughter-in-law. "We feel exactly the same way, Pet. Welcome to our pack."

◆ ◆ ◆

The house was finally quiet, allowing Forrest to put his stocking feet up on the hassock and lean back to read the morning paper. It had been a long and memorable day. Their dear child, Lily, had walked away a happy bride.

Fern Posey sighed, as she picked up her embroidery. "It was a lovely wedding, wasn't it, dear? But I thought…I had hoped…" her voice trailed away.

"I know, dear. You expected the girls to come home for their sister's wedding."

"Yes. Perhaps they did not know?"

"Perhaps," he muttered, letting his eyes skim over the daily headlines.

"We will be grandparents soon," she rambled.

"Not too soon, dear. Give them time to settle in."

She sighed. They weren't getting any younger, and she wanted a grandchild more than anything. "Yes, I suppose you're right. We'll have to wait at least a year or two."

"Yes, dear. Perhaps one of the twins will marry and accommodate you," he snickered, knowing neither girl seemed to show any interest in the subject.

Just then, a light knock was heard at the door.

Fern got to her feet. "Oh, dear, I wonder who that could

be at this late hour? I'm exhausted and you look done in."

"Send them on their way, Mother, and come back and rest for a spell. Maybe I'll rub your feet."

Fern grinned. "That would be heaven. I'll get rid of whoever it is." She hurried to the door.

"Merciful heavens," she declared, as she teetered backward into her husband's waiting arms.

A tall woman with fiery red hair, stood uncertain in the doorway, cradling a small infant in her arms. Tears made their way down her porcelain cheeks.

"Papa?" she whispered.

"Amaryllis?"

AMARYLLIS

She has quite a story of her own to tell and has arrived just in time. Full of surprises, the eldest Posey daughter will take you on a twisty ride full of unexpected pitfalls and victories, proving Lily isn't the only daughter in this family with spunk and wit. Be sure to watch for the second book in the Lovely Bunch of Poseys series.

BOOKS BY ALICE ADDY

Courage Series — Historical

MISSOURI LEGEND
ARIZONA JUSTICE
PENNSYLVANIA VALOR

Birdsong Series — Historical

TRACKS TO LOVE
SWEETWATER
BONJOUR, MY WIFE
IT'S ONLY THE BEGINNING

A Lovely Bunch of Poseys Series

LILY

Immortal Series – Paranormal

THERE'S ALWAYS TOMORROW

Ladies of the Night Series – Paranormal

DARK SIDE OF REDEMPTION
SEEKING REDEMPTION

Novels

LOVING LIBERTY

JEWEL'S GOOD FORTUNE

ABOUT THE AUTHOR

Alice Addy

ALICE ADDY has always been in love with historical romances. Many of her tales spring from stories told to her in her childhood. She proudly claims a famous Missouri bushwhacker as her great-great grandfather, and her overactive imagination fills in the rest of the story. Collecting American antiques also fills her hours, along with her passion for gardening. Colorful flowers and blossoming trees often times find their way into her novels. She believes in setting a beautiful scene for her beloved characters. Readers will also notice her love for children and animals in her books. Hopefully, they will make you laugh, and they may even cause you to shed a few tears, but always, always . . . her stories will have a happy ending. Soon, she hopes to travel extensively throughout the Southwest and the Northern plains. Maybe she will see you, there.

Visit Alice Addy on Facebook

Made in the USA
Columbia, SC
27 December 2021